Acclaim For the Work
of KEN BRUEN
and JASON STARR!

"Two of the crime fiction world's brightest talents, Ken Bruen and Jason Starr, join forces for one of the year's most darkly satisfying and electric *noir* novels…This is one of the top guilty pleasures of the year."
—*Chicago Sun-Times*

"This tense, witty, cold-blooded noir…reads seamlessly—and mercilessly…Funny [and] vividly fresh."
—*Entertainment Weekly*

"Adventurous crime-fiction fans who like their literary escapism totally unrestrained will find this brazenly violent and downright vulgar novel…as filthy as it is fun."
—*Chicago Tribune*

"A full-tilt, rocking homage to noir novels of the 1950s… Hard Case's latest release is smart, trashy fun."
—*Publishers Weekly, starred review*

"Fasten your seat belts, and enjoy the bumpy ride of double- and triple-crosses, blackmail, and murder. If Quentin Tarantino is looking for another movie project, this novel with its mix of shocking violence and black comedy would be the perfect candidate. Highly recomm⸍ terrific summer read."
—*Library Journal, sta*

Leonard drove an old Crown Vic that he seemed to think was some souped-up shit and drove accordingly, siren playing, said, "Man, I never tire of this shit."

The crime scene was a blitzkrieg of cops, civilians, CSI, more cops.

Joe was brought up to speed by the on-site guy who said, "We're hearing PIMP."

Joe looked over a heap of bodies, asked, "A pimp took out all these guys?"

The guy shook his head, explained. "It's a drug. The new kid on the block—well, all over. PIMP is the new drug of choice for the five boroughs."

Joe watched as Leonard ambled over to a basketball court and shot the breeze with the kids gathered there, then walked quickly back, said, "Joe, how you feel about hitting Williamsburg?"

"Why, you run out of wool caps and funny glasses?"

"Got a whisper a dealer is on the corner there, with all the PIMP you can handle."

They blasted over there, scooped up the dealer who was indeed on the corner as reported. Leonard, no frills, picked the kid up, threw him in the back, the kid going, "The fuck, yo?"

Drove to a quiet alley and shook out the kid's cargo pants, packets of dope spilling on the ground, the kid shouting, "Not mine, ain't never seen this shit before."

Leonard made sure no iPhones were around, then gave a slap to the side of the kid's head, not hard but sufficient.

Joe grabbed the kid, shoved him against the Vic, said, "If you want to walk from this, tell us who the main guy is."

The kid, already street legal, said, "Might need that in writing, mothafucka."

Leonard said, "Of course." Kneed him in the balls, said, "Can you read the small print...?"

THE MAX FISHER SAGA
BY KEN BRUEN AND JASON STARR:

BUST
SLIDE
THE MAX
PIMP

SOME OTHER HARD CASE CRIME BOOKS
YOU WILL ENJOY:

FAKE I.D. *by Jason Starr*
JOYLAND *by Stephen King*
THE SECRET LIVES OF MARRIED WOMEN
by Elissa Wald
ODDS ON *by Michael Crichton writing as John Lange*
THE WRONG QUARRY *by Max Allan Collins*
BORDERLINE *by Lawrence Block*
BRAINQUAKE *by Samuel Fuller*
EASY DEATH *by Daniel Boyd*
QUARRY'S CHOICE *by Max Allan Collins*
THIEVES FALL OUT *by Gore Vidal*
SO NUDE, SO DEAD *by Ed McBain*
THE GIRL WITH THE DEEP BLUE EYES *by Lawrence Block*
CUT ME IN *by Ed McBain*

PIMP

by **Ken Bruen** *and* **Jason Starr**

A HARD CASE CRIME NOVEL

A HARD CASE CRIME BOOK
(HCC-123)
First Hard Case Crime edition: March 2016

Published by

Titan Books
A division of Titan Publishing Group Ltd
144 Southwark Street
London SE1 0UP

in collaboration with Winterfall LLC

Print edition ISBN 978-1-78329-569-2
E-book ISBN 978-1-78329-570-8

Design direction by Max Phillips
www.maxphillips.net

Typeset by Swordsmith Productions

The name "Hard Case Crime" and the Hard Case Crime logo are trademarks of Winterfall LLC. Hard Case Crime books are selected and edited by Charles Ardai.

Printed in the United States of America

Visit us on the web at www.HardCaseCrime.com

For all those who did fuck all to help us or give us a review.

DISCLAIMER

*Any resemblance to persons living or dead
is not only intentional but damn necessary.*

ONE

He is a hustler, the guy's a pimp.
But that's not what I'm talking about.
ELMORE LEONARD, *LaBrava*

Max, Maximus, Maximum.

In the bathroom of a tenement apartment in Harlem, Max Fisher stared at his reflection. The plastic surgery had hurt like a son of a bitch and only now was the bruising beginning to fade. What looked back at Max was like Philip Seymour Hoffman after the autopsy. Max, a master of self-delusion, saw a youngish Jack Nicholson, and gave the thumbs-up to the face, went, "Ya still got it, kid."

He was dressed in what used to be called a *lounging suit* but hadn't done any lounging since Sinatra had hit town. It was bright yellow and Max's latest babe muttered, "Looks like a canary's abortion, mon."

Her name was Precious and the fact that she was neither young nor precious was not apparent to Max. She must have been fifty, had ratty gray dreads, was missing a few teeth. She was Jamaican slash West Indian, emphasis on the slash—she'd recently done a sixteen-year stretch at Coxsackie for stabbing her sister in the face.

This was what Max had liked most about her, though—that she had "a past." It was nice to have something in common with a babe. Though Max, of course, had only been in prison at Attica for a few months before he escaped, it was the highlight of his life. He looked back on it the way soldiers looked at war. He'd risen up against the enemy—goddamn Aryans—and defeated all of them. Fuck, where was his parade?

Precious went on, "You're not seriously wearing that, are you? You're going to be chased by a swarm of bees, mon."

Max had been in a daze lately, trying to get his shit together, and he wasn't sure exactly how long he'd known Precious. Three days, a week? She was so annoying he wouldn't have kept her around at all if he didn't need her now for her contacts.

She was going, "Come on, Maxie, I can't be goin' around the city with you, lookin' the way you be lookin', embarrassin' me. And how old is that jacket you wearin' anyway, mon? It looks like something you found in the Salvation Army. I think I seen my uncle Cuvis be wearin' that jacket one time…in nineteen seventy-two. And that color, mon, is so hideous it makes my eyes water from the pain. Nobody be wearin' bright yellow jackets anymore, mon. You're gettin' dressed for a drug deal, not *Let's Make a Deal*."

Precious was laughing now, on a roll, enjoying her own dumb jokes. Great, so now he was dating the Jamaican Don Rickles. How'd that happen?

Max, sick of her lip, went, "I'm sick of your lip. If you knew who you were talking to, you'd realize how stupid you sound. The Max isn't some schmo from buttfuck. The Max knows style. I'm what we Americans call a *trendsetter*. And I don't have to watch Netflix to know that yellow is the new black."

Precious, still laughing, went, "Pa-leeze, mon. You are the most unfashionable man I ever seen. You look like you get dressed in the dark, and go shopping in the dark too."

She continued, clapping, giving herself a round of applause. Meanwhile, Max looked at her stone-faced. He liked that they were both homicidal and that she was big-busted—had to be thirty-eights, E's or F's—and he thought she had a sultry, jazzy look, kinda like a homicidal Whoopi Goldberg. But the cons were starting to outweigh the pros. Her biggest con? She talked too much. Didn't women know that if you want to keep a man around you gotta learn how to—as they say in Ireland—shit the fook up?

What was he doing with this dreadlocked bitch anyway? He had enough problems, he didn't need another one. He wished he could remember how he'd met her.

Shit, his memory was turning into a serious issue. Max had never had great short-term memory—hell, his long-term memory hadn't been so great either—but lately he couldn't remember shit, probably because he'd been coasting on his own latest pharmaceutical high, a new product named PIMP.

PIMP for:

Peyote

Insulin

Mescaline

and a liberal sprinkle of Psychosis.

PIMP had been introduced to him in Portland by a young, long-haired hipster named Sage, who looked like he was right out of *Breaking Bad*, and maybe he was. After Max's big prison break from Attica—yeah, just thinking about those days gave Max some serious wood—he lived in Portland under his pseudonym, Sean Mullin. Figured some tree-hugging city in the Northwest was the last place they'd come looking for him and he got a job working at—where else?—an Irish bar. An out-of-work Irish guy in the U.S., who else would hire him? It was work at an Irish bar or fuck off. As Max often lamented, *we can't all be Liam Neeson*.

So Max grew a gray beard, dyed it red, and gained about fifty pounds. Jesus Christ, he looked worse than Louis C.K. Being a two-hundred-and-seventy-pound Irishman was a good disguise, but being Irish twenty-four/seven he was losing his mind. Jaysus, how did Bono do it? Speaking in that accent all the time —fook, how many times can you say Jaysus in one sentence? How much fookin' Jameson could one man drink? The whole shebang annoyed the shit out of him. Make that the *shite* out of him. Sometimes he wished he'd never busted out of Attica because life on the outside was a whole other nightmare. The lamenting, the self-pity, the depression. If somebody'd told him what it was like to be Irish, he might have stayed in that cell.

Living a fake life was hard enough for anybody, but when you were an extraordinary man like Max Fisher, when you were in the one percent and a mega genius to boot, it was even harder. Talk about riches to rags—he went from running a computer networking business, being a kingpin crack dealer and leading one of the biggest revolts in the history of the American prison system to serving skank beer to wasted frat boys. Some nights, when the college kids were shouting for pitchers of Bud to replace the ones they'd puked, Max wanted to waste all of them. Just go motherfucking postal on their ninety-nine-percent asses. Over the last few years if Max had learned one thing it was that murder was like fucking black chicks—do it once, you're hooked.

One night at O'Hennessy's—can't get more fuckin oye'rish than that, right?—this Kurt Cobain-looking dude started talking to him. He said his name was Sage and Max in his brogue went, "Where's yer mates Parsley, Rosemary and Thyme?"

Friendly conversation at first, then Sage, hair hanging over his face, went smartass: "You're not really from Ireland, are you?"

Max panicked. Had he been made? Yeah, he hated life on the outside, but he wasn't crazy, he didn't want to go back to freakin' prison.

"Ah, yes, me Irish, me Irish," Max said in his shitty fake brogue.

"You're full of shit," Sage said. "I have relatives in Galway, I went there when I was a kid and they don't talk like you do."

"Aye, that's because me from Dublin," Max said. "Aye, like me good mate, Bono."

Sage—drunk, but also definitely wired on something—went, "Galway, Dublin, what the fuck's the difference? I know how Irish people sound and you're not Irish."

Wanting to reach across the bar and strangle the kid, "Want some more Guinness, do ya?"

The guy squinted, went, "You don't sound like Bono."

Getting sick of this kid big time, Max said, "Aye, laddy, why don't you run along now, ye whore's ghost? Good on yah, bollix, fook on a bike." Throwing all the Irish he could think of at the kid, hoping some of it would stick.

But the smartass kid wouldn't let up, went, "What's the deal? Why would a guy go around pretending he's Irish?" Then later, couple more drinks in him, went, "Wait, you look like somebody. Who do you look like? I know I've seen you before."

Max went to take another order, but the kid kept giving him looks all night. Max was afraid the kid was seriously on to him, would blurt out the Max Fisher identity. Max had a flash of himself as Matt Damon, running through Europe, his cover blown. The image invigorated him, reminded him of the player he was—the Max Fisher he'd been repressing since Attica.

Besides, he was in the mood to hit somebody.

So later when the kid went to the bathroom to take a leak, Max followed him in and locked the door. Now he was back in Attica in his head, during the time when he ruled the joint. The fact that such a time never actually existed didn't matter to Max. He saw himself as the kingpin telling his henchmen—that's right, in his mind he'd had *henchmen*—to stand guard outside the bathroom while he beat some Aryan dude to a pulp. But he wasn't fighting an Aryan now in a bathroom at Attica, he was fighting some waify wiseass in an Irish bar in Portlandia. And it wasn't exactly a fight. When they got into the bathroom, Sage went, "What's the problem, bruh?"

Bruh, not bro. What was the world coming to? Sometimes he couldn't keep up, felt like the old man in *Shawshank*. He wanted to leave a note, *The Max wuz here*, and end the misery.

"*You're* my problem," Max hissed, glaring like Dirty Harry.

In Max's case, the glare was bigger than the bite—the bite was more like a nibble. He tried to connect with a hard right, but before he could cock his arm he slipped on the pissy floor, said, "Jesus," then tried to cover and went, "Jaysus," as he fell on his ass, hit his head on the back of the sink.

"You all right, bruh?"

Max looked at the dizzy image of Sage looming over him. The Max down for the count? This wasn't right—this wasn't right at all. Max felt tightness in his chest, went into one of his trances.

He'd been getting a lot of these episodes lately. He'd zone out and an interlude from his past would unfold. Now it was that truly fucked up time when he was an outlaw dope dealer, living off the grid like they said in *Weeds*.

Yep, The Max knew his TV—what else was there to do in freakin' Portlandia? Way before *Breaking Bad*, Max was your citizen turned to the dark side. That time when he was dealing and had to meet with some serious badasses and dude, those dogs were mean, like in your face, biblical fucking stone-cold psychos. In one of his less bright moments, Max had felt it would up his cred to speak Spic. You gonna be down with the *Hombres*, you better sing coyote.

So he got all them Berlitz tapes hooked up, but did a tad too much meth and passed out, Senior Lopez still lecturing to him.

The next day, when he did meet with one particular high roller, the lessons kicked in but the Spanish was high classical Castilian and for some reason stuck on odd directions so he kept rattling to the cartel guy, *"Donde esta el Starbucks?"* and *"Mi aero-deslizador es lleno de anguilas,"* or "My hovercraft is full of eels." Worse, some weird stuff on concerts, as in *"Hay algo mas cutre que hacer air guitar en un concerto?"* Which he would find later meant, "Is there anything worse than going to a concert and playing air guitar?"

To see the expression on the face of a top cartel guy when you spat this shit in his face. Luckily he thought all gringos were crazy and let it slide.

At these times, recalling the glory days, Max would get all choked up thinking about Angela, his soul mate and partner in crime, the love of his life, his *una flor linda*. Or, English translation: treacherous cunt.

He'd loved her, yeah, but he was glad she was dead.

He saw her face before him now, her flowing hair, her intense stare, and then, as suddenly as it had come, Max snapped out of his vision. He saw Sage's hand reaching down to him, and—not beyond a good sucker move—Max grabbed the hand, and pulled Sage down onto the pissy floor.

"The fuck, bruh?" Sage whined.

Max wrestled with him—okay, pulled his hair and scratched at him. After a few minutes of rolling around, grappling with the wasted hipster, Max noticed an extra-large Baggie that had fallen out of Sage's coat pocket, bulging with some white substance. Max's drug instincts kicked in, telling him it wasn't Splenda.

"Whoa, whoa, what's this?" Max asked.

"Hey, give that back, bruh," Sage said, lunging.

Max pushed him away, then examined the contents more

closely. Looked almost granular, flaky, like kosher salt. Wasn't any drug he'd seen before, and he'd seen 'em.

"Let's have a taste, shall we?" he said, more Brit for a moment than Irish, but fuck it. He poked a finger in the Baggie and put a pinch under his tongue.

Holy shit! The rush was harder and stronger than that green drink they once served to him at a Brazilian restaurant in midtown, but that drink must've been laced with something because when he left the place, after half a glass, he tripped over a pile of garbage, needed ten stitches for the gash on his forehead. This feeling was like that, but on crack. Not *actual* crack, because there wasn't crack in this—Max Fisher knew his crack. But something. Was there hash in it? It was a high-low combo all right, like the perfect poker hand. It was hitting him from all directions at once—up, down, sideways. Was he imagining it or was his sphincter aroused? He didn't know what it was, but he was hooked, like when he got his first blowjob, on his twenty-fourth birthday.

He wanted more; *needed* more.

"Come on, seriously, bruh," Sage said.

Max, back to his prison persona, grabbed a fistful of Sage's hair and twisted it, and in his best Bogie said, "Spill it, Sage."

"All right, all right, okay, just quit pullin' on my hair, bruh."

Max squeezed tight.

Squealing in agony, Sage said, "P-P-PIMP."

"Pimp?" Max said. "Your pimp gave it you? Are you some kind of hustler?"

"N-n-no, that's what it's called. It's called PIMP, now can you let me the fuck go?"

Max didn't, said, "Where'd you get it?"

"I made it."

"Made it? What do you mean made it?"

"I invented it. It's…it's my own shit. Now can you please give it back?"

Shit, this kid *was* out of *Breaking Bad*. More importantly, Max was Walter White and this PIMP, holy Christ, this could be his ticket out of Portlandia, all the way back to the top.

Max stood up, accidentally grabbing onto the urinal's flusher and some water and piss sprayed in his face. He didn't care, though—nothing could bring him down from this high.

Still on the floor, Sage went, "H-hey, where you goin' with my PIMP, bruh?"

"I had a rough upbringing," Max said. "My father was killed when I was three, he was a mason and a chimney collapsed on his head." Max didn't know why he was saying this shit—maybe it was some side effect of the drug, making him chatty. He pulled himself together and went, "And my mother, my mother was distant, worked all the time, was never home, but she told me one thing I'll never forget—*always* take candy from strangers."

He kicked Sage in the face and left the bathroom.

Max told the bar manager there was an emergency, left his shift early, went to his apartment and, as that kid book says, "Let the wild rumpus start!"

And, man, did it get wild! The next two weeks were a blur, reminded him of that time in Texas when on a drinking binge he'd gotten, um, a little too close to some Chinese dude. Thankfully there were no Chinese dudes this time, but there was lots of fucking. Max was with the best-looking chickitas he'd ever seen—yep, better looking than the girls at Hooters—and they were in exotic locations—London, Paris, Venice, Attica. Max was in jungles, swinging naked from vines, and fighting in wars. He was partying with the ancient Greeks and he even hung out with Jesus.

PIMP wasn't all sex and fun, though. Before the drug took

hold there was usually a short intense feeling of impotence, Max called it the Bieber effect. Also, once in a while, there was some incontinence, Max called it the Betty White effect. But these periods were always short-lived—or at least in Max's mind they were—and then the shits ended and raging hard-ons took over. Max had the best sex of his life in his mind, banging everybody from Cleopatra to Britney Spears to Judi Dench. Dench was a dynamo and loved it from behind with Max yanking on her hair, glaring back at him over her shoulder, shouting, "Gimme dat big boy! Gimme dat big boy!"

Yeah, this PIMP was some seriously good shit.

The best part was the feeling of power it brought Max. It brought him back to the days when he was the CEO of NetWorld, the computer networking company in Manhattan, and his major way to get off was by firing his employees. Sometimes, just for a rush, he'd fire some technician, usually some Russian, for no reason at all. He'd call Slav or Vlad or whoever the fuck into his office and go, "You're terminated, go home," and feel the rush, like Trump and Schwarzenegger rolled into one. This was like that, but better, because he didn't have to fire anybody, or do *anything*, to feel like he was the baddest motherfucker in the world. He just knew it and that was enough. Was it enlightenment in powder form? Not bad, he could use that. See, Max's mind was already churning, working OT, planning his next move.

Oh, another thing about PIMP—it was addicting as hell. When the contents of the Baggie ran out it was a sad, desperate day. He went back to O'Hennessy's and was told he'd been fired, but he didn't care about that, he just cared about PIMP. He had to find Sage.

It took about a week of searching around, but he finally tracked Sage down, in some rundown off-campus apartment, the back unit of a house.

When Sage opened the door he saw the rage in Max, thought he'd get his ass whooped again, and when Max forced his way inside, Sage pulled a blade on him. Max judged things by the size of his cock and this blade was cock-size, about three and half, okay, three inches.

"Stay back," Sage said, arm with the blade extended in front of him, shaking. "Just stay the fuck back."

"I'm not here to hurt you," Max said. "I'm just here for your PIMP."

Knowing how ridiculous this sounded, but seeing no humor in it because he was crashing from his high and desperate for his next fix. He was damn serious—he'd kill the grungy drug addict, rip the punk's fuckin' head off if he didn't cough up the shit.

But Sage was going, "I'm not giving you shit, bruh. I've been doing some research on you on Google. That's right, I googled your fat, saggy ass and I know who you are. Your name's Fisher, Max Fisher. I know everything about you, bruh. I know about the people you killed, about your drug dealing, and I know about Attica. You're fuckin' homicidal, you're fuckin' crazy."

If he'd still been soaring on PIMP, Max would've taken all of this as a major compliment. Down, he liked being called homicidal, but fat, saggy ass?

"You callin' me fat, saggy ass?" Max asked, glaring empty and psycho like DeNiro at the mirror in *Taxi Driver*. For full effect he repeated, "You callin' *me* fat, saggy ass?" Let it hang there, then added, "FYI, where I come from, back east, all the players carry some extra baggage. Why do you think Tony Soprano had all that street cred? Why did Phil Hoffman get all the great roles? And why was I the CEO of a drug empire? When you've got meat you've got power. It's called being large and in charge."

"Come another inch toward me, I'll waste you." Nerdy white guy trying to be all *Menace 2 Society*.

Half wishing he'd taken out this asshole on that bathroom

floor when he'd had the chance—but not really, 'cause then where would he get more PIMP?—Max said, "Okay, let's say I am who you say I am, though I'm not saying that. But if you really think I'm Max Fisher why aren't you turning me in? I mean, I'm on the FBI's Most Wanted list. You get a reward, what, hundred grand if you turn me in? You gonna tell me you're allergic to the green and white?"

Sage didn't say anything, but it clicked for Max.

"It's the PIMP, isn't it? If you rat on me, then I rat on you." Max smiled. "Well, looks like we have a situation here now, doesn't it?"

The ol' businessman Max Fisher was back in play, and he did what he did best—negotiated a deal. A seventy-thirty split in his favor. Sage would produce the shit and Max would market it. Powder form or pill, user's choice. And as far as ratting on each other went—well, they'd make that risk work for them. Like the U.S. and Russia in the Cold War, they'd each hold something over the other's head. Sage would write down the formula for PIMP and the history of how he'd invented it and sold it to barflies and businessmen all summer, and put this in a sealed envelope; Max would do the same with a confession detailing his crimes; and they'd send the two envelopes to a neutral lawyer, Nathan Schneermesser, Esq., Counselor-at-Law. For a fee, Mr. Schneermesser, Esq., would sit on the envelopes, with instructions to release one or the other in the event something happened—Max's confession if something happened to Sage, Sage's if something happened to Max. A perfect stalemate. Business relationships had been based on less.

With that out of the way, it was time for marketing.

Max had seen *The Social Network*, and knew if you wanted to start a trend, you had to get college kids hooked first. If it worked for Facebook, it would work for PIMP.

He distributed freebies at dorms, bars, off-campus parties, clubs. The kids called Max "Red" 'cause of his beard. The name helped hugely—not Max's, the drug's. Walking past the juice bars of Portland, Max heard, "Gotta get me with some PIMP, yo." Kids were fucking Facebooking and Tweeting about it; PIMP was going viral!

Max, at his core, was a marketing guru, and he knew it didn't matter what you sold, it mattered how you sold it—fuck, look at Amazon. Bezos started with books, cockamamie books, and now people were buying toilet paper from him in bulk—there was a lesson in there somewhere, and your last name had to be Bezos, Trump or Fisher to understand what that lesson was. It was that it all came down to the sell. Max had been watching lots of *Mad Men* and he saw himself as the Don Draper of the new millennium. He knew if PIMP was going to take off, if it was going to rock the nation as the new super drug, he needed a pitch, a tagline, and Max, like Donny D, had one ready to roll.

PIMP: It knows how to take care of you.

Boom, gotchya, slam dunk. Can you say homerun? Winnah winnah, chicken dinnah! He could see the jumbotron flashing, the crowd going wild. In the boardroom inside Max's head, his employees were congratulating him for coming up with that little gem. Then he was on stage, bowing, enjoying the standing O.

Max tried out the line on newbies—in the bathroom at bars and clubs he'd hand out PIMP samples and when a kid said, "Why's it called PIMP?" Max, ready, hit with, " 'Cause it knows how to take care of you." This was perfect because that was what people wanted. Kids today, they didn't want to do any work—they wanted apps to do the work for them. They'd had Generation X and Y, they should call this one Generation Z— for zippo. These kids today had no ambition, wanted every- thing handed to them. Well, PIMP was the perfect drug for

Generation Zippo because all you had to do was pop a pill and chill. *Pop a pill and chill*, there was another one. The brilliance was overwhelming Max now. If he didn't watch out his head would explode.

Then one night tragedy hit—or fortune, depending on how you look at it. Max was at Sage's, picking up some product, when Sage OD'd on PIMP—or maybe he'd been doing coke or shooting up, whatever, but he went into convulsions and then passed out on the kitchen floor. Max considered reviving him, but reminded himself that this was the kid who'd threatened him with that fucking huge knife, and maybe someday would develop the *cojones* to blackmail him, find some way to rat him out to the cops in spite of the fact that "Nathan Schneermesser" was just a name he'd made up, tied to a P.O. Box he'd rented, meaning that Max had the formula for PIMP and Sage had bubkis. So he just kneeled next to him while he was dying, went grim in full brogue like Liam in *The Grey*, and whispered, "You're going to die now, Sage, but it's okay, ya just gotta let go, feel the peace come over you," and then realized, *Eh, who'm I kidding?* and said, "*Adios, muchacho*," and left the kitchen.

Max wiped the place down, filled Sage's car with as much PIMP as would fit, and headed east. First he thought he'd stop in some town in the middle of nowhere and indulge in some local ho action, but the PIMP and the death had ignited something in The Max, and he couldn't resist the urge to shake his little town blues and go back to New York, the big time, and get his whole life back.

Yeah, he knew he was taking a risk going back east. The beard and weight helped, but last time he checked he was number six on the FBI's Most Wanted list—he couldn't just waltz back into Manhattan.

So when he got into town he called in a favor from an old

crew member from Attica. He got the plastic surgery—a botch job, but at least he didn't look like himself, and that was the whole point, right?

Next, to get his business going, he needed to produce PIMP, a shitload of it, and for that he needed *das capital*.

Enter Precious. She claimed she had a contact in the leading Jamaican gang in East New York, Brooklyn. That was good—there were lots of projects there and the second-best place—after a college campus—to start a trend was in the hood. PIMP would be the new Air Jordan, the new hip-hop.

In his room at Precious' Harlem tenement, Max was saying to her, "So who do I talk to?"

"His name's DeMarcus, mon," Precious said.

"DeMarcusmon?" Max asked.

Precious rolled her eyes. "Just DeMarcus," she said. "Mon." He wanted to slap her. So he slapped her.

"Hey, what's that for?"

"A reminder of who's in charge," Max said. Then, "What's he look like?"

Massaging her face, Precious said, "Big, dumb, got dreads."

Thinking, *Kinda like you*, Max said, "So what do I do, just walk in, ask for him?"

"How else you gonna meet the man?" Precious said, as if Max was stupid.

On his way to Brooklyn in a fuckin' Zipcar, Max had a bad vibe and he felt like an idiot. He should've had Precious come along, make the introduction. Old Max wouldn't've made that slip-up. It showed that, far as he'd come, he still had a long way to go.

He should've listened to his instincts because when he got to the place, some kind of warehouse off Utica Avenue, a thin white guy, curly brown hair, glasses—a fucking hipster—put a gun to his head the moment he arrived, took him to a room in the back.

"You DeMarcusmon?" Max asked.

"Do I look like my name's DeMarcusmon?" the guy asked.

Wiseass. These days it seemed like Max was flypaper for wiseasses.

"So what do you want?" Max said, when they arrived in a dimly lit room in the back. The room had no furniture, but there were three big black guys in the room, all with Uzis.

"I want to know all about PIMP," the white guy said. "I want to know where you got it, how it's made, how we can make more."

"Yeah? And what if I'm not in the mood to talk?"

Stuffing the barrel of the gun into Max's mouth so deep Linda Lovelace would've been impressed, the guy went, "Then you die, right here, right now."

Fucking Precious. Another big-busted babe had fucked the Max over.

He shoulda known.

TWO

Someone, somewhere is tired of fucking the hot girl.
CLINT EASTWOOD

Larry Reed was old-school Hollywood, i.e., fuck-all talent but lots of chutzpah. He knew the trick was to blackmail the living daylights out of the real players. He looked like Fatty Arbuckle and indeed had similar tastes. Nearing seventy now, he relied on the little ol' blue pills to keep the L-Rod in gear.

His dick had been working fine of late, but his career was in a tailspin. His last hit had been a Janeane Garofalo rom-com. Yep, it had been that long.

Five years ago he thought he was set for his big comeback. He optioned a pitch for a dollar from some shmuck kid, Bill Moss, who was desperate for a way out of the telemarketing cubicle. Larry talked him into writing on spec, the way a porno producer tells his talent that the first time on the desk is for free and the *next time* you get paid. You need lots of chutzpah to pull off that line but Bill went for it—hook, line, and sucker. Guys like Bill were morons when it came to the business of Hollywood; they believed that they had talent and that it was only a matter of time until their talent was recognized. This was perfect for Larry because Larry only worked with morons; it was the only way to avoid agents and managers and get pictures made.

But Bill Moss, God bless him, knew how to write. The script was called *Spaced Out* and the tagline was "*Alien* meets *Forrest Gump*."

The idea was everything you needed for a big hit nowadays —sexy, high-concept, dumbed down—should've been a slam dunk.

Should've. But this was Hollywood, where there were as many should'ves as there were actresses who'd quit waiting tables to become reiki masters.

The *Spaced Out* pitch: In the not-so-distant future, an Average Joe with a mental disability is chosen by the space program to become the first man on Mars, but aliens invade his ship and terrorize him. It wasn't a horror picture, though, it was drama, because it turns out that one alien is a good alien—"Think E.T. meets Judge Reinhold," Larry would say in the meetings, not realizing that the Reinhold reference made him sound like even more of a dinosaur.

To Larry's unending dismay and kvetching, he couldn't get *Spaced Out* off the ground. It wasn't like the old days in Hollywood when you could go to the Foxes or Paramounts with a stable of projects and they set you up in a bungalow on the lot with a fat production deal. Nowadays they didn't give a fuck about ideas in Hollywood. If you came to them without money and attachments you had bullshit.

For a couple of years he'd had John Travolta loosely attached. Okay, okay, so "loosely" meant that he'd discussed it with Travolta's manager at one of Bryan Singer's pool parties—yeah, Larry had been into dudes for a while, call it "a phase." Larry hadn't gotten an invite, had crashed the party. Hey, Woody Allen says ninety percent of success is showing up, right? When the bouncers were tossing Larry, he'd shouted at the manager, "I want John to be in my movie!" and he thought he'd heard, "Okay, run with it, Lar."

So Larry went around town, telling people "Travolta's on board," but it didn't open the doors he'd expected. Travolta had

had more comebacks than Brett Favre, couldn't he go to the well once more, paint on some more hair, do the combover like that kid in *American Hustle*? He went from meeting to meeting and rejection to rejection and it was getting to be a chicken-and-egg type situation. You can't score when you're desperate— every guy who's ever been to a hotel bar knows this—and desperation oozed from Larry Reed. His marriage to his third wife Bev had been shitty for years, but now it was on life support. One night in the kitchen she screamed at him, "I can't take you anymore, just looking at your old, ugly face depresses me!" Larry had let a comment fly about how she wasn't exactly a pleasant sight either, and that after all the sun damage she'd gotten they should cast her as the next Leatherface, but he got her point. He was a big downer, was even bumming himself out. What had happened to that ol' Larry Reed pizazz? Life just didn't have the spark that it used to have.

But Larry didn't give up, kept pitching *Spaced Out* around town. He thought his big break was on the horizon when Tom Selleck's people had interest. It was about time for a Selleck comeback. So he set up meetings around town. But the plans for world domination hit a snag when he advertised that he had Tom attached. People assumed he meant Cruise or Hanks, and Larry would say, "No, the *other* Tom. Selleck's been on the sidelines for a while, but he's ready to finally blow up in his old age. He's going to be the male Betty White, he's going to bring back the mustache."

Larry's pitch went nowhere. He got the Moss kid to do a bunch of free rewrites—God bless non-Guild writers—trying for a tone change. In one draft, it *was* a horror picture. In another draft it was a bromance. Larry hadn't seen any of those bromances himself—didn't know Jason Segal from Seth Rogen—but fuckit, they were selling.

Well, all but his, apparently. He finally dropped the *Spaced Out* project, deciding that the problem wasn't him or the project, it was that movies were dead. He needed an in to TV, every schmuck knew the big bucks were headed that way. But how did you get into TV if you didn't kiss ass and bullshit your way in? His motto was based on a line he stole from Bob Redford in *Spy Game*, "If it's between you and him, send flowers." Lar had one way or another sent a shitload of flowers.

Now in his West Hollywood office, he stared at the blonde on her knees, doing her best to get him off. The blue wonders were not weaving their magic and he pushed her aside, went, "Eh, fuckit, I'm too creative today to come."

The woman, definitely the wrong side of thirty-five, was relieved, got to her feet and delicately wiped her mouth in a way she hoped came off as sensual. She said, "You are nearly too much man for me, baby."

That lie hovered over them, fighting to find some level of entrance. He lit an Arnie-size cigar, asked, "That a trace of an Irish lilt I'm catching?"

He thought he heard, "That's the very least of what you been catching," and he went, "What's that?"

She smiled, said, "I said I'm from back east, but thanks for asking."

Was he detecting sarcasm? The woman, Brandi Love, was an actress, of course. He'd met her a few nights ago at some party when she'd spilled a drink on his lap and said, "Allow me to wipe you off."

He liked how she'd delivered the line—sexy, yeah, but sincere.

She was Larry's type—not too old, with a big, high rack—so he gave her his usual BS about how he was a "top producer" and needed an executive assistant "to help out at the office," and then he promised her a role in a hot new project, *Spaced Out*, which—bullshit flying now—was "set up at Fox."

As usual, the dumb wannabe had bought all of that crap.

"You can go home early today," Larry said, "and you don't have to come back tomorrow. No offense, but I don't think this arrangement is working out."

"No worries," Brandi muttered. "I'll just poison you."

"What's that?" Larry asked.

"I said it was a pleasure working for you," she said, smiling.

Larry shook his head, thinking, *Psycho actress in L.A.; big surprise there, right?* She was probably addicted to yoga, in A.A., had stalked all of her exes. He sat at his desk, tried to log onto his PC. Shit, these damn machines. He knew how to send email and do that video chat shit, what was it called? Hyping? Yeah hyping, he was great at hyping, but how the hell did you turn the thing on?

"Shit," he said. "Goddamnit. Fuck. Fuck the hell outta me."

"Need some help?" Brandi, at the door, asked.

"No, it's okay." He pressed something; nothing happened. "Goddamn piece of shit."

"You seem a wee stressed," Brandi said.

There was that lilt again.

"Excuse me?"

"Stress, anxiety," she said. "After all, most ED is caused by stress. I mean, I'm sure you don't have a physical problem."

"Whoa, whoa, look here, sweetie." Larry smiled with his new dentures. "Let's make one thing clear, I don't have any problems in that department. The L-Rod goes to the top floor if you get my drift."

"It's on the right."

"What?"

"The switch. It's right there on the right."

Larry pressed the button—shit, it was right there the whole time—and the computer booted up.

"Thanks," Larry said, "normally I don't have a problem turning it on."

"Are we talking about the computer or your cock?"

She said it matter-of-factly, really asking. The kid had spunk; he'd give her that.

"Computer," he said.

"Thought so," she said.

Wait, was this all a put-on? Larry was usually great at reading people—it was how he'd gotten to where he was in this biz—but with this chick it was impossible to tell.

"It's because of my profession," he said. "When you're a big-time producer, it's hard to be—what's the word I'm thinking of—attentive to detail. That's not a word, but you get my point, sweetie. I'm always producing, twenty-four/seven, plotting in my head."

"Right, because you're feeling so creative today."

"Exactly," Larry said. "Exactly."

"Well, I should be going," she said.

"Wait," Larry said, like Travolta's character would have said in *Spaced Out*. *Wait*, when the alien's about to leave the space-ship, after they have their falling out in act three.

Brandi, like the alien, turned back.

"You seem like a good kid," Larry said. "Got more brain on you then most of the girls I usually hire. Anyway, I'm sorry for being a prick. I'm usually not such a prick."

"Oh, I'm not sure that's not entirely untrue," she said, smiling.

Larry smiled with her though he didn't know what she'd just said.

Then he said, "And, yeah, you're right I am kind of stressed out today."

"What's stressing you, baby?"

Jeez, now she was a combo Dr. Phil and his shrink. Two hundred bucks a week and where had it gotten him? He still had daddy issues, still couldn't get a fucking movie greenlit.

"I'm looking for a TV idea," he said.

"That's smart," she said.

"Right, I know it's smart." Larry said, feeling good about himself, who cared if she was bullshitting him? "I mean, I feel like I've been wasting my time, fartsing around with movies."

"You mean like *Spaced Out*?"

Remembering he'd lied to her, he said, "No, I mean that one's coming along, I'm just talking in general. You go to a water cooler today, what're people talking about? TV shows. Not movies. It's *Game of Thrones*, *Homeland*, *Breaking Bad*, binge watching. Old days there were thirteen channels of shit to choose from, now I don't know what's goin' on with streaming, downloading. You heard of Hulu?"

"Yes," Brandi said.

"Fuck, I need to get up on this shit," Larry said. "Every day there's a new term to learn—hashtag, selfie, downloading, uploading. It's a different world out there, and Larry Reed's been in the backseat for too fuckin' long. It's time to take the wheel, baby."

He felt like he was in the third act of another movie—not *Spaced Out*, but that coming-of-age movie he was trying to get off the ground maybe ten years ago, about the high school kids who live on a sailboat for a summer. That line was in the script—*It's time to take the wheel, baby*—which, come to think of it, didn't make any sense because they were on a fucking sailboat. No wonder that piece of shit never got off the ground.

"Maybe I can help you, Larry?"

She was doing that sexy thing with her lips, like Ginger from *Gilligan's Island*.

"I know how to turn on a damn computer," Larry said.

"No, I mean, in other ways."

Yep, she was flirting, and what's this? A little liftoff action from L-Rod?

She came up to him, close enough to kiss, but just stood there, letting him smell her.

Larry said, "Yeah? And what about you, kid?"

"What about me?"

She was looking at his lips. Man, she smelled good. Like tulips, even though he wasn't sure how tulips smelled.

Larry said, "What do you want? You really want to be an actress?"

"Maybe."

"I like that. Honesty. You don't get a lot of that in this town."

"I think I'm good at it."

"Honesty?"

"No, acting. I was in *The Walking Dead*. Took them three hours to get the zombie make-up on and then I was on screen for four seconds before Andrew Lincoln shot me."

"It's a tough ballgame, sweetheart."

"Being a zombie?"

"No, being an actress."

"'Tis true." Sounding Irish again. "Wanted to try for *Game of Thrones*, but they shoot it in the north of Ireland, and there's no fookin' way I'm going back there."

They were about to kiss—Larry's tongue was halfway out of his mouth like a horny frat boy—when she moved away, strutting over to get a bottle of coconut water. What producer in Hollywood didn't have an office stocked with coconut water? Obviously she wanted him to get a good look at her ass. And he got a good look all right. It was a great ass—wide but not flabby like Bev's. With all the dieting Bev did, and all the Pilates and gazoomba or whatever the hell it's called, Larry didn't know why she couldn't get her ass in shape. Didn't she know that cellulite wasn't allowed in L.A.?

Still turned away, she said, "It's probably a blessing I didn't do *Game of Thrones*, I would've been miscast."

"Yeah?" Larry said. "How's that?"

Now she turned back toward him, went, "I could be a great femme fatale."

"I bet you could," Larry said. Yep, definitely getting liftoff— the L-Rod shuttle is preparing to launch—ten…nine…eight…— roger that. He went, "I'll tell you what. You can stay on, working for me, and I'll give you the femme fatale role in *Spaced Out*. I'll introduce you to Tom and the people at Fox."

"Oh, please," she said, more angry than flirty. "*Spaced Out* isn't getting made, it's not set up at Fox, and certainly not with Tom Fookin' Selleck."

The lilt wasn't so sexy anymore.

"What makes you so sure?" Larry asked.

"It's called Google," Brandi said. "If it was really a hot project there would be something about it online."

Fucking Internet. It was impossible to keep a good lie going these days.

"Not necessarily," Larry said.

"You don't have to bullshit me anymore," Brandi said.

Coming clean, he said, "Okay, smarty pants, so if you know *Spaced Out* is dead, why'd you agree to work for me?"

"Maybe it's because I like you."

Larry wanted to believe this lie.

"You're full of shit," he said.

"Maybe," she said, "but not any more than you."

He had to smile. She was moving toward him again, eyes aimed at his lips.

"What if I told you I could get you the next big thing," she said. "The TV project you've been dying for, that could take you to the next level, put you on the map?"

"I'm the producer, you're the blond bimbo. I'm supposed to be promising you this shit, not the other way around."

"You want to hear it or not?"

Oh no, she wasn't going to pitch him, was she?

"It's *Breaking Bad* meets *Pulp Fiction* with an Irish twist."

Yes, she was.

"Sounds like a hit," he said.

"Oh, it will be," she said. "It has it all. Violence, action, humor, sex. Lots and lots of sex."

"Okay," Larry gave in. "What is it?"

"It's called *Bust*."

"*Bust*?" Larry said, as he felt hers pressing up against his chest. "Wait, I read about that in the trades the other day, didn't I? It's the book written by some American girl and a Swedish guy."

"That's the one," Brandi said.

"This is your pitch?" Larry laughed. "The hottest project in town? How're you supposed to get me in on that?"

"Let's just say I know how to get things done." She finally kissed him. Then she reached into his boxers and grabbed L-Rod with a strangler's grip and smiled, but not happily, and went, "Why, what have we here?"

Larry got home to his place in The Canyon at around five-thirty and was planning to take a hot shower—always a good idea after banging another woman; wives, fuck, they were like bomb-sniffing dogs when it came to pussy—and then, after a couple brews and some fast lines, he'd try to figure out how to use his Kindle, get a copy of this *Bust* book. Wait, what was he thinking? He was a Hollywood producer, he didn't actually read. He'd find some reviews, or maybe there were Cliffs Notes.

But when he got in the door he got a slap in the mouth. Managed to see Bev tied to a chair—weirdly his first thought was, *Shit, and she never lets* me *tie her up*, and then a kick in the balls put him on his knees.

When that pain subsided, he looked up at two guys. No masks. Uh-oh.

One was so thin he was practically see-through, tattoos up his arms like the fucking Sunday comics, wearing a black T with the words: NO SHIT SHERLOCK.

The second was as wide as his partner was thin, was something Spanish, not Mexican—Larry, like all Angelenos, knew his Mexicans.

The skinny guy went, "Hey Larry, we're Mo and Jo. I'm Mo."

Mo had some kind of hick accent. Southern, not Texas, maybe Florida. There was something wrong with his speech so it sounded like one of the Waltons with nerve damage.

"Hey, Jo," Larry said to the Spanish guy. "If your name was Curly we'd be the Three Stooges."

Going for a laugh to lighten to the situation, but getting a dumb deadpan glare instead.

"Jesus, how old am I?" Larry said. "Doesn't anybody even remember the Three Fucking Stooges? Come on, didn't you even see the piece-of-shit remake? I wanted my buck twenty-nine back from Redbox."

Mo kicked Larry in the gut and Jo slapped him in the face as Larry went down.

Keeled over, Larry caught a glimpse of Bev bound to the chair. Oh yeah, he'd seen that look before and knew that there would be hell to pay. Even if Larry talked his way out of this, figured out a way to get the guys to leave the house, he wasn't sure he'd be any better off because his wife might kill him herself.

When Larry got some breath back, he choked, "The fuck are you, the Odd Couple?"

Jo took his turn at bat and knocked out Larry's dentures, said

"Need to focus, ol' man, he just told you our names."

Definitely not Mexican. Cuban? Toothless now, he mumbled, "What yah want, asswipe? There's nothing in the house, no valuables. If you want to pay some credit card bills, be my guest."

More glaring from Bev. Shit, she was scarier than Mo and Jo. He knew if she wasn't bound and gagged she'd be tearing into him, going, "Why're you joking around with them? You *trying* to get me killed?" Always criticizing him, taking the opposite point of view.

Mo moved over to the bookcase where an open Sam Adams was resting, took a large swig, belched, said, "This shit is good."

Sam Adams? Larry drank Schlitz. Who the hell had been to the house drinking Sam Adams? Wait, was Bev *cheating* on him?

Then Mo crouched down, almost friendly, close to Larry's ruined mouth, said, "You owe our boss seventy-five large, not including the vig."

Larry managed to move into a sitting position, said, "Fucksake, why didn't you just ask instead of all this *Get Shorty* nonsense?"

Jo asked, "Who's Shorty?"

Mo laughed, said, "You see, Larry, you see what I have to work with?"

Larry thinking, *There's a .357 Magnum in a drawer near where the brew had been resting.* If he could make his way over...

Mo said, "Lookin' for this shit?" and dangled the Magnum off his pinky.

Fuck.

Then Mo sucked on the end of the bottle, making annoying noises, asked, "Where's the cash at, my man?"

"Cash? You must be making a mistake, I'm the last guy on this block who has cash."

"That's not what the boss be sayin'," Jo said.

"The boss?" Larry said. "Who's the boss? Please tell me it's Tony Danza and this is all some fuckin' joke."

"Y'all think you funny," Mo said.

"Y'all?" Larry asked. "There was only one of me, last time I checked." Larry smiled.

"That's what's goin' on?" Jo said to Larry. "You laughin' at us, man? You think we clowns?"

Larry said, "Look, Puerto Rican Joe Pesci, first of all, I don't know who the fuck you are or what the fuck you want from me. I'm Larry Reed the movie producer, not Larry Reed the millionaire. Second of all, you seem like a smart young fellah, you think I really would keep that kind of dough here?"

Mo raised his hand and Larry flinched. Mo smiled, said, "Relax, man. Trust me, if I really wanted to hit you, you wouldn't have time to duck." Then cold cocked Larry, said, "See."

True enough, Larry hadn't.

Jo said, "I look Rican to you?" Then, "If you ain't got the green, we gotta be mean."

The fuck was he talking about?

This: "We gonna take your wife with us, have us all a *party* and you can get her back when you bring us the seventy-five K."

"Bring it. Bring it where?"

"You find out," Jo said. "And you call the cops, you find your wife in the L.A. River with the rest of the dead fishes."

He stuck out his long tongue, looked like Gene freakin' Simmons, and gave Bev a porno style kiss over the bandages, and then he and Mo lifted the chair.

"Whoa, the fuck you doing?" Larry said, upset that they were taking the club chair he'd paid two hundred forty-nine bucks for at Crate & Barrel, then it hit that they were taking Bev away with it. He fought off the thought of, *Take the cunt, she's all yours*, and went with, "Hey, where the hell you takin' my wife?"

He felt like he was in a movie—he was the good guy, the hero with a set of skills. They were fucking with the wrong guy. He was ex-CIA, ex-DEA, ex fuckin' *something*.

At the same moment, Jo fired the Magnum and pain exploded in Larry's thigh. In agony, he looked down at the bloody gash, just glad L-Rod wasn't harmed.

Then, still like he was in a movie, a horror flick now like the shitty ones he used to make in the seventies, he watched the guys carry his wife out of the house.

THREE

Never let those fuckers tell you what to write.
EDWARD BUNKER

The way *Bust* happened:

Paula Segal, tired of her career as a midlist crime fiction writer, had written a draft of a Max Fisher true-crime story called *The Max* that had gone nowhere. Her agent told her that the book was too dark, too unrelenting, and would never sell to a "big five" publisher, so she paid a company a few hundred bucks to format it, paid another couple hundred for a cover—a mocked up image of Max's infamous mug shot—and put it online herself with a new title, *Max Fisher: Uncensored*.

It sold sixty-four copies, and that was after hours of tweeting and blogging and, okay, *begging*. Paula didn't get why the book wasn't taking off, why Tarantino wasn't calling. Wasn't self-published supposed to be the new black? She thought this was the book that would propel her to the next level, but instead it had solidified her rep as a has-been, a loser.

Paula had her faults—she was addicted to coke and sex, just to name two—but she'd always been an optimist, especially about her writing career. She'd always believed that somehow, someway, she'd make it to the top. She'd be the writer with thirty backlist books at Barnes & Noble, obnoxiously taking up half a shelf, and other writers would whine, *It's so unfair, why won't my publisher give me the Paula Segal treatment?* Yep, Paula believed it was only a matter of paying your dues, kissing the right asses, going to the right Mystery Writers of America events, buying enough drinks for Otto Penzler, and, oh yeah, writing good books, and her career would eventually skyrocket.

Well, that fantasy was as dead as an independent bookstore in Manhattan. Four long, unpublished years went by. Agentless, at the end of an inheritance from her grandmother, and living on a Facebook friend's couch in Williamsburg, she was questioning everything. With all her whining and bitching she felt like one of the fucking *Girls*. Maybe she wasn't a good as she thought she was, maybe she'd never had a serious chance of making it and had been kidding herself all along. Maybe she'd let the early success, the award nominations and a few nice words extracted from a mediocre Marilyn Stasio review in the *Times* go to her head, and it had been the all-too-common case—in the literary world—of early ripe, early rot. It had been ages since that Barry Award nomination for a book in her P.I. series at St. Martin's Press, when she'd been on top of the world.

As a last-ditch effort to salvage the Max Fisher story, her career and—who was she kidding?—her life, she emailed her literary idol and old friend Laura Lippman, asking Laura if she would appreciate the honor of co-rewriting her self-published true crime book as a novel. In her delusion, Paula seriously believed Lippman would have to be an idiot to not jump at the chance and was shocked when Lippman ignored her notes, which, in retrospect, was not all that surprising since the last time she'd seen Lippman at that B&N in Manhattan, security had to remove Paula from the store. Bounced from a bookstore—oh, the irony!

But Paula didn't give up trying to contact Lippman. She friended her on Facebook under a fake name—Megan Abbott. She knew Lippman had blurbed one of Abbott's books and would accept the request.

Lippman did but only to IM: *I know who you are and if you don't stop harassing me, I'm calling the police.*

Paula IM'd back, but Lippman had already blocked her.

Well, looked like the Lippman bridge had officially been burned. The last kick in the balls, Paula saw that Laura was co-writing with Reed Farrell Coleman. Coleman? Seriously? That guy truly had no shame, was there anyone he wouldn't co-write with? Was he through writing with the Irish guy, the friend of Colin Farrell? What the fuck ever.

Paula felt dissed, marginalized, was ready to quit writing, or even jump from the Williamsburg Bridge.

Then, one morning, she had an idea that would change her life forever.

Swedish books were all the rage. After Stieg Larsson mania you just put an unpronounceable name on the cover, set the book in twenty-below weather in Sweden, and boom, Knopf was wining and dining you, David Fincher was filming you.

Simple, right?

She remembered how Max Fisher had told her that he'd learned Spanish from Berlitz tapes, so, inspired by the Max, she got Berlitz Swedish tapes. The first three words she learned:

book was *boken*
bestseller was *saljare*
money was *pengar*

Shit, she was gonna make some serious fucking *pengar*. So much that someday Lee Child would be coming to *her* parties at the mystery conferences.

"Show me the fucking *pengar*!" Paula shouted so loud her roommate banged on the wall.

She stayed up all night, reading translations of Swedish literary blogs. She came across info about an apparently bitter,

shunned writer named…wait for it…Lars Stiegsson. At first
she thought, okay had to be a dumb joke, like the Drunk Otto
Penzler Twitter feed. But, nope, turned out Lars Stiegsson was
the real deal. Claimed he'd written *The Dragon with the Girl
Tattoo*, and Larsson, a rival from grade school, had ripped him
off, trying to capitalize on the Lars Stiegsson name recognition
by knocking off Lars' work, and his name.

Sounded crazy, insane and Paula wondered if the years of
rejection and torment she'd experienced as an ex-St. Martin's
Press author had finally taken its toll on her, if she'd officially lost
it. But, nope, it was all true. She did more research, discovered
that Stiegsson had written twenty-seven crime novels pre-Stieg
Larsson. Stiegsson claimed that Larsson had read an unpublished manuscript of Stiegsson's *Girl Tattoo* and was so jealous
that he penned *Dragon Tattoo*. Larsson got the last laugh from
the grave of course, as his books sold tens of millions of copies,
and Stiegsson had disappeared from the publishing scene.

As dawn approached, an idea was forming for Paula, a way to
get to the top of the mystery genre.

Stiegsson was near impossible to contact. Some in the blogo-
sphere even speculated that he was dead. Then Paula met up in
Manhattan with an old friend and ex-flame from her straight
days—British noir writer Maxim Jakubowski. If you needed a
contact to the underworld of crime fiction, Jakubowski was
your go-to guy. Sure enough Maxim had an email address for
Stiegsson and Paula was able to contact him at his home in
Oxelösund, Sweden. They exchanged a few emails and then
arranged a time to Skype.

Paula was wearing something low-cut, showing lots of cleavage.
She was surprised at how decrepit Stiegsson was—scraggly beard
and deep circles under his eyes. In the publicity photos on his
old books he was always smiling and looked so debonair. She half-
wondered if she was Skyping with Stiegsson's Unabomber brother.

"It's so great to finally meet you," Paula said. "I'm so excited about the prospect of co-writing with such a respected Swedish author."

Stiegsson maintained his sour glare and asked, "Is there money in the deal?"

"Yes," Paula said. "I mean no. I mean not yet. I mean, I have several publishers in mind, it's really just a matter of finding the right fit."

"You don't answer question," Stiegsson said. Then he said very slowly, "Is...there...money?"

"Yes, there's *pengar*, there's *pengar*," Paula said.

Stiegsson's glare asked, *Who are you kidding?*

Figuring she might as well shoot straight with the disheveled Swede, Paula said, "Okay, there's no publisher yet, but with a writer of my caliber teaming up with a writer of your caliber there will certainly be lots of interest."

Stiegsson was staring grimly. Did anybody ever fucking smile in Sweden? If you tickled a Swedish baby would it glare back at you?

Finally Stiegsson said, "So I will get this straight. You have no money, you have no publisher, and you expect me, Lars Stiegsson, to write book with you?"

"Yes," Paula said.

"Why you want me?" He leaned closer to the camera, making him look even uglier. "You're famous American writer, friend of Laura Lippman. Why not ask her? Why not Dennis Lehane?"

"Actually I considered Den," Paula said, "but we had a, well, falling out. Something about how he thought I was stalking Laura. I *was* stalking her, but that's a whole other story. Besides, I think Den is too much of a moralist for this tale. I think your existential edginess would be a perfect fit for the material."

She tasted vomit.

"Stop shitting in my pants with me, or shitting with the bulls or however you Americans say it," Stiegsson raged. "You want me because I'm Swedish. Because you think it will sell your stupid little book to have Swedish name on cover."

"That's not the only reason," Paula said, hoping the bullshit wasn't too obvious. "I also am also truly a big admirer of your work."

"My work," Stiegsson spewed. "Name one book of mine you know."

"*Freeze My Margarita*?" Paula said. Wait, shit, that was Lauren Henderson. "Or, no, I mean, *The Black Rubber Dress*?" Shit, Henderson again.

"You don't know my books," Stiegsson said. "My books never been translated. You know why? Because Stieg Larsson stole everything from me. I knew Stieg when he was poor homeless man, penniless, has no books. He see me, Lars Stiegsson, with great success, and what does he do? He steals everything from me."

Paula could barely understand what this grizzled nut was saying, but she said, "I know exactly where you're coming from. But that's precisely why you need to do this book. To prove that you're the real talent, not Stiegsson, I mean Larsson... You know what I mean."

"You know," Stiegsson said, almost smiling, "you are very attractive woman."

Oh gawd, the little Rumplestiltskin wasn't hitting on her, was he?

"Usually Lars not attracted to American women, usually Lars only like Mediterranean women, the dark skin, not bullshit pale skin like here in Sweden. But you're beautiful pale woman. You know who you look like?"

"Kate Winslet?" Paula asked.

"No, Agnetha Fältskog."

Jeez, did Swedes actually like ABBA? Who'd ever said, I love ABBA?

"I love ABBA," Paula said.

Fingers crossed. Legs? Not so much.

Stiegsson beamed, made him look younger. He said, "I once listened to 'Dancing Queen' four hundred sixty-eight times in one day. The song, it saved my life when my mother died."

He was doing something with his hands off screen. Jerking off? Ohmigawd, not another Max Fisher.

"I have so much respect for men who love their mothers," Paula said.

Stiegsson grunted—either coming or clearing his throat—then said, "You like ABBA, that's good thing. But not good enough. You get Swedish authors, Americans cream selves, your book become bestseller, no?"

The fuck was he saying?

He added, "As your President Kennedy said, 'You know what you get from Lars Stiegsson, but what does Lars Stiegsson get from you?'"

"If you're angling for a blow job, it ain't happenin'," Paula said. "Not with this chick anyway."

Steigsson raged, "I'm not talking about stupid blow job, I'm talking about stupid book. I'm Swedish author, but who are you? Just some American with books from St. Martin's Press. Lars Stiegsson does homework, yes?"

Trying not to get defensive, Paula said, "Look, I admit I don't have a resume as impressive as yours, but I'm widely considered to be one of the rising stars of crime fiction. I'm noir, but noir with a soft edge. Otto Penzler told me he's a big fan. I had to say, 'My eyes, they're like up here, Otto,' but he seriously thinks I have talent."

She thought, *Hear that and weep muthahfuckah*. Wondering

if the Swedes had such a term, she'd have to download a Swedish dictionary from the app store. Then hello, light-bulb moment, worthy of her being on *Ellen*. She said, "I love tennis."

He was lost, said, "I don't know from…"

She nearly said, *Speak fucking American.* Jesus, it was bad enough that the likes of Rankin, Hughes and company refused to write in real English, i.e., USA English, hello, but a Swede who didn't know about tennis? Seriously, apart from fucking Bjorn, ABBA and suicide, what had they given the world? Okay, okay, not that she was moralizing, she left that to the Lippmans of the world and their ilk, but really, when you'd given the planet little else but shit music and a surly tennis player, could you really afford to be judgmental?

She said, "I'd like to have a discussion about tone. I'd like the book to be a paean to noir, to illustrate the neo-noir deconstruction of post-modernist genres. To demystify the whole concept of the legacy of Goodis, Willeford, Thompson, Guthrie, and Aleas, to bring out all the shades of noir, as a palate of such dark delicacy that Lee Child and his crew throw down their mega-million contracts and gasp, 'I want me some of that shit, nigger.'"

So, okay, they wouldn't phrase it like that, but she added, "I hope we are on the same page, Mr. Stiegsson."

Silence.

She was delighted, knew she'd got the great man, that her humble treatise had been received with warmth.

She took a deep breath, figured, that was the first step. She was on her way. Should she leak the story to the blogs, get a buzz going? Or was it too early? Probably be better if she and the Swede wrote something first.

"Why don't you sleep on it," she said, "let me know what you think in the morning. But I know you're going to love it. This could really be an important opportunity for you, a chance to show the world that Lars Stiegsson is a writer to be reckoned with. A writer that, no offense to your departed colleague, can kick Stieg Larsson's pussy ass. You know you want to." And then she disconnected before he could say another word.

Switching apps on her phone, she recorded a voice memo for herself:

"Get fucking ABBA greatest hits."

Jesus, that was punishment, no one could say she wasn't prepared to suffer for her art.

She added:

"Get Swedish dictionary."

Later, at a bar in Bushwick, into her third cosmo, she slurred:

"And check out the tennis players. The Swedish ones."

FOUR

How's everything in the pimp business?
TRAVIS BICKLE

Max never, ever, forgot a grudge or a slight. Back in his day, the freaking glory days, when NetWorld was riding high, he'd considered at one point offloading the whole set-up. Like that dude who'd sold off his Internet company and got like billions and went off and set up a publishing company.

Like that.

Max had put out feelers and gotten a nibble from Nick Dunne, who was buying up networking companies around the country. Dunne was a minor Trump, just had a little combover where The Donald had a freaking field. Max, at that time, was covering his bald spot with spray-on hair and sometimes when he got nervous and sweated, the hair would like melt and drip down onto his forehead and ears. Not exactly a great impression at a power lunch; he should've just worn a yarmulke.

Dunne had seemed seriously interested and after tense negotiations and all that due diligence, he had summoned Max to his apartment, on fucking Central Park South. Trying the old power move of trying to intimidate a potential business partner with his digs. Max knew this move well, he'd done it often himself throughout his career as a businessman and then later as a drug dealer, but Max could usually intimidate with just a look, the way a wolf looks at you before he attacks.

"A wolf doesn't need to growl, Mr. Dunne," Max said.

Dunne seemed confused, went, "Excuse me?"

Max didn't feel like explaining it to the wannabe. He'd find out soon enough.

Max was steel on the outside, but he was a bit nervous. He knew because, shit, his hair was melting. If this guy bought the company, Max would be richer than fuck, Caymans here he comes. Dressed to impress—a suit from Lagerfeld, shoes by some Italian hairdresser, and an appropriate air of humble submission. Gotta be up front with the bullshit, right?

It had started not bad, ultra-dry Martinis, a zing to the olives, lots of chat about summering in the Hamptons. Precious wasn't the first to call Max "Maxie" because Mr. Dunne had gone, "So Maxie, may I call you that?"

Max, not above brown-nosing for a deal, said, "Mr. Dunne, you may call me anything your heart desires."

Puke, right?

Dunne had smiled, the smile of a Great White, all teeth and ice. He went, "The thing is Maxie, your company is actually quite a good fit for my portfolio."

Who except Patrick Bateman can say *portfolio* with a straight face? Max smiled in what the self-improvement tape swore was a winning way, humor tinged with gratitude.

"But see the problem is..."

And the muthah made Max wait, asking, "Wanna hazard a guess as to what the problem is?"

Max had no idea, said, "I have no idea."

And Dunne was on his feet, near yelling, "See, that's the problem right there, you have no idea, about anything. The problem, Maxie, is you. I wouldn't take your company for a stale bagel if you were the lox, if you get my drift."

Max had excused himself to take a leak, on the verge of apoplexy. The bathroom was gigantic and that made Max even crazier. He did some five or so fast lines, well, ok, maybe a tad more. The voice in his head, the one true voice, going, *The fuck you saying to me? Yah fink*. Brit tones slipped in when Max was overwrought. He continued, *You think you can talk to me like I'm some kinda...* He was lost for a term, then thought: *minion...*?

But this was before Max's ultraviolent drug-dealing days, when he let the bullets do the talking, so to get his revenge on Mr. Dunne he took a more subtle approach.

The day after the lunch powwow he sent the secret video he'd shot of Dunne on one of their nights on the town a few weeks earlier. Max always knew that to get ahead in the business world you needed the ammo for extortion ready in hand, and he always prepared in advance. The footage had been taken mostly in the fantasy room at Stringfellows and showed an increasingly wasted, bare-assed Mr. Dunne getting spanked by various strippers. From a contact/mole Max knew at Dunne's company, he obtained—for a price, and what a price, but it was worth it—the email addresses of Dunne's entire client list. He then anonymously sent the video off to them in a group email with the subject heading: NICK DUNNE TAKES A BEATING. A few months later, Max was adding Mr. Dunne's clients to his own portfolio.

Moral of the story: Nobody fucks with The Max and escapes unscathed, and he'd ruined enough lives to prove it.

Now, with a gun halfway down his throat, the same Fuck-With-The-Max-The-Max-Will-Fuck-You-Back-Harder attitude boiling up in him, Max knew he was going to give Precious and her friends some payback—it was just a matter of when and how. First, he had to get out of this mess. Unfortunately there was a how to be figured out here too.

Then it came to him.

Max had had a heart condition for, like, ever. His cardiologist had told him to lose twenty pounds or else about eighty pounds

ago, and yet Max was still alive and ticking. Ma
PIMP was like Drano for the arteries? Anyway, I
ried heart pills with him, just in case, and he'd
episodes by now that he knew more than enough

He held his breath to make his face go red, started convulsing,
let some saliva dribble down his chin like Leo in *Gilbert Grape*,
and then let his head go limp. Silently cursing the cut to his
palate he'd given himself while fake-convulsing with a gun in
his mouth. Fuck, that shit *hurt*. That *better* have been convincing. Fuck.

One of the dudes holding an Uzi off to the side went, "Yo,
you better chill with that shit, I think you killin' the mothafucka."

The thin white dude removed the gun from Max's mouth
said, "You gonna play ball and tell us how to cook up the PIMP,
yo?"

Max let his knees buckle, his tongue sagging from his mouth.

Another of the Uzi guys shouted, "Nigga's dying, K."

Believing it, the thin guy said to Max, "Shit, you okay, man?
Can you hear me?"

Perfect—he knew if he let The Max die he'd never crack the
PIMP code.

Max was gasping, barely said the word, "Water."

"Get the man some water," an Uzi dude said. "The fuck you
standin' there?"

One of the thugs arrived with a glass of water. Max managed
to get a pill into his mouth, making the struggle look good—
where was his Oscar?—and then clutched the glass of water.

He'd seen enough attacks at Attica to know exactly what to
do next. Gulped a sip of water then smashed the glass against the
wall, holding onto the bottom of the glass, and then rammed
the shard into the thin guy's neck.

_lood splurted—bingo.

During the shock, Max kneed one of the thugs in the balls, grabbed the guy's Uzi, and went *Pulp Fiction* on him and the rest of the room. He fired like *Mad Max 2*—or was it *Rambo III*?—till the clip ran out. He was firing on empty for a minute before he realized it was done. Standing in the carnage, with smoke, cordite, and the copper scent of blood all round, and not even a sound, not even a siren…yet.

Time to get his Rambo ass in gear. Checked his watch, allowed two minutes to raid the dead. These Bloods were carrying serious weight, in Rolexes, bulging wallets, diamonds and, sweet Mary and Joseph—his Irish persona still kicking in—and lots of dope.

Max went outside, squinting against the sunlight. The Boyz n the Hood were still doing the corners gig, Jesus, how passé was that? Max, flying on PIMP and some margaritas earlier, marched up to a brother, shouted, "Where Demarcusmon at?"

The guy stared at him, showing gold teeth—was he smiling? "Demarcus? Over there by the Caddy."

Max blew the smiling asshole's head off, scattering his friends.

Then he strode toward the big man. He was marching to a whole other deadly drumbeat, in his own movie that laid waste to the disbelievers who dissed The Max.

Precious wasn't kidding when she said Demarcus was big. Jesus, the guy had to be six-eight, three hundred and fifty pounds.

Max went to him, "What up, Black?"

The enormous dreadlocked man turned to face Max, not in a hurry, gunfire notwithstanding. This wasn't a man who got bothered by a little thing like gunfire. A smile already creasing his scarred handsome face, he was going, "The fuck you…?" when The Max shot him in the balls, then moved over, shot him in the face, turned, shot the lieutenant, who was going for his piece, in the side, then turned in whiplash movement—Jeez, that

PIMP gave you some moves—and shot the guy on the corner. Then bent down, frisked Demarcus, found stash of cash, dope, and turned with the U, mowed down any brother who moved.

As the smell of cordite and utter disbelief spread over the street, The Max began to stroll down among the fallen bodies, putting a *coup de grace* in any mother who moaned, then turned, shouted, "That all you got? Spread the word you corn pickers, I own this fucking town."

He piled everything into the white Caddy. Now a siren was blaring. He put the white in gear, cruised outa there like the King of New York.

His mowing down of the hood kept replaying in his demented head. He reached down as he put distance between him and the cops, unwrapped a shitload of PIMP. Pulled over, snorted four or five lines, punched the wheel as the PIMP hit, shouted like the anorexic pirate in that Hanks movie, "I'm duh captain now!"

Yeah.

In my fresh ride, blasting de hood, wasting dem there mutha-fuckas.

Yeah, he was down. Then up. But mainly he was rich.

He needed a pad, many women. As he pushed the pickup, he thought, gotta get me some Hank Williams, a coon dog, a Winchester instead of the two fluffy dice hanging in the back window. Pulled over at a convenience store, he was suddenly ravenous. Man, wasting dudes was like, exhausting. Needed some serious death-rate carbs. He was getting out, the Uzi still slung on his shoulder, and he thought, *Uh-oh. Not smart.*

He reached in among the litter of guns, jewels, and dope, left the Uzi on the pile, and selected a fat wallet brimming with Franklins. Shoved that in his back pocket, grabbed a Heckler, put that in his waistband, tight fit but he got it in there, then strutted towards the convenience store, thinking, fook, he might take it down, depended on whether they had Grey Goose or not.

Later, he sold the Caddy to a shady lot in Bed Stuy, piled his loot in a beat-up pickup he'd taken in part-exchange. The dealer, a wiry one-eyed huckster, looked at The Max, handed over the cash, said, "Got some freight there buddy."

Once Max would have been intimidated by this but now, he whipped out the Uzi, got right in the loser's face, asked, "You ever see me?"

"N-n-no…n-never."

Max was on fire with power, pushed, "You want I come back, pop a cap in yer sorry ass?"

No, he'd prefer not.

Max went Clint, said, "Don't have me come back here, punk."

Riding back to Manhattan in his pickup, Max was crashing fast. He pulled over, snorted a couple lines to pump himself back up, then continued back to the city.

He parked on the street in Harlem near Precious's, got into the building when someone was leaving. Went up to her apartment, busted down the door, knowing no one gave a shit in this tenement, doors got busted down here all the time. He heard the shower running. He approached like Norman Bates.

"Maxie, mon, you're alive!"

"Yeah, but you're not," he went, and blew her away with the Heckler.

FIVE

I admire a man who can throw a saddle on a gift horse.
HOUSE OF CARDS

Joe Miscali had started out of the 1-9, back in the day when a cop wasn't too pushed on procedure. Meaning you could beat the livin' daylights out of a perp and not have to justify it.

He was almost a caricature of the beat cop. OD'ing on jelly doughnuts, caffeine way beyond ulcer alert, stomach bulging against his shirt—white of course, and soiled.

If he'd read books, he'd have read McBain. Though not Irish himself—he was 100 percent Italian—he had adopted the code of the Irish cops. Summed up in three basic tenets:

Fuck 'em
Fuck 'em twice
Fuck 'em all

Life had never been good for Joe, but it had been worse lately. He'd recently had his second quadruple bypass in three years, his ex-wife was engaged—to a fucking opera singer—and he couldn't remember the last time he'd made a bust.

On top of all this, he was depressed, popping Prozacs like sucking candies.

He was off his game in every way possible and it wasn't like he deserved it. Rumors were going around that he was getting soft in his old age—fifty-four now, thinking about taking an early retirement package next year. He hadn't minded the talk when he was the star of the department, had all the street cred.

But lately he'd lost his edge and everything was going steadily to shit.

Joe carried a Glock but hadn't actually fired it on duty in years. Like a lot of Homicide cops, he arrived after the deed was done. But he dreamed of using it, on Max Fisher.

Years back, he'd gone on a routine wife-murdered call with his ex-partner, Kenneth Simmons. Little knowing they were about to embark on a crusade that would end with Kenneth six feet under and Joe wishing he was down there with him. The husband, Max Fisher, was the killer. No freaking doubt. But as it was to be with all things Fisher, it was complicated.

Not least by a psycho named Dylan. A stone-cold Irish freak, ex-IRA madman who, get this, dabbled in poetry, and, oh yeah, murder.

Enter stage left the femme fatale, Angela Petrakos. She would by turns enchant, infuriate, and intimidate Joe. But, fucking Fisher, he was the one who'd haunt Miscali forever. He was the fuck-up that started Joe's downward spiral. Joe had gotten bad info on a drug deal and while he had half the NYPD staking out a location in Staten Island there'd been a bloodbath in Queens. Okay, it wasn't as bad as Clinton missing Osama, but it had been his personal shitstorm. He could have gotten Fisher that day and saved dozens of lives, but instead the ass-clown got away and went on to kill again.

It seemed like it was over when Fisher went down for first-degree murder, got shipped up to Attica for thirty-to-life. But then came the news of the prison break, and that Fisher was missing. A manhunt ensued, but it seemed like Fisher had vanished. Some presumed he was dead, may have even been killed by a member of his own crew. Joe hoped a body would be discovered, maybe Fisher had even offed himself. But, nope—no body, no Fisher. He was convinced Fisher was still out there and would someday, somehow bite him in the ass again.

And the case was still open. There were occasional reports of Fisher sightings, leads in Phoenix, St. Louis, Florida, various parts of Mexico, even one in Thailand. The most credible was the sighting in Florida, Boca. Joe had flown down there on the NYPD's dime, only to discover that "Fisher" was actually Donald Goldenberg, a divorce attorney. Miscali wound up using Goldenberg to handle his divorce, figuring he could do worse than a Jewish lawyer from Boca. Figured wrong as Goldenberg bungled the case, costing Joe thousands. Joe blamed Fisher for this, too.

Joe's C.O., tired of the Fisher obsession, barked at Joe, "Get the fuck over this and go catch me some rugheads."

Like that would happen.

Joe Miscali was about to knock off his shift when his new partner, Leonard, hollered, "Got us a live one." Paused. "Well, a dead one actually."

Joe was bone weary, sighed, "No one else catching?"

They went up to Harlem. The beat cop led Joe and Leonard to the scene. A busty black chick, a three-time loser named Precious Orange, got her brains blown out in the shower.

NYPD's version of Dexter was there, said, "Looks like it was Norman Bates with a Heckler."

A few minutes later, they got a call from Brooklyn, as it looked like the same weapon had been used in a mass drug-related shooting in East New York.

Leonard said to Joe, "Guess we're going to sunny Brooklyn."

Joe groaned.

Leonard drove an old Crown Vic that he seemed to think was some souped-up shit and drove accordingly, siren playing, said, "Man, I never tire of this shit."

The crime scene was a blitzkrieg of cops, civilians, CSI, more cops.

And it being Brooklyn, a hotdog vendor.

Joe was brought up to speed by the on-site guy who said, "We're hearing PIMP."

Joe looked over a heap of bodies, asked, "A pimp took out all these guys?"

The guy shook his head, explained. "It's a drug. The new kid on the block—well, all over. PIMP is the new drug of choice for the five boroughs."

Joe watched as Leonard ambled over to a basketball court and shot the breeze with the kids gathered there, then walked quickly back, said, "Joe, how you feel about hitting Williamsburg?"

"Why, you run out of wool caps and funny glasses?"

Leonard didn't get it, said, "Got a whisper a dealer is on the corner there, with all the PIMP you can handle."

They blasted over there, Leonard hooting and yapping, making Joe's head ache even more. They scooped up the dealer, who was indeed on the corner as reported. Leonard, no frills, picked the kid up, threw him in the back, the kid going, "The fuck, yo?"

Drove to a quiet alley and shook out the kid's cargo pants, packets of dope spilling on the ground, the kid shouting, "Not mine, ain't never seen this shit before."

Leonard made sure no iPhones were around, then gave a slap to the side of the kid's head, not hard but sufficient.

Joe grabbed the kid, shoved him against the Vic, said, "I've had me a long day, my freaking head is like, about to explode, so if you want to walk from this, tell us who the main guy is."

The kid, already street legal, said, "Might need that in writing, mothafucka."

Leonard said, "Of course." Kneed him in the balls, said, "Can you read the small print?"

The kid didn't have a whole lot, had only once seen the main man, said, "He looks like that dude in *Hunger Games*."

Leonard looked at Joe who tried, "Donald Sutherland?"

Nope.

Then the kid said, "He got like an Oscar for playing a faggot."

That was lost on them.

The kid sighed, dumb fucking cops, then said, "Hey, the dude like OD'd, you know, it was in the news an' shit."

Joe went, "Heath Ledger?"

"Damn," the kid said. "Don't y'all got cable or all you white people just be watchin' Netflix?" Then he got it, spat, "Hoffman, with like a cat's name before it."

Leonard, delighted, said, "Sylvester?"

"Fuck, man," the kid said. "Y'all be on PIMP like all the hipsters?"

Then Joe said, "Seymour."

The kid went, "Duh."

Joe made a note of this, his gut churning. This whole case was bringing up a familiar sick feeling, but he wasn't sure why.

They got in the car, threw the dope in the trunk. The kid moaned, "Hey, you can't leave me without my product an' shit."

Joe said, "You're right, here's something you can sell," and flipped him a rusty St. Christopher medal he'd found on the street.

Leonard cackled and as they drove off, he said, "That was like, low, man."

Joe nearly smiled, said, "What can I tell you? I'm a piece of work."

A couple weeks later, the suspect was still at large in the Harlem and Brooklyn shootings, and the Commissioner was coming down hard on the whole force, demanding an arrest. Joe was regretting his fifth coffee of the day, his gut felt like something putrid had curled up in there and died. He did what you do, began to chew on a jelly doughnut, mix it up.

Leonard sat on the edge of his desk, said, "You see the cooler of brews the new next-door tenant sent by?"

Joe, uninterested, went, "New tenant, huh?"

"Yeah, he's throwing a little shindig for some movers and shakers, asked us to drop by, grab some eats."

Joe smirked, said, "Partiers kissing ass with hot dogs so we don't bust 'em, eh?"

Leonard stood, pushed, "Joe, c'mon, don't be always hard-core, lighten up. Me and the guys going over there now, why not tag along?"

"Can't see how it could in any way be of interest to me."

Joe didn't go.

A few hours later, Leonard came back, could barely stand.

"How was it?" Joe asked.

"Fuckin' great, my main man." Leonard tried to give Joe a high five, but missed, stumbled. Then he regained some balance and slurred, "Never saw the host though. Wall ta wall people in d'ere."

Leonard already had his dick in his hand, on his way to the bathroom.

When Joe left, the party was still raging, hip-hop blasting. A party like that, right across from the precinct? Joe didn't know who the host was, but he knew one thing—the cocksucker had some pair.

SIX

All of us that started the game with a crooked cue,
that wanted so much, and got so little,
that meant so good and did so bad.
All of us.
JIM THOMPSON

Larry got a smarmy doctor, Dr. Hoff—The Hoff, he called himself—to make a house call. Hoff was at one time attached to a major studio until he, um, *overprescribed* to a *Batman* actor and the guy bought the farm. Now he supplied Larry and other players in the biz with an abundance of scripts, and not the Final Draft variety.

Hoff examined the gunshot wound, went, "Not serious."

Larry wanted to wallop him, said, "Not fucking serious for *you*. It hurts like a son of a bitch."

A pause as they both knew this meant, Vike.

Hoff, wanting to at least feel appreciated, said, "Gunshot wound, you know I'm supposed to report this."

Larry slapped him on the side of the head, said, "Yeah and I'm supposed to helm the next *X-Men* but like that's gonna happen."

Hoff handed him a couple of scripts, asked, "You going to report it?" He looked around, asked, "And, by the way, how's your wife? Haven't seen the little woman in a while."

Something in his tone whipped Larry's head around. He snapped,

"What's that mean?"

Hoff sighed, went, "Well, it's called manners, or even consideration."

Larry took a long moment, wondering, *Is the Hoff fucking my wife?* Did they have a fight, a falling out, leading to the kidnapping? One time—maybe three months ago—he recalled Hoff calling his house, Hoff sounding surprised when Larry picked up.

"But why did you say you haven't seen in her a *while*?" Larry asked.

"Because I haven't?" Was Hoff confused or pretending to be confused?

"But you made a point of it. So I'm wondering why that is. If I haven't seen somebody in a while I ask, Hey, how you been? I don't make a point of saying it's been a *while*."

"I...I'm not following."

"You drink Sam Adams, Doc?"

"What?" Hoff asked.

"Sam Adams. It's a beer."

"I know it's a beer. Why do you care what kind of fucking beer I drink?"

"Hey, manners, Doc, manners," Larry said.

"I don't drink beer," the doctor said.

Lying? Yeah, probably. Larry knew the face of a two-shit liar. He saw it in the mirror every morning.

Larry stared at him, went, "You know anything about two guys, Mo and Jo?"

Hoff squinted, went, "Who?"

"Mo and Jo. You know, as in bad mojo."

The doc gathered up his stuff, muttered, "Story of my life." Then added, "Better double on the Vike. I don't wanna know what happened to you, but it's fucking with your head."

That evening, Larry, coasting on a Vike, called Brandi, said, "Come by my place."

She was surprised, asked if his wife minded.

Larry giving a bitter laugh said, "She's got a whole load of other shit on her mind."

When Brandi arrived, she was dressed in Lindsay Lohan mode, i.e., almost nothing and strutting it. Larry had wrangled some of the blue magic pills from the disgruntled doc and was indeed The Rod.

After the third round, she said, "Now that's A-list baby." She cooed and purred and added, "You're the Hollywood sign, sugar."

He poured them some lethal shots of tequila, said, "So *Bust*, what's the story?"

"I already told you."

"Tell me again. I'm a movie producer, I have fucking A.D.D. You think I pay attention to a pitch the first time around?"

She outlined the plot, about Max Fisher and Angela Petrakos, the drug dealing, the serial killing, the prison break. "It's got it all. And best, it's true."

"Jesus Christ, what's wrong with these people?"

Brandi glared at him. "I thought you wanted crime stories."

Larry shrugged. "Does she have to be half-Irish?"

"What do you have against the Irish?"

"I don't know, but I think she'd be sexier if she was, I don't know, Spanish. Maybe we could attach Salma Hayek."

Larry didn't care about the story, only the box office numbers, but he, yeah, okay, he wanted a shot at banging Salma Hayek.

"She's Irish and she's staying fookin Irish." Don't-fuck-with-me tone.

"Okay, baby, okay," Larry said, not wanting to fuck with her. "Okay, so how'm I supposed to get the rights?"

Brandi smiled, the hook, said, "First off, my name isn't really Brandi Love."

"Somebody in Hollywood with a fake name, wow, shocking. What, you think my name's really Larry Reed?"

"What's your real name?"

"Laurence Olivier Horowitz. No, shit, my mother was a big Olivier fan, loved him in *Carrie*, not the *Carrie* you're thinking of, another fucking *Carrie*. Me, named after a B-flick. Shoulda known, right?"

"I don't get it," Brandi said. "So why don't you use the name Laurence Olivier? If my name was Marilyn Monroe or, fook, Marilyn Manson, I'd fookin use it."

"Thought about it," Larry said, "but it's too British. Nobody trusts a Brit in Hollywood—why do you think Piers Morgan got voted off *Celebrity Apprentice*? Besides, Larry Reed, is snappy, it's cool. When you hear Larry Reed, you think Lou Reed. It's called subliminal influence. I'm serious, don't laugh. A name says a lot about a person."

"Well, I'm afraid my name isn't the only thing I lied to you about," Brandi said.

Here we go. After his last girl on the side said that to him he wound up having to go to the Hoff to treat a bad case of syphilis.

"You don't have syphilis, do you?" he asked. "'Cause I don't think you get immune to that, like chicken pox."

"Nope, no syphilis," Brandi said. "That I know of anyway. But I hope you've had genital herpes."

Was she joking? He couldn't tell. He forced a smile, hoping so.

"But it's my background I haven't been entirely truthful about," she went on. "It's true I'm an actress, but I've mostly done porn, and there's a reason why I changed my name, and it wasn't for my acting career. At least not initially."

Larry, still thinking about herpes, wondering if that's why

L-Rod had seemed kind of itchy this morning, couldn't follow what she was saying.

"Okay, okay, so who are you?" he asked, agitated.

"Angela. Angela Petrakos. And don't let the Greek exterior fool you, I'm like one of those Oreos they serve on St. Patty's Day—green on the inside."

The fuck was this crazy chick talking about?

"Am I supposed to know an Angela Petrakos?" Larry asked.

"Have you been listening to a fookin' word I'm saying? *Bust*. I'm the star of *Bust*, that fookin' book by Stiegsson and Segal, it's all about me. It's my life. Max Fisher, you might know him as The Max, is my ex. But that's another story. Or part of the main story, depending how you look at it."

"Hold up," Larry said. "You're saying you're a *character* in this novel?"

"It's not a novel, it's my life," Angela said. "These people, these writers, are fookin' criminals, they stole my life. I deserved that money, it's mine, fookin' mine. Fook, the pain I've met falling for the wrong men—Max Fisher, Thomas Dillon, Slide—yeah, *that* Slide—Sebastian, Rufus—and I'm not getting' a fookin' cent of it?"

"Okay, back up, back up," Larry said. "I wanna make sure I'm getting this straight. You're in this book so you think, what, that entitles you to a piece of the TV show?"

"Not just a piece," Angela said. "A fookin' chunk."

"Sweetheart, that's not the way it works," Larry said. "The producer, I remember now, I think I saw in the trades, it's Darren Becker. He probably optioned the book or, knowing Darren, purchased the rights outright."

"I don't give a shite who purchased them," she said. "Where I come from in Ireland we pay in cash and possession is eleven tenths of the law."

Larry shook his head, as in, *Did I need this shit today?* and said, "I don't need this shit today." Added, "I don't think you get the way things work in this town, sweetheart." Talking down on purpose to the ditzy broad. "This isn't fuckin' Bollywood where they fuck buying the rights and steal the damn book. If Becker has the rights to the book now, it's his, he owns it. No one else can make it except Darren Becker."

Larry went to sit where his favorite club chair, the one from Crate & Barrel, had been, and fell onto his ass.

"Jesus Christ," he said. "I think I broke my hip."

"Only thing you'll break is my eardrums with yer whining," Angela said. "Get the fook up, ye wimp."

She was psycho and bitchy as hell but, yeah, he was kind of into it. She'd look good in some tight black-leather getup, holding a whip.

"Up," she barked. "You need to help me with this situation."

Larry struggled to his feet and said, "I have another situation here, a little more important than making a TV show. As you noticed, my wife isn't home."

"Yeah, I noticed your wound before, too," Angela said. "Figured you offed the cow."

Was she kidding?

"She was *taken*," Larry said, "and unfortunately I'm not Liam fuckin Neeson, or his stunt man, so I can't exactly hunt down the guys that did it."

"Who took her?" Angela asked. She seemed comfortable, like she was in her element, talking about kidnapping.

"Mo and Jo," Larry said.

"Like the Three Stooges?"

"It's two people, not three, and there's no Stooge named Jo." Was he seriously having this conversation? "Actually I think my doctor might be in on it."

"Your doctor?"

Larry grabbed the empty bottle of Sam Adams and said, "See this? This is evidence. I think she was fucking somebody behind my back."

"Your doctor."

"Probably."

"And I thought I attract the crazies."

Ignoring this, Larry went. "They want seventy-five K and I think these guys are serious. I'm worried they might be raping her as we speak, and I'm broke, have nada, ziltch, bubkis. I put up a good front with my whole aura of being a high-flying producer, but I'm behind on my office rent and home mortgage, have credit card debt up the wazoo. There's no way I can come up with that kind of cashish."

Angela sat in a leather chair, put her feet up on the ottoman, expanded her chest, and said, "Well, it sounds like you need a piece of *Bust* then, don't you?"

An idea was hitting Larry—maybe crazy enough to work.

If he could get his eyes off her tits he might even be able to verbalize it.

Finally he said, "What if you went to Darren Becker's house? Darren's a player. If you get close to him maybe we can blackmail him, that's the way anything gets done in this town." Then he shook his head. "Ah, fuck, it won't work."

"Why not?"

"Darren's gay, or at least partly gay. I saw him at one of Bryan Singer's pool parties."

"What were *you* doing at the party?"

"I was just, um, experi…never mind. But I guess the question is, could you seduce a half-gay guy?"

"Not a problem," Angela said. "A few weeks ago in the bathroom at the Chateau Marmont I scored with Bret Easton Ellis."

Thinking about it more, Larry knew what to do. Larry had known Darren forever. Darren had had a few sex scandals over the years; he'd gotten out from under them, but he didn't need any more bullshit on his plate. Larry could see him going for this.

"If the seduction doesn't work, just tell him who you are—Angela Titcockass, or whatever the fuck it is. If you threaten a lawsuit, going to the trades, he'll freak and agree to go into business with us. You get me attached as co-exec of *Bust* and then I can sell a percentage of the film, points to private investors. With a little luck I can drum up enough to get my wife back."

"This sounds great," Angela said, "but why do you need me? Why don't you blackmail him yourself?"

"Me and Darren Becker, let's just say we have a history," Larry said. "In other words, I think you'll make a better impression."

"Okay…" Angela said. "But you're forgetting one thing."

Larry was confused.

"Hello?" Angela said. "My role?"

"Oh, you'll get a part on the show, sweetie, don't worry."

"If you think I'm going to go over there, seduce this fookin' guy, for a *part*, you're mad. I'm a player, goddamn it, not a whore. Well, I have been a whore—but not anymore, I'm a Hollywood player now, and ya better get used to it, I'm co-executive producing with you, Larry."

"Whoa, baby, take it easy there, using your brain like that, you might pull something." He smiled, loving how fucking witty he was, making a crack he'd made thousands of times before. Then said, "What do you know about producing, sweetheart?"

"After spending a few days with you, I apparently don't have to know much. At least I know how to turn on a fookin' PC."

"Okay, okay, you can produce, you can produce," Larry said, just wanting to shut her the fuck up, the Irish accent grating on him. He figured they could deal with it later and he'd rip the dumb bitch off on the points. He'd drop her down to associate producer, or the ultimate bullshit, co-producer.

"That's not all," Angela said. "If I'm going to sleep with him I'm going to star in the show too. No one can play Angela better than me."

"Honey," Larry said. "Producing's one thing, but I have no control over the casting, that's up to the studio and the network."

"A moment ago you were promising me a part on the show!"

"A part, sure—not the fucking lead. I can get you an audition, but that's it."

"You mean I have to audition to play myself?"

Larry smiled, went, "Welcome to Hollywood, sweetie."

SEVEN

Women can be tricky.
NORMA BATES

In the cab to Darren Becker's house in the Hollywood Hills, Angela was dressed in a black faux-leather short skirt, white silk top, and black-patent drill heels, and felt almost like in the glory days of real hotness. A surge of confidence was aided by a few fast lines of coke. Time to manipulate and seduce.

"Fookin A," she said, an in-joke to herself, a dark legacy from the days she first encountered Max Fisher.

Phew-oh, a time that was. A blend of hot sex, wild schemes, and of course Dylan. Ah, the mad Mick. If he was capable of loving anything save his shitty poetry, it might well have been Angela. Too many years, too much poverty, too many escapades had blotted out the negative side of the crazy Irishman, so that now she tended to color him as *a lovable scamp*—a psycho scamp, but lovable. It was one of the myriad lies she sold her own self just to keep some semblance of sanity. And all the years of utter mayhem that slid down the pike after—jail in Greece, a savior who was a dead ringer for Lee Child, and then being shot in Canada by the dead ringer...

Drink Canada Dry. She had sure tried to.

Literally at death's door, she had been rescued by a mammoth guy who made his living pretending to be Bigfoot. And she'd thought, *Once, just fooking once, couldn't Brad Pitt be in her rescue*, but no, the freaking luck she had, she'd gotten Bigfoot.

He took her to a local hospital with a story of how a Bigfoot hunter had shot at him, but hit her instead. They had to remove one of her lungs, but in the end it was the Bigfoot guy who really took her breath away. He was such a sweet guy and, silver linings, he was big in other departments—turned out the big feet, big cock adage was true—and she almost forgave the insanity of being shacked up with an urban legend. It may even have lasted for a time but wouldn't you know, the guy was so convincing that a mild accountant from Toronto bagged him on a slow weekend.

On the phone to his wife yelling, "I tagged Bigfoot."

She going, "Try tagging your big mouth."

So Angela, sighing anew, took the stash of cash Bigfoot had amassed and went to London. She hadn't been charged with any crime, no one knew she'd helped Max and his gang escape from prison, so she was free and clear, bought a one-way ticket for London.

One-way because she knew there was a good chance she'd wind up in jail her own self.

She was hunting for Sebastian, Lee Child's psycho double. After he'd shot her, and she was lying on the ground at that gas station, bleeding out, she'd remembered how in bed, when they were in love in Greece, he'd once called her an "Irish guttersnipe." He'd said it in a sexy way, as in, "Take in every inch of me, you bloody Irish guttersnipe!" and admittedly it had excited her when he was, as he used to say, rogering her—but, as far as Angela was concerned, relationships were all fun and games only till you lose an eye…or a lung. In other words, when somebody shoots you, the game shifts from romance to vengeance. She promised herself that if she survived she wouldn't rest until she hunted him down, killed him like one of the quails he'd claimed he'd shot, growing up in the English countryside.

Was it true? Who knew what was real and what wasn't with Sebastian? The man had more stories than Joran van der Sloot.

After months of traveling around England, sick from the food, she had no luck finding Sebastian and her cash was dwindling. When you're down and out in London, unless you are George flipping Orwell, all you get out of it is utter desperation. Angela had a bedsit in Earls Court. It has been written that those whom God forsakes are given an electric fire in Earls Court.

Amen to fucking that, Angela would have said, but her mouth was full of Asian dick. Not by choice but for money, a low-level porno, shot by Russians for the Chinese market. Gawd, don't you love the free economy?

The Russian director was shouting, "Brandi, look like you love dis ting!"

Yeah, they'd named her Brandi Love, she could put a little smiley face on the *i* if she wished. She made enough money to get by, shooting a series of these, featuring "Brandi with Ginger."

Ginger wasn't Ginger, and maybe not even female, but for art, hey, who cares? What Ginger had was a supply of coke which got them through most of the shoots. Angela wanted to go to L.A., take her newfound acting talent mainstream. She had the chops, and if Glenn Close could still cut it, hell, she had a shot her own self.

Ginger managed to get her a passport but alas put Brandi Love on it. When Angela had enough cash put by, she stole Ginger's purse, thus netting a cool grand and a haul of coke.

The experience with the porn shoots got Angela thinking about a career in film and TV. She'd always wanted to act, and don't they say all actors are great liars? If there was one thing she was good at...

So it was sayonara London, hello L.A.

On the flight out of Heathrow, she thought about Ginger,

whom she'd liked—but not enough to really give a fuck.

At passport control, the official had seen number two of the *Brandi with Ginger* series and, starstruck, said, "Never met a real porn actress in the flesh. Wouldn't've thought you girls use your real name."

Angela, barely able to credit her luck with this schmuck, cooed, "Bet you'd like to play Ginger's part…"

And was waved through, thinking, *Sex flies*.

Like so many before, Angela arrived in L.A. with big dreams and a big bust, but when your tits sag you can get surgery—not much to do for a fading dream.

The first few weeks in town were the same old, poverty, bad dire sex and desperation. Killing time when cash was so low became an art form. Plus, she still had to stay hip to the scene if she was to lure a guy with serious clout. One evening she was so desperate she even went to a bookstore reading, the last refuge of the penniless and the deranged. It was for a mystery writer named Bob Steel. Quite a respectable crowd had showed, which suited Angela, but she had to wait until after for the wine to be served, so they could flog more books.

Bob was a card, as in hilarious. Angela knew this as Bob said so, twice. He then thanked

His wife

His agent

His publisher

His typist

His gardener

His neighbors (named them all)

And just about all of his high school.

Oddly none of the above had been able to tear away from busy schedules to attend.

Then he read the first five chapters of his book, titled *Steel or Die*. The blurb by some Irish guy said he was the new Lee Child, and even just hearing that name again gave her shivers. The chapters were long and Angela felt Child had no immediate cause for concern. When it was finally over, Angela rushed to the wine table and downed two cups of some putrid plonk, appropriately served in the little plastic cups used for urine samples. Looked to see if there were any eats and came face to face with Bob.

He seemed overjoyed to meet her, gushed, "So, how did you like the book?"

"Riveting," Angela said.

He filled her cup, leering slightly, said, "My Amazon rating is seven hundred ninety-eight thousand and the book has only been out a few months."

Angela figured she needed two more cups of the awful wine to help her sleep, so asked, with absolutely zero energy, "Got any movie interest?"

His eyes widened. "You think it would work as a film?"

"No doubt."

Then he frowned, went, "Thing is, I don't know if I should go with the straight movie deal or hold out for a TV show."

She managed, "Be sure to keep control of the character, I mean, a creation like Steel, they will all want a piece of him."

He was nodding furiously, then said, "I think maybe I'll do fifteen in the series, then go for a standalone."

Jesus, she thought, said, "What the world is crying out for."

Angela didn't buy Bob's book, but another book caught her eye—a towering pile of a new book called *Bust*, published by Hard Case Crime. Angela was familiar with Hard Case. Years ago, when she was Max Fisher's executive assistant—didn't those days almost seem quaint?—she needed some cash and posed for one of the covers. She liked the cover of *Bust*—an image of a camera and a surprised old guy and a sexy woman in the lens. The scene seemed familiar somehow, but she wasn't sure why. She wasn't planning to read the book but, fuck it, she bought it.

Bob followed her out of the store, going, "Wanna go for some brewskies? I'm paying for my own tour but, hey, long as we discuss the book, beers are tax deductions, right?"

Later, in a side street, as he anticipated a BJ, she kneed him in the balls, took his wallet, said as she weaved away, "Deduct that."

Sadly, Angela was making more from these hustles than she was from her acting. Aside from a half-day shoot in *The Walking Dead* and a few lines in a dreadful revival of *A Long Day's Journey into Night*—they wanted her for her American/Irish accent—she hadn't gotten any work at all. Money tight, she had to work part-time for an escort service. She didn't mind the screwing—compared to Russian/Chinese porn it was like free money—but the insults got to her. Guys thirty years older than she was, calling her a MILF? It made her think of her own long day's journey into what was shaping up to be a cold, bitter night.

Then, on yet another sun-filled morning in L.A., Angela was at her local Starbucks near the strip. Behind her was a long-haired guy with hip shades. She wondered if Starbucks had mass-produced this guy and planted him in the corner of every branch. Going for that hip draw of, *Hey, you too can be a writer*.

When the guy left, giving her a radiant smile that said, *Yeah, we both know I'm hot to trot*, Angela noticed he'd left behind a copy of *Variety*.

She had begun to flick idly when she saw a big announcement of a major TV deal for a hot new bestseller, *Bust*. She remembered it was the book she'd bought, so she read on.

"Jaysus wept!" She shouted so loud the other writers in the

store looked up from their laptops to see what the fuss was about.

Angela read the story at least ten times, to make sure she wasn't missing anything. But she wasn't: *Bust* was *her* story. Paula Segal, that little tramp from New York, had teamed with some Swedish writer to write the book, which was now being "fast-tracked" for a TV series. Lionsgate was the studio and a guy named Darren Becker was the Executive Producer. It was like a feckin' nightmare or a joke—a joke with no punch line.

Later, Angela read more about the project online. There were rumors that Ethan Coen would write the pilot and David Fincher would direct, and she watched a video on YouTube from *CBS Sunday Morning* of the Swedish guy—can you believe that fookin' name?—Lars Stiegsson. Angela had heard about him from Ginger; he'd once had a notorious legendary rep in the porn industry, but she'd had no idea that he was a crime writer. Jaysus, Mary and Joseph, seemed like you could throw a dead cat and hit a crime writer these days. Watching the interview, Angela tasted vomit as Stiegsson tearfully told his story of how Stieg Larsson had ripped off his whole career and how fulfilling it was to now, years later, finally hit it big with *Bust*.

Angela read the book in one setting, amazed at how well Paula, that cunt, and the Swedish pornographer had captured the entire story. It was all almost exactly the way it had happened. A few names had been changed, some of the dialogue had been altered, but the major events were all there. In particular Angela loved the chapter where she tried to dissolve Dillon's body with Drano in her Gramercy Park studio. Angela felt they'd really captured the psychosis, delusion, and rage that had been boiling inside her at the time. She read these passages aloud, feeling like she was back there, living it.

While Angela admired the novel, the reality of the current

situation was setting in—Angela was a third-rate escort, sucking off the dregs of Hollywood, and Segal and Steigsson were making millions on Angela's life story.

She had to find a way in.

A few days later, at a dull party in Santa Monica thrown by Charlie Sheen's dogsitter who, of course, was also a screenwriter, she met an old, sleazy producer, Larry Reed. Hard to find one of those in Hollywood, right? She hoped he could help her get an in on *Bust*, or thought at the very least he'd be an easy score. She'd work for him for a while, suck him off a few times, then rob him blind.

It seemed to be heading toward the "rob him blind" option until he invited her to his place and told him a crazy story about how his wife had been kidnapped and he badly needed money— the sort of money *Bust* could give them both. He came up with a crazy, desperate plan to get in on the deal. While Angela didn't give a shite about Larry Reed, or his kidnapped wife, she thought it was worth a shot. She had a feeling that this was her last shot. It was *Bust* or bust.

Angela arrived at Darren Becker's, the driver letting the fare slide in return for her fake phone number.

It was quite an estate, had to be twenty rooms. Tall bushes, a brick pathway leading to the house, a Merc and Caddy in the drive, probably for show. There was probably a pool, guest house in the back, maybe Kato living there. Angela wondered what movies this guy had done to get a set-up like this. Darren Becker. She'd never seen the name before she'd read that *Variety* article. But he had to be somebody, somebody worth getting close to.

Rang the bell and Christ, heard *Tubular Bells*, who the hell even knew what it was outside of Irish writers. The door opened to a surfer dude, seemed to be in his early twenties, with a mop of shaggy blond hair, cut-offs, and washed-out blue eyes. Thrown for a moment, she faltered, "Um…Darren Becker?"

One-hundred-watt smile and, "Was me when I woke up."

She was thinking, the wonders of cosmetic surgery, and said, "Larry Reed sent me over to discuss a terrific movie opportunity."

The guy seemed like he wasn't totally up to speed—with anything—said, "Well, let's get your sexy self inside."

And, no fooling around, she went for it, going, "Wouldn't mind your own sexy self inside me."

Took a moment for this to sink in, then the grin again and, "Works for me."

Right there in the hall, they got to it and moments before the, um, bell tolled, she heard, "The fuck is this?"

A man in his late fifties coming down the impressive stairway, dressed like, yeah, a movie guy. Shades hanging from the collar of the white angora sweater with rolled-up sleeves, the de rigeur outfit for moguls of a certain vintage.

The guy underneath her, managed, "Dad!"

She thought, "Oh fuckit."

Managed to stand, get her clothes in some sort of order, said, "Mr. Becker, I admit I thought if I could charm the son, I might actually seal the deal with the dad."

Becker considered, obviously thought this was horseshit, said, "This is horseshit," and had his cell out.

"Who are you calling?" Angela asked. "The police?"

"Worse for you. Private security. Ex-Oakland Raiders."

Okay, a setback, but Angela was sometimes at her very best at these moments of imminent unraveling. She rushed, "I look familiar to you?"

Angela didn't think the call had connected yet.

"What?" Becker asked.

"My stage name is Brandi Love, but my real name is Angela Petrakos."

Becker was squinting. "You audition for me?"

"Hello, I'm in the fookin' book you're producing. Is the cliché real? Doesn't anybody read books in L.A.?"

"Honest answer? I haven't read a book since *The Firm* in 1991. When you make it as a producer you hire people to read for you. It's called coverage."

"Well you'll cover your eyes when you hear this. The book is based on me, my life, and if you produce it, it's slander. I'm lawyered up."

She was throwing all the *Law & Order* she could think of at the guy.

But it didn't seem to be working because Becker said, "Good, you'll need a team of lawyers to get out of this. Too bad for you Marcia Clark's writing mystery novels these days." Into his cell, Larry went, "Hey, yeah we have a situation here…" He was right up in her face now, but said to his son, who was still bottomless, "Go fuck some waves." He waited until the son had slouched away, then into the phone he continued, "Yeah, there's a woman at my place, she broke in and she won't—"

"A Bryan Singer pool party ring any bells?" Angela asked.

Becker was staring at her, slight look of uncertainty, then granite. "Don't know what you're referring to."

Angela heard a voice on the phone, a woman saying, "You still there? Mr. Becker? Mr. Becker?"

He ended the call.

She pushed, "Oh a very wild party, back in the day and the photos, damn, they are…loaded."

He considered a bluff, stonewalling, then caved, asked, "Whatchya drinking?"

He poured her a Jameson, straight, and a Bud Light for himself.

As he handed her the drink, she glanced at his hand, the one with the thick wedding band, and said, "You don't want your wife finding out about your pool party days, I'm sure."

"Actually my husband Ron gave me that ring," Becker said. "I've been divorced from my ex-wife Ellen for twelve years and honestly I don't give a shit what you know about me and Bryan Singer. You wouldn't believe how many A-listers were at those parties. It's like prohibition days in Chicago when the Mayor was drinking with the rest of the town at the speakeasy."

"Last I heard, fucking underage boys is against the law," Angela said.

"Can't be proven," Darren said, "but I don't want to waste my valuable time and resources defending myself against false allegations. I'm sure you don't need big legal bills in your life either. And heaven knows I don't need any hiccups in *my* life right now. I'm doing everything I can to make *Bust* happen."

Angela knew he was playing it cool, not wanting to let on, but he was terrified.

"Sounds like you want to make a deal," Angela said.

"Depends," he said. "What's in it for you?"

As they say at Hard Case Crime—time for the Money Shot.

Angela said, "You bring me and Larry Reed on board as producers and you have my word, I'll keep my mouth shut."

Darren waited then said, "You're out of your fuckin' mind."

Angela downed the Jameson like a marathon runner downs water, then headed toward the door, "I'd keep my eye on the headlines if I were you."

"Okay, let's relax here," Darren said, cutting her off. "No

need to threaten each other. There's always the middle ground, right?"

"Nope, no middle ground," Angela said. "I'm in or my next visit's to Nikki Finke."

"There's no way I'm going into business with that loser Larry Reed. The whole town knows he's poison, the *Cooler* of movies. He hasn't had a hit since that Janeane Garofalo rom-com in the nineties."

"Are you suggesting what I think you're suggesting?" Angela asked.

"I'll work with you, but not Larry. That's my final offer."

Angela thought it through for maybe two seconds. Cut Larry out? Why not? The bastard had been ready to fire her yesterday, kick her guttersnipe arse to the curb, till he needed her, of course.

"Fine, Larry's out," she said, "but there are two conditions— I want the same deal you get with the network, and I get to audition to play myself in the show. I know that no one could play that role better than me."

"That can be arranged," Darren said.

They shook. Darren's hand was small and in Angela's experience the ol' adage was true. She felt sorry for Darren's husband.

Though who knew, maybe Darren was strictly a catcher.

"Looks like this is the beginning of a beautiful friendship," Darren said smiling.

Angela, smiling with him, thinking, *Or not.*

EIGHT

If you remove noir from the mystery novel
you're left with a vague cut above chick lit.
KB AND JS

Paula was over the freaking moon. You spend years being fucked over and, more importantly, passed over and then, out of nowhere, a call, to say, "We would like to publish your novel, *Bust*."

From Charles Ardai himself. Oh heavens to Ardai-betsy. This was it, the break she finally had almost given up on.

Paula had met Charles a few years ago at a meeting of the Outdoor Co-Ed Topless Pulp Fiction Appreciation Society, a bunch of girls who got their tits out in city parks and such, supposedly as a feminist statement but really because they were bi as all get-out and wanted to bang each other. She'd lounged around topless in Central Park with the other sexy babes, reading Lawrence Block, James M. Cain, and Christa Faust. Charles showed up to deliver the reading material. He was a classy guy—she only saw him drool once or twice—but they didn't talk books at all, and at the time she never dreamed she'd ever be published by Hard Case herself.

The publication news was even sweeter because just a few months earlier she didn't think the book would get written at all. Working with Stiegsson had been a nightmare, with the little Rumplestiltskin's constant fretting and middle-of-the-night texts and e-mails—*We must change this line of dialogue, Max Fisher would never say this; I must write the sex scenes because*

I understand heterosexual sex much better than you do—it went on and on. The Swede couldn't write Irish *or* American dialogue, so Paula had to do all of the heavy lifting, and, worst of all, he was humorless, as bleak as Stellan Freakin' Skarsgard. Paula, of course, was known for her sardonic wit. Marilyn Stasio had used the word "droll" in that *Times* review, David Montgomery had called her "witty" on his blog, and in declining a blurb request Charlaine Harris had written Paula that one of the books in her St. Martin's series "made me chuckle." The only one who disagreed was some putz at *Booklist* who'd called her humor "forced," but that guy didn't know noir from shinola.

Oh, the other thing with Stiegsson—he was constantly trying to have cybersex with her. In the Skype sessions he'd say, "Please, one time, your naked breasts, I save screenshot." No matter how many times she told him she was gay it didn't seem to register. Didn't they have dykes in Sweden?

Though there were times she regretted the decision to write with the horny Swede, they somehow hit their stride in the book while writing the chapters with Dillon and Angela—Stiegsson, maybe from personal experience, did write great psychos—and they seriously got in gear writing the chapter where Bobby Rosa, the paraplegic, busts into the hotel room and takes the damning photo of Max and Angela. That's when Paula sent Lars an excited email of her own in the middle of the night—*I have the title: how about BUST???*—and after that the book seemed to take on a life of its own.

As the publication date approached, expectations were low. Lars wasn't even planning to come to America for the book launch as there was no money for a tour. Paula had done many St. Martin's tours, on her dime, for low-print-run books, and knew this was a surefire way to get dropped *and* go broke— a double kick in the cunt. Charles had arranged for a few features, including one by Tom Callahan in *Penthouse*. Paula was disappointed that they didn't ask her to pose in the buff— it prompted her to write a long tirade about ageism in the pictorial biz on her blog—but it was a nice shout-out for the book.

Then came starred reviews in *Publisher's Weekly*, *Kirkus*, and even one from the noir hater at *Booklist*. Thanks to Ken Tucker, the book was number one on *EW*'s Must List and the TV rights were purchased by Darren Becker, an A-list Hollywood producer, and the show was immediately set up at Lionsgate, the studio behind some of the biggest TV shows and movies—*Mad Men*, *The Follower*, *The Hunger Games*, *Blitz*.

A few days later, a call from Janet Ortiz, Paula's new literary agent: "I have some great news for you, Paula. *Bust* is debuting at Number 7 on *New York Times* bestseller list."

Paula wasn't shocked. The news really only proved what she'd always known about herself. For years she'd been a literary sensation trapped in the skin of a midlist author, and now this was her time to shine.

With number one on the list in sight, Hard Case had arranged for Lars to come to the city after all, for press interviews and to read at the Barnes & Noble at Union Square, and then go on to events in several other cities.

Paula got a call from Charles: "Can you turn *Bust* into a trilogy?"

Paula replied: "Does Reed Coleman co-write?"

Paula revealed that *Bust* would become a trilogy in a *New York Times Magazine* feature, saying that the second book in the series would be called *Slide* and the third *The Max*. Hard Case was already busily designing the covers.

The day Darren Becker's check cleared, it was goodbye Williamsburg couch, hello loft in DUMBO. And it was goodbye IKEA, hello Bobby Flay's decorator.

Celebrate? You better fucking believe it. Dressed to kill, short black leather mini, the drill heels, white silk top and short leather jacket, looked in the mirror, cooed, "Girl, I could bed you myself, you hot author, you."

There were rumors *Bust* was the frontrunner for the Edgar Award for best paperback original, and Paula was already preparing her speech, a blend of humility and humor, finishing with, "Lippman, you my bitch now."

At a bar in Bushwick. Dangerous? She sure hoped so. Had her can of pepper spray and a cute silver .22 she'd got from a Russian wino. She knew about the bar from *Crimespree Magazine*, Jon Jordan wrote how Open Road Media used it to film mystery writers at play.

What-the-fuck-ever.

Place was hopping. She ordered a large vodka, slim-line tonic, moved to the rear to see if maybe she might set a scene from *Slide* in here. A sharp-looking guy literally handed her a joint as he cruised by; it was that kind of evening and she thought, as she inhaled deep, she might persuade Charles to have the next launch party here, get that street vibe jumping. Show that even though she was literary now, she could still slum it with the mystery writers.

Her mind was on overdrive, she could already see Stephen King writing an intro to the ninth edition of *Bust*, or Stevie, as she would then be calling him.

Then she felt eyes on her and turned to see a goth, or at least a chick in all black, glaring at her.

The fuck with that.

Paula was armed in every sense. As a now-successful writer, she was bulletproof, snarled, "Help you with something?" Paused, then added, "B...I...T...C...H."

The woman—girl, really—moved closer. She had jet-black

hair, deep brown eyes and a body to melt for. She asked, "Did you just call me *bitch*?"

Paula felt a frisson, as the A-list might term it, cooed, "Just to get your attention, babe."

Indecision hovered over the girl for a moment, then curiosity won. She asked, "Are you like...somebody?"

Paula gave her best smile, part warmth but mostly manipulation, said, "Oh, you have no idea."

The girl seemed to visibly relax, said, "Oh good, I'm somebody too."

Paula seriously doubted it, the chances of two celebrities in one dive, like, hello?

But she was feeling mellow from the weed, so went, "Really..." It came out almost British: *Railly!* "...and pray tell, child, who that is?"

Summoning up all her energy, the girl said, "The forgotten one, the invisible member of the most famous American family."

Paula thought, the *Obamas*? No. Surely not the Brady Bunch? No, those chicks had to be grandmothers by now.

She fake yawned, went, "I give up."

The girl stared at her dainty feet, whispered, "Kat...Kat Kardashian."

Paula would've laughed, thought it was a bad pickup line, if, holy shit, the chick didn't look like a combo of Kim and Khloe and a little Kourtney in there too. And, yessirree, she had the family big ass. Paula was a fan of a nice *derriere*.

Though it was still hard to believe to believe that a Kardashian was out looking for rough trade at a dyke dive bar in Bushwick.

"You're really one of them?" Paula asked.

Kat rattled off a story of how she'd been estranged from her family for years.

"I wasn't into money and material things so they rejected me. Since high school I've been living on a kibbutz in Israel.

You don't believe me, look…" She took out her iPhone and thumbed through old photos from her childhood and, son of a bitch, there was the young Kat, with Kim, Khloe, Kourtney, and the dad—the one whose claim to fame was that he'd helped Marcia Clark fuck up the O.J. case—on exotic beach vacations and ski trips. There were more recent pictures of her on a kibbutz, hugging a rabbi.

"Fuck me," Paula said, double meaning intended.

On cue, Kat rested her hand on Paula's thigh, and said, "Oh, don't worry, I will, honey."

Paula hadn't picked up anyone at a bar in a long time. The last time she'd tried was at a bar in Attica, New York, when she went up there to visit Max Fisher. Attica, not exactly a party town, and worse, a lesbian-free zone, at least on the night Paula was there.

During a break in the action at the loft in Dumbo, sweaty bodies intertwined, Kat asked, "So who are you?"

"I told you…my name's Paula."

"I didn't ask you what your name is. I asked you who you *are*."

Bitchy, yeah, but sexy.

"I mean you have to be somebody," Kat went on. "Kick-ass apartment, view of the Brooklyn Bridge. Please, just don't tell me you're a Hilton."

"Do you know *Bust*?" Paula asked.

"I know yours now," Kat said, squishing closer.

"No, I mean the bestselling novel, *Bust*, soon to be a TV show from Lionsgate Entertainment."

"Oh, that *Bust*," Kat said. "I think I read a review in *People* while I was tearing out the cover story on Kim and Kanye."

"It was reviewed in *People*?" Paula, asked, full of shit. She'd fucking memorized that rave even though she'd said in the *Times Mag* story, "I never read my reviews." The moral? Don't believe anything you read in the *Times* even if it isn't by Jayson Blair.

"Yes, and it was a good one too," Kat said. "I think I've seen that book on the front page of Amazon."

"You probably have," Paula said pseudo-modestly.

"And you wrote it? Are you serious?" Kat's face was glowing. "Wow, it looks like I'm the starfucker, not you. I just *have* a name, but you *are* a name."

"No, you are the name, hon," Paula said, as it hit her that this was it—the final piece of her puzzle of literary domination.

If anybody wanted to make it to the top these days, if you wanted that extra jolt of cachet, you needed to have a relationship with a Kardashian on your resume. Even if you break up, a Kardashian in your past could help catapult you, or at least get you a reservation at a hot restaurant, sipping the wine right alongside Donna Tartt and Jay McInerny. And not just literary fame—fame fame. Move over Ellen and Rachel, the world of gay women was going to have a new spokeswoman. Hell, it was only a matter of time till Paula had her own TV show. Hello, red carpet. She'd call her show *Paula* and it would become the new *Oprah*.

She turned Kat onto her back and was on top, pinning her down.

"What're you doing?" Kat asked.

Paula kissed her hard, went, "Sealing the deal, you naughty kitty Kat, you."

A few days later Paula arrived arm in arm with Kat at the Barnes & Noble on Union Square for the big reading/signing/discussion of *Bust*.

Here she was, back at the store she had been tossed out of when she'd sort of, well, assaulted Laura Lippman, but now she was returning, as a literary star herself. She'd have to put this in the next book.

Of course Paula was dressed to impress. Hot pants were back, where had they gone? A tight two-sizes-too-small T-shirt that would look like she and Jennifer Aniston hung out and swapped clothes.

The store was crowded. Didn't they say reading was dead? The news hadn't filtered down to these yuppies. Mind you, they were reading but not fucking buying, unless it was a triple grande light decaffeinated vanilla latte. But they were reading, and they were here in the store. What Paula didn't get was why people weren't swarming her. Didn't they read *Penthouse*? It was hard to believe that everyone was like her and just looked at the pictures. Where were the cameras? With a Kardashian in tow the masses were just letting her, like, pass by?

For a fleeting moment it occurred to her that she was behaving a lot like Max Fisher. Was it possible that, like many authors, she'd become too close to her subject? She'd come to know Max so well—his delusional thoughts, his megalomania, his addictions. It was why she'd been able to pull off writing Max as a character, getting in his head, making him seem so real. But had she gone too far? Had she crossed the proverbial line and actually *become* him?

But like Max would, she shrugged off these concerns with, "Ah, fuck it," and continued through the store.

Heading up the escalator, it was hard for Paula not to get sentimental, but she couldn't cry in front of the public and photographers—there had to be photographers around somewhere, right? She went up to the top floor to get a peek of her adoring fans. Would she have more than Hillary Clinton?

Whoa, what the fuck, she had maybe fifty people here, and some were in chairs, drinking coffee and reading magazines, and may not have come for the reading. While fifty people was forty-nine more people than she'd had at the last reading she'd done when the publicist at St. Martin's Press was setting up her events—and the one attendee was the publicist herself—for a bestselling author of her caliber it was a disgrace.

"This is a disgrace!" she shouted.

"Calm down, baby," Kat said. "All will be well. Everyone's probably at the coffee bar."

It was so soothing to have a Kardashian by her side. Kat was like the pony, leading the racehorse to the starting gate.

There was Charles Ardai engaged in a conversation with Lars Stiegsson, taking about porn, or whatever straight men talk about. Paula blew a kiss to Charles, but he was too engrossed to notice her. Paula's agent Janet came over to Kat and seemed enamored when she heard the word, "Kardashian."

"Where are my fans?" Paula whined to Janet. "Where are my handlers?"

So much for soothing.

"I'm not sure," Janet said distractedly. Then to Kat, "So what was it like on the kibbutz?"

"Never mind, I'll do it myself," Paula said, and stormed away.

This was perfect—a tantrum, that's what all the celebs did, right? Maybe she should start toppling bookshelves, kicking and punching security. It would be very AlecBaldwinian; was TMZ here? In the aftermath, she could blame her fame, then admit she had a problem and check in for some rehab, and then get out, pull a Lindsay, and go on a coke binge. Or what was that new drug she'd read about, the one related to those shootings in Brooklyn? PIMP. Yeah, PIMP. She'd go on a PIMP binge.

Paula returned to the ground floor, still surprised she hadn't already been stopped numerous times for autographs, and sashayed to the information desk. That's right, *sashayed*, because she was the new female literary star and that meant she could be as big of a sexy tart as she wanted to be. Goldfinch that.

She approached a lanky James Bond type at the desk.

The guy said, "Help you?" The accent was southern, and it sounded polite but not interested. The clothes weren't speaking to him, probably one of those schmucks who did stuff to sheep. She adopted her best little-girl-lost voice, never failed, whimpered, "I'm Paula Segal. I'm reading here tonight."

Being modest about it, but not because she was feeling modest. Saying with her modesty that I'm such a big deal, I can afford to be modest.

"Oh wow," the guy said. "It's an honor to meet you. I'll get the Events Manager, but first…" He reached under the desk, brought out an advance copy of *Bust* and said, "Signature only."

"Selling it on eBay, huh?" Paula asked.

The guy's face flushed as if she had nailed it.

As she was signing the book, she asked, "Where you from?"

"Florida panhandle."

Yep, definitely a sheep fucker. Good thing Paula wasn't wearing wool, the guy wouldn't be able to control himself.

Paula was waiting for the Events Manager when she saw a fat guy in a crumpled suit chewing on a disgusting cigar and staring at her. She knew he wasn't about to make her the next supermodel, gave him the finger.

He smiled and she thought, *Whack job*.

He came over, said, "A moment of your time, Paula."

Was he a fan? And with no book, of course? Did they even *sell* books at this store anymore, or was it really a giant coffee bar? And where was her publicist to protect her from this vermin?

"I can't sign now," Paula said.

"I don't want you to sign anything," he said.

"What the hell's wrong with you people?" Paula screamed. "Don't you understand that this is a bookstore? Meaning a store that sells *books*?"

He showed a badge, went, "Joe Miscali, Manhattan North."

The name registered. She knew Miscali, of course, as she

knew all the major players in Max Fisher's life. He was the
partner of Kenneth Simmons, the cop who was killed by Angela
Petrakos' boyfriend. Simmons was a major character in *Bust*.
While Miscali appeared in *Bust* as well, Paula had renamed him
"Fusilli," a shout-out to her writer friend, Jim Fusilli.

She shot back, "A little out of your jurisdiction, aren't you,
officer?"

She had no idea if this were true but had seen it on *Law &
Order* and had stolen it for the book.

He smiled, displaying nicotine-stained teeth, said, "Max
Fisher." Added, "A moment of your time."

Could she refuse? Sure, but then what? Besides, she was
curious.

She muttered, "Okay," and he led the way to, naturally, the
coffee bar.

Paula was definitely more curious than upset. Why was Miscali
asking about Max Fisher? Fisher was officially on the Most
Wanted list, but she hadn't heard about any Fisher sightings in
years.

"Get yah?" Miscali asked.

The future Pulitzer winner said, "A decaf frappe."

He almost sounded friendly, said, "Take a seat."

She did. Noticed a long-black-haired guy in the corner, rattling like a demon on his laptop and stopping periodically to
laugh out loud then re-attack the keys with ferocity. Now that
was the kind of guy she wanted to write with, not Stiegsson,
whining about how it was too dark in Sweden to write, or whatever his complaint du jour was. Maybe when she got to book
four in the series—she needed a good, snappy title for that
one—she'd look this guy up.

The cop was back, placed the coffees on the table with two
wedges of carbo nightmare Danish. Like she could, and watch

the shit go right to her hips? No way, Jose. Not when she was looking to get into talk shows.

He said, "I shouldn't," then took a massive bite out of the Danish. "Oh….ugh…holy fuck, that's good." Then he wiped his mouth with a napkin, said, "Okay, to business. Where's Fisher?"

"Why would you think I know where Fisher is?"

"You wrote a book about him."

"*About* him. Why does that mean I know where he is? And he's presumed dead, isn't he? Is that what you are now, a ghost detective?"

Unamused, he said, "Have you had any contact with him since the Attica riot and his escape or not?"

She was astounded, said, "I'm astounded."

He wasn't buying. "You were part of his…circle before all the smoke in Canada."

She composed herself, which meant she pushed her rack in his fat face, said, "I'm a writer, I write about lowlife, I don't hang out with them. Well, aside from those Irish writers who come to mystery conferences, but you get my drift."

"Yeah? You got a big book out there. Looks like you got lucky, huh?"

She was livid. Did Laura L. have to endure this kind of condescending attitude?

She tried for haughty, went, "I'm working with a European writer now. Maybe you saw his name on the posters in the window. He's upstairs right now, in fact."

"I'm not interested in the Swede, honey, I'm interested in you."

"Are you harassing me, Officer?"

"Excuse me?"

"*Honey?*"

"Huh?"

"You called me fucking honey."

"Jesus, it's a figure of speech. It's not like I called you a whore for fuck's sake. Tell me, when exactly was the last time you spoke to Fisher?"

She refused to answer this. She looked over at the long-haired guy. He was still banging on the keys, oblivious to the world. Her type of guy. If she were straight she would've been all over him.

"I'll ask you again," he said through a mouthful of Danish. "When was the last time you saw him."

"At Attica," Paula said.

"I mean since then."

"I haven't seen him since then. I thought he was dead like everybody else."

"He's not dead."

"How do you know?"

"A hunch."

"That's how you investigate these days? On hunches?"

"I'll do my job and you do your job."

"I want to do my job. My job is to greet my fans."

"Some job."

"What's that supposed to mean?"

"I mean you get one lucky hit, you get some PR, and you think you wrote the next *Godfather*."

"I don't think it, *honey*, I know it."

"Where the fuck is Fisher?"

"Okay, I admit it, I know where he is." Paula paused then said, "He's hiding out in Pakistan. Maybe you should send Kathryn Bigelow to go get him."

The cop was standing, put his card on the table, said, "Fisher will show up, especially now that your book is out." He'd said *book* with total disgust, as if it were the name of a disease, and now added, "Fisher is predictable, he'll be in touch, always returns to those he knew. When he does, call me."

Then he was gone, leaving her with the remains of the Danish staring at her. She resisted for all of a minute, then snatched it, swallowed half, drooled, "Oh God, that is *so* good."

The sugar high only lasted a brief time but during the buzz, she wondered, *Was Fisher actually* alive?

NINE

Max had lived in some shitholes in his time, try eking out a living in a bumfuck cell in Attica. So now, now it was live large.

PIMP was bigger than Max had ever imagined. His "It takes care of you" slogan was catching on, dealers all over the city using it to lure in customers. Max hired the fucks who'd worked for the scumbags he took out in Brooklyn and ran his business like an army. The business blew up faster than fucking Shake Shack. He was the general—you better fookin' believe it—and he had his colonels, lieutenants, etcetera below him, all the way down to the dealers on the streets. After his bloody rampage in Brooklyn, Max was a freakin' urban legend. They were calling him "The Red Devil." The Max had a nickname! *Another* nickname. Fuck, it was like he was the villain in some comic book, but better, because there was no superhero to catch him.

Max was riding high, but he'd had enough lows in his life to know how things could go from sixty to zero in a hurry. He was cocky, fuck yeah, but he was also as paranoid as that kid in charge of North Korea. Nobody except his most trusted highups got any face time with him, and even they didn't know his true identity.

With PIMP money flooding in, he'd bought a loft-style apartment—get this—across the street from the Manhattan North precinct, where that prick Miscali worked. While in jail, Max had read all the great true crime books and one of his faves was

Where the Money Was by Willie Sutton. When Willie was *numero uno* on the *Mas Wanted* list, he holed up next door to a police station in Brooklyn. The rush he must've felt, saying fuck you to the cops every time they walked right by him! You had to have some *cojones* to literally bring it to the enemy and Max and Willie were true *compadres*.

At Attica, Max had made many great contacts, including a queen who once decorated for Bernard Madoff. Out now, and Max had employed him to decorate. The guy had a lisp—not because he was a gay guy trying to blend in, an actual lisp—and a whole shitload of gratitude. He said to Max, "Darling, I am *tho* indebted."

Max, thinking "put-on" and tiring of it, had said, "Yeah, whatever, now dazzle me with excess. Exceth. Whatever."

And dazzle he did.

The loft was ablaze with white light, white leather furnishings, white floors and a huge bay window. That looked down at the precinct. Sometimes for kicks—in between visits from hookers—Max would use high-power binoculars to watch Detective Miscali and his partner going in and out of the precinct. What a total Fuck You, but it wasn't enough. Sometimes Max, with dark sunglasses on, would take a stroll right past the precinct. A couple times, he walked past Miscali himself, and the dumb prick had no clue.

One evening, Max invited some of his new buyers over to his place for a shindig. One of the crew, an intense black guy with Jay-Z moves said, "The fuck is with all the white, yo?"

Max, like a Tony Soprano, read into this, thought the guy might be implying he wanted to make a move.

Max smiled, showing him some more of the white, and went, "New beginnings, a virginal setting."

The guy said, "Man, you a crazy mofo living cross five-oh."

Max didn't like the crazy jab, showed disrespect, so he had a couple of his lieutenants slit the guy's throat and dump him in landfill.

Later that evening, Max was chilling with some PIMP and a ho when Slav, one of his colonels, came and said, "Visitor to see you. A woman."

"You know, no *visitors* get face time with the Red Devil."

"She said she knows you from Attica."

A woman from Attica? The only women who'd visited him in prison had been Angela and Paula Segal, that lesbo writer.

Max, sensing there was more to this, agreed to let her in.

The woman—longish gray hair, a nice body, though no rack there—entered as the hooker exited.

The woman said to the hooker, "May Jesus have mercy on your sinful soul," and then Max got a good look at her face, thought, *Shit*.

"How'd you know I was back?" Max asked the nun.

She had ferret eyes, levelled them at him, said, "God told me."

Uh-huh.

Max, in a robe like Hef, drained his champagne, counted to five, asked, "Did God mention me by name?"

She gave a knowing smile, the one exclusive to zealots and groupies, said, "God has oh-so-special plans for those who mock His Name, and you would do well to remember He knows all."

Max, not missing a beat, asked, "He knows who's gonna win the third at Belmont?"

Max joking around with her, trying to loosen the nun up, but knowing he was in some deep shit.

Back in Attica, before Max rose to prominence, came into his own, he'd been shit scared. No idea of how he'd survive at a notorious prison, and especially survive a giant of a black man named Rufus, who on Max's first day had promised to make Max's ass his "own sweet booty."

Sometimes clergy came round to visit—nuns, pastors, rabbis, undercover Scientologists, trying to lure the cons into their respective scams. Usually they got lots of interest as it meant time out from the cell and you could usually hit the pious up for cigs, Hersheys, mags and hey, even some off-color sex talk in the form of confession.

Max had drawn the nun, went by the name of Sister Alison. She'd opened the chat with, "Call me Ally....God's own wee pally."

Trace of an Irish lilt hidden amid the bullshit. The Irish seem to have the patent on the whole nun gig, as they knew how to scare the shit out of you better than anyone. Max was terrified for another reason—because yet another Irish person had entered his life, and this always led to some sort of disaster.

But he'd assessed her, then gone ghetto, said, "Babe, you a playa, a crazy bitch, but you got it goin' on, know what I'm sayin'?"

Stone-faced, she said, "I see from your file you are a very dark sinner."

Max, knowing the power of repentance, as a tool of holy manipulation—fuck, he'd prayed in the courtroom every day— bowed his head, said, "I wanna be good." Using the submissive voice he'd been taught by a vibrant dominatrix in the Bronx.

The nun asked, steel amid the piety, "Are you prepared to take the steps to salvation?"

Hmm, Max thought. Said, "I need to be chastitied."

"Excuse me?"

"I mean chastised. I need to be chastised."

He saw the color rise in her deadly pale face, spread all down her neckline, as she went on, "And will you follow my guidance?" Was that a *purr* crawling into her voice?

Both of them a little breathy now, he said, "On my worthless knees."

So was born a very unhealthy dialogue that kept Max in heat until he managed to break the fuck out of the joint.

He hadn't really given her a whole lot of thought until she turned up at his party. Now she gave him the special nun glare, full of malevolence and viciousness. She asked, "These good folk out there don't know who you really are, do they?"

Max, flustered, tried to rally. The weight gain and red hair and plastic surgery had worked until now.

He tried, "I think you might be mistaking me for somebody else."

Didn't realize he was shouting until the burr of conversation died down around him. He cleared his throat, asked, "Who did you think I was?"

She gave an evil smile, said, "You want to get on your knees, Max?"

Fuck.

He said, "Might I get you a drink?"

She grabbed his arm brutally, hissed, "Cut the horse shite, Max. I'm not going to blow your act if…" and smiled sinfully.

Now he eased up a notch. A deal. Deals were his thing. And they weren't in freaking Attica now. He asked, "What you want… bitch?"

Let her know he was now The Man.

She stood back, surveyed him. Then, "Looks like you have a heavenly business going here. Half a mil for starters."

He laughed, said, "That all?"

"For starters, yes."

Max was still smiling but knew then he'd have to take the cunt out.

TEN

Joe Miscali was at his desk, having his usual heart-attack break-fast—two eggs Benedict, with sausage and bacon on the side—when Leonard came into his office and went, "You don't want to read Page Six of the *Post* today."

Joe took a huge breath, rolled his eyes, thinking, *Ah, fuck me, what now?* Saying, "If it's about me I don't wanna hear it."

"You?" Leonard said, sarcasm dripping, like why would they bother to write about Joe Miscali on Page Six. "No, it's not about you, but it's about somebody you know."

Agitated, Joe snapped, "Stop fucking with me, I'm in the middle of breakfast here, all right?"

"Testy today aren't we?" Leonard said. "Well, you're really gonna be on the rag when you read about the new Max Fisher book."

That name, Fisher, brought up acidy eggs Benedict. Another Max Fisher book? There was the instant book, right after Max's arrest, written by a couple of reporters from the *New York Post*. Then one by an American guy and an Irish guy that got a few reviews and disappeared. Joe had thought the Fisher literary trend was finito.

"*Bust* is on the *Times* bestseller list," Leonard said. "Ahead of the latest Jack Reacher. Can you believe it? *Bust* above Reacher? I bet Lee Child's flipping out."

Joe started to choke, had to take a big swig of coffee to get a hold of himself.

Joe read:

WE HEAR that Paula Segal and Lars Stiegsson will read from their bestseller BUST, about Manhattan businessman turned homicidal drug dealer Max Fisher, tonight at seven p.m. at the Barnes & Noble at Union Square.

If Fisher was alive, maybe Miss Writer Broad knew where he was hiding out.

So Joe went to the store, found Paula at the information desk. It was easy to spot her, she looked just like the pic on her website, except, what was the word? Snooty. Yeah, she looked snooty.

They had coffee and Danish and she was one of those lesbos with a chip on her shoulder. He called her "honey" and she flipped out, acted like he was trying to fuck her. Christ, in 1997 you couldn't stick a broomstick up a perp's ass, and now you couldn't call a witness honey? What was next?

She claimed she hadn't had any contact with Fisher. He thought she was full of shit.

He caught some of the reading, Paula and the midget Swedish nutjob taking turns. Paula read the section where Kenneth Simmons, Joe's partner, was killed by the Irish psycho. Paula looked right at Joe a couple of times as if saying, *This one's for you*.

It made Joe sick that people were lining up, buying this book, and, worse, that it was going to be a fucking TV show.

Joe left the store, but lingered outside, double parked in his unmarked. When Paula and Stiegsson left with a few other people and hopped a cab, he tailed them to the Soho House. Snooty literary people hanging out, for fuck's sake. He waited there till Paula and a dark-haired women left, arm in arm, kissing while waiting for a cab. Jesus Christ, Paula was a carpet muncher, no wonder she had a thing against Joe, a manly cop.

Joe tailed the cab to Brooklyn, Dumbo. It was a clear night, full moon, maybe the werewolves were out. Joe had been hoping Paula would lead him to Fisher, but after waiting a couple of hours, pissing into a Pepsi bottle three times—his damn prostate —it looked like she was in for the night with her girl toy.

On his way back to the city, Joe hit a diner near the Manhattan Bridge for his second dinner of the night, deciding he wasn't going to give up on Fisher till there was a dead body. As he wolfed down two cheeseburgers, onion rings and a large chocolate milkshake, he just hoped the dead body wasn't his own.

ELEVEN

Can we talk about something other than Hollywood for a change?
We're educated people.
GRIFFIN DUNNE IN *The Player*

Back in the glory days when Stallone was a star—yeah, that long ago—Larry had a partner named Jerry Yarmolowitz, Jewish guy. That's how Larry would introduce him to people, go, "Meet Jerry Yarmolowitz, Jewish guy," and smirk, getting a kick out of it every time, a Jew so jew-y he didn't even bother covering it up, while Larry had quietly Ellis Islanded *Horowitz* into *Reed*.

He and Larry were the new kids on the block and some early successes had critics comparing them to great double acts:

Lennon/McCartney
Scorsese/De Niro
Jagger/Richards
Bruen/Starr

Plus, these guys were tight. Not just professionally but buddies outside the job too. They'd fly to New York, hang at the Mansfield, drink until dawn, hit on hot waitresses, and score on the ponies. And through it all they worked on their projects nonstop. Larry was all about character but if you wanted the plot to jell, then Jerry was the go-to guy.

A true study in contrasts, Larry was all mouth—fuck this, fuck that—and on speed to get everything done. His mantra might have been, "Yeah, that's great, what's next?"

Jerry put the M in mellow, laid-back, no fuss, his mantra seemed to be: "Let it slide."

And they were fun to be around, got people caught up in their shared energy. Weirdest thing was they looked alike— same graying hair, same pot belly, same bald spot. An exec once cracked, "Who are you guys, the Glimmer Twins?" and the name stuck. They even called their company Glimmer Productions.

Then came two pivotal moments. The first was the arrival of a movie script, *The Wallace Tapes*. This seemed to be a sure-fire hit but turned out to be a *Heaven's Gate* clusterfuck of bad management, worse timing and budgets that went ballistic. Larry, always the savvy dude, cashed in his shares, got out before the shit really hit the fan, but neglected to tell Jerry. Neglecting to tell—that was the second pivotal moment.

Jerry, believing that their friendship could turn anything around, stayed until the bitter end, a premiere in Boise. He lost everything. Things were so bad he even contemplated writing a mystery novel for quick cash. But some shred of dignity still remained and he took a job as a dishwasher at a diner, and at last disappeared in to the great anonymity of Manhattan.

Worse, in interviews, Larry dissed him, going, "Thing is, ol' Jerry lost control. Instead of *writing* the plot, he became the plot. He never understood the basic principle of cut and run."

Even Michael Cimino referred to Jerry as the guy "who made *Ishtar* look profitable."

Larry's wife, in rare moments would ask him, "You ever think about Jerry?"

Larry, on his B-movie uppers, would snort, "Jerry, Jerry is history."

But now, in traffic, on his way to a lunch thing at Musso & Frank's on Hollywood Boulevard, Larry wondered, *Could Jerry have kidnapped Bev?* Jerry was a Sam Adams drinker, used to drink the shit like water, so there was that. And he had boat-loads of motive for revenge.

So Larry did a little research. Well, called a neighbor who had a twelve-year-old kid who knew how to use the Internet, was some kind of genius with Google.

Larry went, "Hey, can you have Kyle do me a solid?" Larry had just heard this phrase used by some kid at his chiropractor's office and felt hip using it himself. "Can he research Jerry Yarmolowitz, the ex-movie producer, and see what he finds out?" His neighbor wrote back a few minutes later, informing Larry that Jerry had invested in a start-up during the tech boom, cashed out, and was currently living in a villa in Greece.

This news established two important things for Larry:

One, the idea of Jerry's involvement in Bev's kidnapping was probably what the mystery writers call a red herring.

Two, he had to be some kind of idiot, wasting his time fartsing around in the fucking movie business.

TWELVE

If you want to make God laugh, tell him about your plans.
Woody Allen

YOU GOT SIX HOURS LEFT

The note Larry found stuck to the windshield of his car when he left Musso's.

"Christ," Larry said, ripped up the note, the way he'd rip up a parking ticket.

He'd just finished a power lunch with Eddie Vegas, young guy who'd invested in a couple of Larry's film projects that had failed to launch. Vegas, like the whole town, believed that TV was the place to be.

Vegas wasn't from Vegas, he was a young Spanish guy from the hood, about thirty, kind of looked like John Leguizamo, and Larry had no idea how some Cheech from East L.A. got the last name Vegas. Honestly Larry didn't give a shit about him, except that he a) had money and b) was willing to invest in practically any film project. As they say at Santa Anita—nice perfecta.

Larry hadn't heard back yet from Angela yet, but he was taking meetings on the project, being proactive, figuring if the Irish bitch couldn't pull off the deal, he'd go to Darren and blackmail the child-molesting fudgepacker himself.

"Tellin' you right now, bro," Vegas had said. "This *Bust* shit sounds cool, but it better not die like those other two shits you put me in. I got a three strikes rule, man. Two strikes, Eddie be cool, but Eddie don't strike out, *entiende*?"

Larry didn't *entiende*. He didn't know what the Latin fuck was talking about—he just wanted the kid's money and he'd say anything, tell any lie, to get it.

"No, this is a different kinda situaton," Larry said. "This deal's solid, as close to a slam dunk as you can get."

"Yeah, that's what you was sayin' 'bout *Spaced Out*."

"*Spaced Out* was an unfortunate, isolated situation," Larry said. "We would be at the premiere now, talking to Melissa Rivers, if Tom didn't fuck us over."

"Tom Cruise was gonna be in it?"

"No, Tom Selleck. But as a fortune cookie I got once said, *The wind of one door closing opens another*. If *Spaced Out* got going maybe we never get involved in *Bust*, and ten, twenty years from now, when *Bust* is hailed as one of the greatest TV shows of all time, right up there with *Bonanza*..." Shit, that made him sound old. He said, "I mean *The Sopranos*. Yeah, *The Sopranos*. You're gonna be thanking God I got you in on the ground floor of it."

"What about *Prison Break*?" Vegas asked.

"What prison break?" Larry asked.

"The show *Prison Break*," Vegas said. "*Bust* gonna be like that?"

Larry remembered *Prison Break* now, with the cop from *Friends*. He said, "It's funny you mention *Prison Break* because this film has a prison break in it. It's about Max Fisher."

This got Vegas's attention. He leaned over the table, his half-eaten T-bone, and said, "The white dude who busted out of Attica? The motherfuckin' businessman?"

"Yeah, that's the one."

"Yo, why didn't you say so?" Vegas said. "Oh, shit, I been hearin' stories 'bout Max Fisher for years. Motherfucker's *stone* cold. A'ight, kid, a'ight. You makin' a show about Max Fisher, you put me down as Executive Producer, I'm down with that shit."

Another great thing about Eddie Vegas—he was a handshake deal kind of guy, and he paid in cash. He told Larry to meet a friend of his at nine tonight at the parking lot of the In-N-Out Burger on Sunset and he'd give him 75 grand, the "investment capital" Larry claimed he needed to get *Bust* going.

So Larry was flying high until he got the note on his windshield. He'd gotten several similar notes over the past couple of days:

> *WHERE'S THE FUCKIN MONEY*
> *MY FRIENDS ARE KEEPING THE BITCH HAPPY*
> *YOU COULD'VE AVOIDED THIS LARRY*
> *GIVE ME THE MONEY AND THIS ALL GOES AWAY*

Like that.

This was more frustrating now, though, because now he had the fucking money coming, but he didn't know where he was supposed to bring it.

He looked around in every direction—maybe the note had just been left—but he didn't see anybody suspicious. Who was he kidding? This was L.A. *Everybody* looked suspicious.

He still had no idea who the hell was behind this. It was obviously somebody he'd fucked over somehow, but that narrowed it down to about half the city. The notes were all on the same type of index cards, handwritten in the same type of block letters. He probably should've saved the notes—they were evidence after all—but he was a busy guy, he had a TV show to get rolling, and he didn't have time for this Sherlock Holmes bullshit.

To the parking attendant—Jesus Christ, the blond kid didn't look like he was old enough to fucking drive—Larry said, "Hey, did you see anybody near my car?"

"Huh?" The kid looked out of it, with a dumb smile. Maybe he was on that new drug that Larry had read about in the papers, the one spreading around the country, the one they were calling "the new crack." What was it again? PIMP. Stupid fucking name for a drug. Who came up with that?

"When I was eating," Larry said to the attendant, "somebody put a note on my car. Who was it?"

Still an idiot smile, then, "Sorry, sir, I didn't see anyone come near your car."

Then Larry realized the kid wouldn't help him even if he had seen anything as Larry stiffed him on a tip every time he parked here. He was lucky the car still had hubcaps and the windshield hadn't been smashed.

He paid, without tipping, and drove out of the lot, edged into the near-standstill traffic on Hollywood Boulevard. Larry wondered if this was all a game, some kind of practical joke. Who knows? Maybe Bev was in on it? He remembered reading the coverage on *Gone Girl*. Isn't that what happened, the wife getting revenge on the husband for being such a prick? Well, maybe the same thing was happening to Larry because he'd been at least as much of a prick as that guy was. Yeah, this theory that Bev was behind it was starting to make a lot of sense. That's why they didn't tell him where to bring the money, give him any contact information. Maybe it was like in *The Game*, that Michael Douglas flick. Maybe if this was a movie that ugly guy, good actor, had banged Madonna, the fuck's his name? Sean Penn, yeah, maybe Sean Penn was behind this. Maybe Sean Penn was the one fucking Bev. In the movie, they'd be cutting back and forth between Larry, trying to find his wife and scrounge up the ransom, and Penn and Bev plotting. Whoa, Jesus Christ, Larry was seriously thinking now, because that's what geniuses do—they thought. After *Bust* got going, he could develop this story into a movie—*Taken* meets *The Game* meets

Gone Girl. Holy shit, what a fuckin brilliant idea. He pulled over, took out his phone, wanting to leave a voice memo to himself. He said into the phone, *"Taken* meets *The Game* meets *Gone Girl,"* but, shit, he couldn't figure out how to get the voice recorder to work. On his sixth try he got a message, "Your call to Morocco can't be completed as dialed."

Eh, never mind, he decided. After all, brilliant ideas are never forgotten.

In twenty minutes the traffic had moved about three blocks when Larry got a call from Mickey Downing, an agent from ICM, and put him on speaker.

"Make it real," Larry said.

"You fucking cocksucker," Mickey said. "You useless fuck hole."

"Whoa, Ari Gold, chill out," Larry said.

"You fuckin' prick face," Mickey said. "You stupid fuckin' smoldering piece of horse shit. You useless fuck. You're as useless as the piece of skin between my balls and my ass."

"Hey," Larry said, offended, "don't call me stupid."

Still fuming, Mickey went, "You rub egg in my face, I'm gonna rub diarrhea in yours. I'm gonna smear it into your face till you choke on it. I'm gonna make you choke on my fuckin' diarrhea till you die, Larry."

Larry, wondering *Did Mickey Downing kidnap my wife?*, heard traffic noise in the background, Mickey doing work in his car too like the fucking Lincoln Lawyer. People complain about the traffic in L.A., but if people weren't in traffic all day nobody would ever get anything done.

"Whoa, what did I do?" Larry said, wondering if this was part of *The Game* too, another twist in the plot?

"You told me you're EP'ing *Bust*, that's what you did," Mickey said. "So like a moron I take that to mean you actually are EP'ing the project, and I bring it up at a staff meeting and my co-agents start sending the scripts to talent. I hear Paul Fuckin' Giamatti's loving the book, wants to be Max Fisher. I got Paul's manager calling me, asking when the script's gonna be finished, shit like that, so I call Lionsgate. I go, 'What's up with *Bust*?' and the exec there sounds surprised, is like, 'What do you mean?' and I tell him that I got a call from you, you said you're EP'ing, and they have no idea what the fuck I'm talking about. They say, 'Larry Reed? We wouldn't let Larry Reed anywhere near this project. You think we're insane?'"

"You serious about this?" Larry asked.

"About calling Lionsgate?"

"No, about interest from Paul Giamatti."

"Are you listening to a fuckin' word I'm saying?" Mickey screamed. "Lionsgate says you're not on this project, you've never been associated with it. Meanwhile, you have me going around town, sounding like a fuckin' asswipe."

"Whoa, slow down," Larry said, "there must be a misunderstanding. Maybe Lionsgate didn't hear about my involvement in the project yet from Darren Becker."

"No, actually Lionsgate said that Becker is Co-EP'ing with some chick I never heard of, Brandi Love, sounds like a fuckin' porno name."

"Brandi Love's *my* partner," Larry said.

"Look," Mickey said, "I don't know what the fuck's going on, but I feel like a fuckin' idiot, believing Darren Becker and Lionsgate would ever go into business with you."

"I'll call you right back," Larry said.

Mickey was saying, "You better fuckin'—" when Larry hung up on him and called Angela.

She picked up, saying, "Brandi Love Productions."

Jesus Christ.

"You got us in with Darren, right?" Larry asked.

"Who is this?" Angela said.

"It's me, Larry Reed."

"Who?"

"Larry Reed. Your producing partner on *Bust*?"

"Oh, I'm sorry, I'm in a meeting right now, can I—"

"Whoa, what's going on?" Larry said. "Just heard through the grapevine that Lionsgate's not aware of my involvement in *Bust*, but I know that's a mistake because they know *you're* involved."

"I'm sorry, you can leave a message with my assistant," she said, and hung up on him.

The Irish bitch hanging up on A-list producer Larry Reed? Was she serious?

"Are you fuckin' kiddin' me?" Larry screamed.

So much for mellow-yellow Larry.

He called back, maybe ten times, kept going straight to voice-mail.

Larry didn't like this, he didn't like this at all. He was the big-time producer, the player. He was the one who was supposed to do the fucking; he wasn't supposed to *get* fucked.

Okay, he had to steady himself. Jesus Christ, where were his fuckin' Ativans? He'd deal with *Bust* later, first he had to get Bev back. Whether she was maybe in on it or not. But how was he supposed to pay a ransom when he didn't know who to pay it to?

Doctor Hoff. It had to be him, he was the Sean Penn, the mastermind of the plot. He was fucking Bev and they decided to do a fake kidnapping, squeezing 75K out of Larry, so they could get away somewhere. Maybe Hoff got in deep with drug dealers, figured this was his only way out.

Larry drove across town to Hoff's house, made good time—under two hours.

When Hoff opened the front door, Larry forced his way inside.

"Hey, what's going on?" Hoff said. "If you're looking for some more Vike, I really don't think it's a good idea for you to take any more. I mean, I don't wanna wind up sharing a cell with Michael Jackson's doctor."

Larry was staring at the doc. Something was off. The guy had been acting squirrelly, fidgeting, unable to meet Larry's eyes. Plus, Larry's gut was telling him, *The schmuck's guilty*. Larry didn't get to survive all these years in lotus land by not being able to read betrayal. His motto was: *Some can read the writing on the wall. Others put it there*.

"I have your money," Larry said and waited for a reaction.

"Money? Money for what? You mean the bandages for your bullet wound? Your insurance is covering it, right?"

Larry went for the jugular, shot, "How long've you been fucking my wife, Doc?"

The doc, nervous, went, "Come on, Larry, I have my own bitchy wife I can't stand, why would I want to fuck yours? I mean, when you already have one minivan do you go out and buy *another* minivan?"

Larry's gut was shouting now, he pushed, "Come on, where is she? Your basement?" He shouted, "Bev, can you hear me! Bev!"

"Can you keep your fucking voice down, you're gonna scare the poodles."

"Fuck your poodles." Larry grabbed the doctor. "How's my wife holding up?"

Doc had the grace to at least act confused, said, "Holding up, you mean the boob job I referred her for?"

Larry felt a wave of bile and rage, near shouted, "I'm warning you, I've had a bad day and it's getting worse, so don't fuck with me, Doc!"

The doc made the fatal error of looking to his left. Larry had read in his psychology manuals that this was the sure sign of lying.

Or was it to the right?

Aw fuckit. He lunged at the doc, got him in a headlock, shouted, "Where is she?"

The doc, surprising Larry, managed to do a body turn and shuck him across the room.

Larry landed hard, maybe cracking a rib, got to his feet, said. "Been working on some martial arts shit, huh? Is that your drug connection too? That why you're extorting money from me, to pay the fucking Chinese?"

The doc, all his pent-up frustration from over the years coming to a head, sneered, "I think you've officially lost it, Larry. You crossed a line. You are in a world of hurt now, big boy."

Larry reached for an antique vase on a pedestal by a wall, hurled, and it connected, smashing Hoff's nose and remaining intact—the vase, that is.

Hoff, blood streaming down his face, whined, "You broke my nose! Why'd you *do* that? The rhinoplasty was a bar mitzvah present from my Uncle Marvin."

Larry jumped at him, got him around the waist and they fell through a glass table, rolled across the room, glass cutting them both.

Hoff was first to his feet.

Larry, a little slower, put up a hand, said, "Enough, I give up."

Doc, a nasty smile leaking through the blood, suddenly like the poster of *Die Hard*, said, "Too bad. 'Cause there's more where that came from."

Larry, letting his body slump into the defeated mode, limped to the desk, said, "Let's have some drinks, and we can work out this misunderstanding."

Doc was coming up behind him, one arm raised. Larry spotted

an ornate letter opener on the desk, snatched it up, and, turning, plunged it deep into the doc's chest.

Doc looked stunned but Larry didn't let that stop him. Rearing back, using all the force of his right hand, he hammered the hilt of the letter opener home, almost burying it in the doc's chest. The Doc uttered a small *oh!* and crumpled to the floor.

Larry saw the fall in capital letters, as if it was a hot script, then kicked the body twice for luck and badness.

It hit—*Jesus Christ, what the fuck did I do?*

He got on his knees, like he was in that movie with Jon Voight, and said, "Champ, wake up, wake up, Champ."

Shit, he'd snapped. Say it was an accident, self-defense, he'd say the doc came after him with the letter opener and Larry had to wrestle it away. But would they believe it? On *C.S.I.* didn't they always figure out the truth? But that was a TV series, a fucking procedural, the truth had to come out. In real life lies held up, like Jodi Foster in *The Accused*. Wait, that movie was about a rape, not a fucking murder. Wasn't there a Harrison Ford movie where this happened, where Ford been accused of a crime he didn't commit, or didn't mean to commit?

He took out his phone, said, "Idea for thriller. Harrison Ford is accused of a crime he didn't commit."

He had to sit down. As he did, the phone beeped. Automatically he picked up, the opposite of how he felt, said, "Make it real."

A voice said, "You got the money yet or we gonna have to kill the bitch?"

The voice sounded familiar, but Larry wasn't sure why.

Took Larry a moment to regroup. He said, "Look, the boss is dead, it's fuckin' over, so let my fuckin' wife go."

Silence, then, "The fuck you talkin' about?"

It was Mo or Jo—the skinny one, not the Spanish, non-Mexican guy.

Tired of being manipulated, Larry said, "Look, the game's over. You can tell my wife that too because I know she's in on it."

"Man, you crazy," the guy said.

"You don't understand," Larry said, "the boss is gone now. I killed Geronimo."

"What?"

"The guy you're working for, Dr. Hoff. Bill. Or The Hoff, as he called himself."

"Hef? Like *Playboy*?

"No, *Hoff*, like the guy who was fucking my wife."

"The fuck is Hoff, man?"

Larry, a dread slithering along his spine, tried, "Your boss?"

"My boss is right here next to me, yo."

Shit. Had Larry killed the wrong guy?

"Hey, Larry? You ready to play some ball now or what?"

This was a nightmare to end all nightmares. But—silver lining, he could use this twist in the movie too. Killing the wrong man? Oh yeah, people would eat this shit up.

THIRTEEN

Maybe my future starts right now.
JOHN GARFIELD IN *The Postman Always Rings Twice*

Mo had it all figured out. Once they got the money from that Larry Reed motherfucker, they'd take out the boss too. Hell, why the fuck not? Mo liked even numbers a lot more than odd. Mo never was too good at math in school—or maybe the problem was he wasn't in school all that much at all—but he knew 85K split two ways was a lot more than 85K split three. But can you even split 85? He thought you could only split even numbers. Fuck it, man, if there was an extra dollar, he'd keep it, and they'd go down to Meh-hee-coe. Man, eighty-five thousand dollars is like a million pesos down there. Money's worth more below the border, he didn't know why everybody didn't want to move down there. Why waste your time with dollars when you can have pesos?

Mo's plan: they could use some of the cash to buy a ranch-type hacienda or whatever they were called, then use the rest to see how they might take on part of the cartel's business. Stay small but profitable. He'd need Jo for the heavy lifting, the guy was dumb as shit, but you don't got a wingman, who else gonna take out the trash?

But Jo, man, he'd been sniffing round Larry Reed's wife, going, "Can't wait to taste a piece of that meat" and "Bet the lady be tastin' sweet" and "There's a sweet hole down in that basement and I'm gonna plug it."

Disrespectful-to-women shit like that.

Mo was southern, and all southern boys are gentlemen. He didn't mind that talk when it was for show, like at the producer's house. But that was just to put on a show, to scare the dumb guy.

Mo went to Jo, "You talk to your momma with that mouth?" and Jo said, "If I wanted to fuck her, I would."

Jo was so stupid, it was impossible to have a sensible conversation around the man.

Mo was from Tennessee, hundred miles outside Memphis. Mo was the type of guy who'd kill a man who looked at him funny—and he had, seven times. Make that eight—there was that guy who gave him queer looks at that honkytonk back home. But women, man, he didn't never kill none of them. Women were sacred to Mo. He didn't understand how any man could ever hurt a woman. Women were a gift from God. Just look at them—how soft and gentle they all were, with all them curves. A woman was like a beautiful white mountain. Not that women had to be white, he wasn't no redneck—at least not when it came to fucking. He'd fuck any woman, no matter what color. Like at ho houses, some guys would only pick the white girls, but Mo went black, Chinese, Mexican, didn't matter to him. But most of the guys Mo knew growin' up went around hating niggers.

That's one reason why Mo took off for Los Angeles. He had big dreams and he knew none of them would come true if he stayed in the back country with a bunch of morons his whole life.

The thing that surprised Mo most about L.A.: there were just as many morons out here as back home. Different kind of morons though, 'cause back home people were dumb and knew it, but out here people were dumb and acted smart. Putting on a front, always like a movie camera was going and they were, what, actors? Mo could see through all that fake though. People out here with their clothes and their cars and their perfect teeth, acting like they knew everything about the world. Whenever Mo saw one of them Hollywood dickbags he would be laughing his ass off inside, knowing the truth even if nobody else did.

Mo made money like he'd been doing back home—little dealing, little protection, little GTA. Only had to kill people once in a while. Struck out twice but, like a cat, he was good at burying his shit, and he never went down for killing nobody.

Mo had met Jo on a job, hired to kick the shit out of some dumb Hollywood fuck who owed money for coke. Mo thought Jo was all right, except for the way he treated women.

Driving in Santa Monica, passing a pretty blonde in a bikini, Jo yelled out the window, "Yeah, baby, sit on my face with that shit, I wanna taste you."

Mo grabbed Jo, nearly crashed the damn car, said, "The fuck you talkin' to her like that for? That there's a woman. She's sacred, man."

"You crazy, yo?" Jo said. "Almost gettin' our asses killed just 'cause I was talkin' to a bitch."

"Tellin' a woman to sit on your face ain't talkin' to her," Mo said.

"Where I come from it is," Jo said. "Different rules in Colombia, kid."

The fuck did that mean?

Mo said to Jo, "The fuck does that mean?"

Jo said, "Go down to Colombia someday, you find out."

This was the kind of stupid talk that made Mo's head want to explode. The man wasn't even from Colombia and he was talking about Colombia rules? Jo was *part* Colombian and part something else, maybe American Indian, and was born and raised in goddamn Phoenix. Mo's family went back to France, but you didn't hear Mo saying, "Different rules in France."

Shit.

So now when Mo told Jo to chill with the nasty talk about the producer's wife, and Jo went, "Different rules in Colombia, kid," Mo was ready.

Went, "I don't give a shit what the rules are in Colombia, where my people come from in France, we respect women. When I fuck a woman, I thank her afterwards, call her ma'am, even if she is the biggest ho at the ho house. You understand what I'm sayin' to you? You have a woman tied up in your basement, you understand that even though she's a hostage, she's still a woman, and as a man you respect that, 'cause that's what men do."

Jo stared at Mo, dumb look, then went, "You some kinda faggot?"

Mo punched Jo in the face—heard the crunch, saw the blood. Man, Mo loved red, had to be his favorite goddamn color.

Then he grabbed a sixer from the refrigerator, settled in to check out some Netflix.

FOURTEEN

Neo-noir is suicidal loners and unhinged nymphos
with nothing but past and no future.
KURT BROKAW

"Executive Producer."

Angela rolled the words round in her mouth, like a cinematic blow job, but one she'd initiated. She checked the mirror, and fuck, she already looked different. She had a sharp, stately look, like Michelle Obama—well, Michelle Obama with makeup. Hmm, maybe Executive Producing and acting was just the beginning. Maybe after a few blockbusters, and Oscars, she could announce she's leaving acting and producing to embark on a career in politics. Hey, if a foreign bodybuilding maid-fucker could be governor, why not her?

With producers and a studio on board, all they needed was a writer. Angela, wanting to flex her power as Executive Producer, announced to Darren Becker, "I want to bring in my guy."

They were in Darren's home office, posters from *Casablanca*, *Vertigo*, and *Titanic* of course. Were they in every producer's office? Larry'd had the same posters in his office.

"Who's your guy?"

Angela was lost, didn't actually have anyone in mind, then on a whim, said, "He wrote a script I was involved with while I was working for Larry."

"Whoa, I told you, no Larry," Darren said. "The guy's the kiss of death. If Larry gets involved this project will sink so deep James Cameron won't be able to find it."

"This has nothing to do with Larry," Angela said. "It's the screenwriter of a script I loved, but the project fell apart. *Spaced Out*."

"Who's the writer?"

"Bill Moss."

"Never heard of him."

"Exactly," Angela said. "I know Larry didn't pay him anything."

"He wrote it on spec?" Darren laughed. "Moron."

"Right," Angela said. "So if we offer him to write for minimum he'll be over the moon."

"Love it," Darren said. "You're already thinking with your producer's hat on. Try to keep costs down and fuck the writer, that's the way to do it. But how do you know he's right for this? I mean *Spaced Out* was a space movie, right?"

"I'm telling you," Angela said, "it's the cosmic twin of *Bust*."

"I'll get coverage on the script asap," Larry said, "but Lionsgate has some ideas themselves, heard Ethan Coen's name kicked around. But Coen's quote is a fortune. They'll like that we can lowball this…what'd you say his name is?"

"Moss," Angela said. "Bill Moss."

"Mr. Spec," Darren said, and left the room shaking his head and laughing.

Angela knew it would put her in total control of the project if she got the job for her guy, but how to get him? Like the old joke, the bimbo goes to Hollywood and sleeps with…*the writer!* Hey, they say there's truth in every joke, right?

Angela was imagining the look on Larry's face when he read that Bill Moss was writing *Bust*. It would be another kick in the balls, and that's the type of ego-driven head game that the New Angela thrived on. That's right, Angela was a player now. Suck on *that*, Larry Reed.

But this was what an Executive Producer took care of. Smooth and cajole. Get them together in a room and she'd weave her witchy spell. Getting Bill on the phone, not so easy. Had to go through a manager and two agents, but Angela slalomed through the obstacles like a Hollywood pro.

They met at the Chateau Marmont. On the way in she spotted several hot Hollywood couples: Will and Jada, George and Amal, Leo and Tobey, the Teen Mom and James Deen. Clint was at a table with some young blonde, and was that Al Pacino in the corner or was it some other guy with too much plastic surgery? Angela made these star sightings with her peripheral vision, of course. She wasn't some wannabe; she was one of them now. Let them stare at her, and she knew they were. They were all thinking, *Is that Brandi Love, the new A-List producer I heard all the buzz about?* She was surprised Leo wasn't rushing over, asking for an autograph.

She sat at the table, and in true Hollywood fashion ball-busted the waitress, demanding room-temperature water with a slice of organic lime. When the waitress brought the water she had a sip, then grimaced and said, loud enough that those around her and the lurking paparazzi, could hear, "This is not room temperature. It's seventy-seven degrees here, and this water is seventy or below."

The waitress, an obviously frustrated, jealous actress, apologized and went for a new glass.

Then in walked a guy, long hair uncombed, unshaven, wearing old jeans and a hoodie. Was the restaurant about to be robbed?

"I'm Bill Moss," he announced.

Didn't have the A-list look Angela was expecting, but what did she expect from a mere writer? She was the Executive Producer and he was merely the talent. It was okay for him to look like shite. Besides, Angela had screwed worse—she saw a flash of

Max Fisher, fake hair melting, dripping down his forehead, but struck it from her mind quickly.

Her first words to Bill Moss: "You are going to be shit rich."

It was a grabber.

First his grim face nearly smiled, then settled into constant disbelief, and he said, "Yeah, right, and the check's in the mail, just like Larry Dickfuck Reed, when he promised me Guild minimum and the first rewrite, and he didn't pay me jack shit. He jerked me around for years when that project was in development, told me it was my ticket out of the telemarketing cubicle, and guess what, I'm still in the telemarketing cubicle."

She turned on the full-heat voltage, right in his crotch space, asked, "You want to hear me out or not?"

Managing to make that sound like, "You want to fuck me every which way but loose?"

The waitress brought a water. Angela sipped it and muttered, "Acceptable."

Bill ordered a lemonade.

Then Angela said, "I just need your focus." Again with the subtext of, *Put it to me, big boy*.

You want to hook a writer, quote lines from his past glory, can't fail. It didn't. He actually let his body move from tense to interested, asked, "So you really liked *Spaced Out*, huh?"

She looked on the brink of multiple orgasm, gushed, "Liked... liked? I got down on my knees and worshipped that script. When the alien says to the hero, 'I feel your pain. Your pain is my pain,' I wept buckets."

"Wow, really?"

Sold.

She ran an outline of the *Bust* story, then the hook, "It needs a writer of extraordinary sensitivity and vision to bring this to glory."

She thought she may have overpitched but there are two types who will buy this shite fully—writers and wannabe writers.

He was on board. Asked, "That fucking piece of shit Larry Reed won't be involved, right?"

"No, I guarantee it."

"Am I gonna have full freedom?"

She smiled, asked, "Is Barack black?"

Bill was getting into it, promised, "I'm right on this sucker."

She fluttered her eyelashes, said shyly, "You *are* the man, Bill."

And he fucking believed that too.

She had asked him, "How do you define film?"

Not that she gave a toss but she felt it was vague enough to sound like she knew what she was asking and because he was the kind of gobshite who loved abstracts.

He didn't disappoint, went into a long spiel about post-structuralism and the use of prism as a channel to postmodern parody.

She battled not to yawn.

In an attempt to be clearer, he tried, "The writer Stuart Kaminsky, his son Peter wrote, 'If there was a hell, he had a one-way ticket, and if there was any argument he had with Satan about the matter, all Satan had to do was say, "Roll the film and show that scene from the bathroom."'"

She couldn't help it, went, "Wot?" in faux Cockney as the whole gig seemed to require absurdity.

He said, "The world is divided into those who hear this and nod and those who ask, 'What bathroom scene?'"

What choice did she have? She nodded.

Later, leaving the restaurant, Angela called Darren on her cell and gushed, "I got Moss."

"Great news," Darren said, "and the timing's perfect. I got

great coverage on *Spaced Out*, and I agree, Moss is perfect for *Bust*. Also, I heard through Lionsgate that for some reason Ethan Coen doesn't want to be in business with me. But, hey, it's Ethan's loss. I'll be sure to thank him when I win my Oscar."

When Angela clicked off, she saw a familiar face, staring at her in the lobby of the Chateau. Was it Lee Child?

The guy saw her noticing him and rushed away. Angela went after him, but when she got near the escalators, he'd either gone into an elevator or left.

The truth was setting in. It was actually him—the man who'd shot her and left her for dead in Canada was now here in L.A. Definitely not Lee Child, but when she found him he'd wish he fookin' was.

FIFTEEN

The best the white world offered was not enough ecstasy for me.
Not enough life, joy, kicks, darkness, music. Not enough light.
JACK KEROUAC

Sebastian, a name to reckon with.

You'd think, right? 'Twas a curse and a blessing that he looked like Lee Child. While ol' Lee's star was in the ascendency, so was Sebastian. But, oh dreary me, now Lee was losing his grip. *I mean*, Sebastian pouted, *that bloody Jack Reacher movie.*

Sebastian looked in the mirror, he still was *hot*, wasn't he? So okay, a slight pot belly, gotta cut down on those pints of bitter. As if a Brit could. It was enshrined in the constitution that an Englishman must down pints of the swill and eat Yorkshire pud at every opportunity. It was also enshrined that a handsome British man with no wife must be in want of a good fortune.

Sebastian came from a reasonably wealthy family, i.e., they could afford to play polo but not quite afford to fund Sebastian's lifestyle. He was a writer, with stunning plots, descriptions, gripping narrative style. So okay, get petty, he hadn't actually written down any of his masterpieces, but gosh, a chap had to live, experience the planet. And did he ever! On the lam, on the loose in Greece, a few years back, he'd met an American babe, Angie. The moves he put on her, he was astonished at his own charm. You got it or you don't. He had it, in bucketfuls. But she turned out to be a complete nutter, a psycho of epic proportion. He shuddered to think of it now, helping the mad cow throw a dead body over the cliffs of Santorini.

Write that.

He'd managed to get away from her, until the dead guy's insane brother recruited him to carve revenge. He'd managed to blot the whole crazy sordid affair from his mind, almost. The years in between had been lean, and *Darling*, he gasped, *he wasn't getting any younger*.

The big Four Oh was beckoning and he hadn't a pot to piss in. The days of marrying a debutante were gone. Those gels were marrying Americans! Horrors indeed.

For several years he lived in London, hiding out too from many assorted creditors, and working, yes, working. One had to earn a crust. It was what made the Empire great. He was in Earls Court, in a call centre, trying to swindle ordinary Johns out of their pensions. His track record wasn't exactly lighting up the skies and the boss, a Paki, had the bloody cheek to suggest that he hit the targets or hit the road. That someone from the Colonies would have the effrontery to speak to an Englishman thus!

The situation worsened. The Paki suddenly appeared over Sebastian's shoulder one day, screeching, "Facebook! This is how you waste my time, you…" He reached for an English description, found, "…wanker!" Then commanded, "My office, *now*."

And Sebastian found the old forgotten rage of the Angela era, tired of being the fall guy, of forever hustling for a break. His growing anger was fueled by the looks of the other drones in the centre who looked on him with, was it pity?

He was God's own Englishman, by Christ, he would not be talked down to by a shitheel who should be grateful to even grab a job as a bus conductor. His temper was ignited by the fact that being fired, he'd again be scrambling for nickel and dimes. Enough.

The Paki led him into the office, closed the door, began, "I must say…"

Whatever it was was lost as Sebastian hit him on the chin with a Golden Award Statue for Sales that had been perched, pride of place, on his desk. It knocked him back against the board of projected sales for the first quarter. And lo, Sebastian came alive. All the groveling, the desperate kiss-ass existence, the fucking Facebook insult, why wasn't he up there with Katy Perry, who had eclipsed Obama on the site? Where was his share?

Sebastian strolled over to where the fallen Paki lay, kicked him in the head, asked, "So, who's the wearing the knickers now?"

Pulled the desk drawers open, found a bottle of Teacher's, twenty Valium, one thousand pounds sterling, five hundred dollars, and a well-thumbed copy of a trashy paperback called *Fake I.D.*

Put the lot in a bin liner (except for the cash), moved back to the man on the floor, and asked, "Got a wallet?"

He did.

Holy Queen, three thousand in cash.

The man began to rise, blood dripping from his chin, spat, "I make sure you go to prison for life, yes, life, you piece of Rawalpindi sewage."

Sebastian had no idea what this meant save that the foreigner was insulting him. He grabbed him by his non-UK throat, hissed, "We might have lost the World Cup but by all that's English, we never, never lose our dignity, so swallow this, you fucker."

Managed, with great difficulty to force the phone receiver down the guy's throat, not an easy task but got there, and as he watched the guy finally succumb to his death rattle, said, "Hello, call waiting."

Added, as the guy went still, "Your call is important to us, please hold while we try to transfer you to another operator."

Headed out, cash leaking out of every pocket, stopped, said to the waiting faces,

"You've all being given a bonus and the rest of the day free."

Marching out of there, a ticket back to America and maybe a fast few vodkas were his next, well, *call.*

But Sebastian didn't make it 'cross the pond, popping in at a travel agency on Goodge Street instead and purchasing a ticket to the Canary Islands. An Englishman needs his holiday.

A few weeks later, Sebastian returned to his Britain homestead, broke, but rested. What next? He didn't think applying for a position in the phone industry would work out very well. How would he respond to the interview question: "So, why no recommendation from the previous job?"

Over the years in a pinch he'd made some good dosh by impersonating Lee Child. He'd set up tables at flea markets, with a stack of Reachers, claiming he was Lee, signing books with a forged signature that would've made Tom Ripley proud. Oh, and yes, he did roger a few fans along the way—thank God for the Reacher Creatures!

The authorities caught on to the scam, though, and he did a few months at a dreary prison near the border of—the horror, the horror—Wales. Whatever proper Englishman didn't believe in hell hadn't been to a football pub in Cardiff.

When he was released, he was lonely in that peculiar English fashion. He missed cricket, warm beer, Yorkshire pud, London fog.

Now, he had never played cricket, drank only gin 'n tonic, wouldn't quite know what Yorkshire pud even was, and he certainly had never seen London fog outside of a Jack the Ripper movie. But Sebastian had public school looks, i.e., ripe for buggery, and was British as British got in the eyes of non-Brits. Was that the key to success? If you can't be big at home, go abroad. Knock 'em dead in Japan. If that fails, try Germany. It was what the U.K. crime writer Simon Beckett had done and, get this, even more than Lee Child, Sebastian was Beckett's spit. Crikey, it seemed as if he could do a spot on for any of these English writer chaps. If he grew a mustache and told some old jokes he could pass for Mark Billingham.

As it turned out, impersonating Britain's own Simon Beckett, Germany's number-one bestselling author, wasn't such a bad thing when you were desperately short of cash, prospects and plans. He was in the small town of Kuhn, a short ride away from Frankfurt, and the locals were delighted to have a celebrity among them—he embellished ol' Simon's C.V., claiming he was the grandson of Samuel Beckett. He regaled the peasants with tales of sitting on Samuel's lap as a child, and how he was indeed the inspiration for the character of Godot in *Waiting for Godot*, enduring the shame afterward when the frau of the bookshop informed him that Godot never appears in the play. Bloody Irish writers, always with tricks up their treacherous sleeves.

Sebastian was doing well, but living on very extended credit and time was running out, especially as the real Simon Beckett was due at the Frankfurt Book Fair in a matter of days.

Sebastian was shacked up with a *frauline* named Franziska, a slip of a thing with long blond hair. She was increasingly anxious to see Sebastian/Simon's new book. He could only stall for so long. Sitting at a writer's desk she had provided, he looked like an author. Had that studied appearance of seeing beyond. Plus the slight air of disdain common to the best literary people. He was chewing on a pencil, longing for a pack of John Player's.

Franziska called out, "Simo-o-on, how is it going?"

The German accent, as soothing as a swift kick in the balls. Holy mackerel, he had better write something.

To while away the days, he'd been cruising U.K. dating sites. Maybe salvation lay there. He had put on his profile: *An understated intelligence with a smoky allure*. Women, the poor things, were hopelessly attracted to enigmas, especially ones they couldn't solve. He had only two requirements, two essential things he desired in a woman—cash and stupidity.

He hadn't reckoned on the forthright replies of the U.K. online-hunting female, the kindest of whom replied, "You freaking wanker!"

For diversion, Sebastian was checking his Facebook status. He had a wonderful profile on there and nearly three thousand friends. No fans, alas. Then in the current feed he saw a friend had posted a link to a news story about an upcoming TV show based on a crime novel. The show was called *Bust*, based on the bestselling book, but not by Lee Child or Simon Beckett, so—really, now—how good could the bloody thing possibly be? For the past several years, Sebastian had only read books by Lee and Simon—Brits must support their own, by George!

Then he recognized one of the authors' names—an American, Paula Segal. Good heavens! She'd been a bit player in the whole post-Greece saga, and he muttered, "Barely worth a footnote, in the grand, dark scheme of those iconic events." Sebastian had a way with words, was always able to capture the essence of a moment with his linguistic gift.

He continued to read of the impending production with mounting hope and adrenaline. He'd never for a moment considered raking over that time to make money, mainly relieved that he got away with his life. But here was Paula Segal, crowing on about her collaboration with some Swede; they'd written the Max Fisher story. He was outraged. He'd been there, nearly lost his balls, and if anyone had the cojones, the sheer detachment, to write in a cool and elegant fashion about the Max Fisher saga, it was him. On impulse, he put Fisher in the search machine and Holy Moly, not only did Max Fisher have a Facebook page, he had nearly a quarter of a million fans.

That elusive animal, hope, began to sing her alluring song, and Sebastian thought, *Hmmmm, you think? Maybe*.

❖

Sebastian borrowed two thousand euro from Franziska to pay for hospital costs for his sick mum—his mum was alive and well, on to her fourth husband, living in the north of England— then ditched her at a circus on the outskirts of Stuttgart.

A few days later in Berlin he'd met, via a dating site, an aging American actress. She looked sort of like Bette Davis before *Whatever Happened to Baby Jane*. So yeah, ugly, but with some moves. Of course she fancied his "like, adorable accent." Plus, he had dropped vague hints to his being 978th in line for the throne. Her current name was Jane Bemore—as in, *Can a woman of advanced age be more gullible?*—and she had provided the one thing Sebastian needed—a ticket to L.A.

So he did the deed. Yup, rode that baby until she cried. He cried too but for different reasons. And bingo, she, post-coital glow, whispered, "My gals would love you back in L.A."

Done deal.

Sebastian had visions of him and Jane in first class, sipping champers, slipping her the mucky under rich duvets as the stewardesses eyed him with—let's just come out and say it—awe.

But at Frankfurt Airport, Jane cooed, "My sweet Lord-baby, there has been a slight hitch, no business class I'm afraid."

Fuck, bloody fuck and thunder. He rallied, said with his stiff upper lip, "We shall make the best of it, ol' gal, slum as if we meant it."

Thinking he was unduly witty under the circumstances. She rubbed his cheek with her Madonna-like withered hands, fluttered, "Oh you lovely silly man, *I'm* in business class."

Sebastian learned all over again the humiliation of being fucking nobody and resolved there in the lobby of the German departure lounge, "I will be a bloody contender, I will get a slice of movie action if I have to kill somebody."

He tried for an upgrade at the gate, but his upper crust accent held no weight with the frau from Lufthansa.

The flight was awful, just poverty with wings. And he watched as they drew the curtain on Business Class as Jane and others freighted smoked salmon, champagne—on frigging ice too! And, oh Jesus, oysters. Economy class got plastic sandwiches and dire coffee, with a fee for headphones to watch Adam Sandler in some ghastly two-year-old flick.

Sebastian fumed.

Beside him was a fat guy from Ohio, who had been to the Frankfurt Book Fair. The guy babbled on about hot books and hotter chicks, and Sebastian suddenly perked when the guy mentioned book rights for an international bestselling novel named *Bust*.

It was a sign. An omen, a nudge from dark forces that he needed to get his shit together.

In L.A., Jane asked if he'd like to go for a drink before he headed off? Meaning, hit the road cowboy.

He kissed her hand, said gallantly, "It has been fun, madam, but I feel I should go meet someone who is not getting the old-age pension."

Then he hired a cab to follow her Town Car home. Watched her have the driver carry suitcases into her pink chateau. He let her get settled, i.e., remove the layers of shite on her face, drop some of her anti-aging pills. He was seriously enraged, the cunt had used and abused him, and in an Irish accent, from his Angela days, he swore: "I will not be fooking cast off."

His comprehensive education not a complete waste, he jimmied the back door, moved silently towards the lounge where she was predictably watching one of her old movies, circa 1968. He grabbed her from behind, muttered, "Your contract has expired, love."

But who knew the old buzzard had so much spunk? Fought like a lunatic and they fell, struggled, smashed, nigh death-danced all over the lounge, with glass, ornaments, cushions flying. She nearly got the upper hand too, having kneed him in the balls. But instead of delivering the *coup de grâce*, she opted for a speech. Fucking actors, can never resist a scene. As she intoned, channeled a very bad Desdemona, he reached for a poker and smashed her face, over and over, until he sighed, "Who knew she had so much blood in her?"

He ransacked the place, got money, jewelry and even the keys to her sporty Monte Carlo. As he crunched out over the broken glass and debris, he looked back at the twisted body, said, "Been fun, doll," and headed out to be a star.

Having read online that *Bust* was being produced by Darren Becker, Sebastian began stalking the chap. He followed him and his lover—yes, Becker was indeed a shirt lifter, but who wasn't in this place?—to his office, to the studios, to tennis, to the gym, and to various high-end restaurants. Darren was living the life Sebastian was desperate to live, and would be living soon.

Sebastian had read that *Bust* was in need of a screenwriter.

Deciding that it would be best to meet Darren naturally, Sebastian used a stalker's trick he'd read about once in some thriller he'd nicked from Waterstones, and got a job working at Darren's gym.

One morning when Darren arrived, Sebastian was there, handing him a towel saying, "Darren Becker, is it?"

Darren squinted, said, "You are…"

"Sebastian. We met, oh I don't know when was it, ten years ago?"

"We did?"

"You said you were a huge fan of my writing."

"I did?"

"Yes, you called me the next Beckett, I believe it was. Not Samuel, Simon of course. Well, hardly matters now, does it? I happened to hear through the ol' grapevine that you're producing *Bust*, and I just want to throw my hat into the ring, so to speak."

"Is this some sort of joke?"

"Pardon?"

"I have no idea who the fuck you are, some fucking towel boy at the gym."

Americans and their horrid manners. Why Sebastian had always thought they should've banned John McEnroe from Wimbledon.

Properly, Sebastian said, "I told you, I'm Sebastian...Sebastian Child. Perhaps you know my brother, Lee? As in Jack Reacher?"

"I hated that fucking movie," Darren said, trying to get by Sebastian.

Sebastian wouldn't move, said, "I haven't had my big break yet, but I assure you nothing will get in my way."

"Maybe Lee'll let you write the next Reacher," Darren said, "but there's no way in hell you're writing *Bust*." He pushed by Sebastian and headed to the steam room.

The next day, Sebastian was unceremoniously fired from the job at the gym and knew Becker was behind it. He resolved right then that he'd kill the bastard, preferably in some homoerotic way, the way Tom killed Dickie in the Ripley film. But how would he get Darren out to sea in a rowboat to crush open his skull with an oar? Well, he'd have to sort that part out, wouldn't he?

A couple of days later, he was waiting outside Darren's house in Beverly Hills, when he couldn't believe his bloody eyes. It

couldn't possibly be her, after all these years, could it? After all
he'd shot the mad Irish cow at point-blank range in the chest,
left her for dead outside the gas station in Canada. But it was
her—same blond hair, same luscious bosom. He should've
expected she'd survived. The Irish, they're so dreadfully hard
to stomp out. The Brits had been trying to off the lot of them
for years by secretly urinating in exported Guinness, warming
it up properly, but the Irish suckers keep popping back up like
roaches post-apocalypse.

When she entered the house, he rushed over to peer in through
a window. Good Christ, she was servicing Becker, bringing flash-
backs to Sebastian's own time with her in Santorini. Ah, the
memories of young love! It made sense that she was getting it
from Becker as Sebastian well knew that if anyone could turn a
gay man, it was her.

Sebastian did the only sensible thing under the circumstances—began to diddle himself. He was British, so he felt
shame for the act, of course, and moaned "So sorry" as he came
all over the bushes.

Later, 'round lunch time, Angela headed off and Sebastian
pursued. He had so many questions and so few answers. What
had Angela been doing all these years? How had she wound up
in L.A. with Darren Becker? Did she have some involvement
in the TV show?

He followed her up to the Chateau Marmont. Finally, a
proper establishment, Sebastian was back in his element. He
trailed, watching as Angela was seated at a table, and then as
some horrendously dressed man arrived. Crikey, he was in
trainers!

An hour later, Sebastian was in the lobby, momentarily distracted, when he was suddenly face to face with her. The rage
in her eyes terrified him and instincts screamed, *Run!*, so he

slipped away. Obviously she hadn't forgiven him just yet for that shooting business in Canada. This complicated things, but he knew he could win her over; after all, the Sebastian psychopathic charm was impossible to resist.

As always, all he required was a plan.

SIXTEEN

*The deal with noir is
whoever you meet on page one is completely fucked
and it's only going to get worse.*
JIM NISBET

Larry was sitting in the In-N-Out Burger on Sunset, nursing a cup of truly shit coffee, looked like the spillage from the Gulf of Mexico, when two cops entered, fucking CHPs.

One was younger, crewcut, Larry could cast Newman in *The Hustler*. The other was mainly bald but blond, maybe a Redford type, so it would have to be present-day Redford, i.e., Redford with the fucked-up looking face.

Larry was so nervous he felt like he was going to puke the coffee right back into the mug. They were here for him, he was sure of it. They weren't looking at him, they were looking up at the menu, but they were just playing cool. Any second now they'd attack him, pin him to the floor and cuff him like he was in a fucking rerun of *COPS*.

They must've found Dr. Hoff's body; why else were they here? Larry knew he couldn't survive prison, he'd have to go out *Bonnie and Clyde* style. Only problem was he didn't have a gun. Well, he'd do something, throw the coffee in their faces, to incite them and get shot. It could be like that movie he'd fast-forwarded through the other night—*Fruitvale Station*. Cops these days were trigger happy and—who knows?—maybe they'd even make a movie about Larry, he'd be a fuckin' martyr.

But the cops didn't attack Larry or try to shoot him. They

bought their burgers and shakes and returned to their patrol car without even looking at him.

Larry knew he wasn't exactly in the clear. He was in some shit up to his eyeballs and there was no way out now, he was D.O. fuckin' A. He'd left Doctor Hoff's body in the house with the letter opener still in his chest. He'd developed enough cop projects over the years to know how to wipe down a crime scene, and he'd spent a couple of hours cleaning up prints and any other trace he was there. But he'd also developed enough crime shows to know that it was only a matter of time till he got caught. In procedurals there was always a bust at the end, and cops these days with their fucking forensics, databases, DNA and whatever other new bullshit had come down the pike were so far ahead of the criminals it was a miracle half the country wasn't in jail. He didn't think he was on any surveillance video, but he knew they'd catch on to him eventually and his only chance was to run.

Before leaving, he'd smashed some breakables, ransacked the place a little to make it look like a robbery. In the bedroom, he found some cash, about five hundred bucks, in a sock drawer and thought, *What the fuck?* and pocketed it. After all, he was already a killer, on his way to hell, so what did he have to lose?

And he'd run. But where had it gotten him? Now he was down to his plan B, or was it C or D? He was losing track.

His brilliant plan was to meet Eddie Vegas's guy at the In-N-Out Burger and get the seventy-five grand. He'd then hand over the seventy-five grand to the kidnappers and get Bev back. Then—assuming he hadn't been arrested or killed by this time— he and Bev would fly to Brazil. He had some moolah offshore, not enough to finance a movie but enough to survive for a few years. By then hopefully he'd drop dead and not have to come up with another plan to make money.

He knew the odds of this working were slim to none, especially since he still had no way of contacting the kidnappers. He considered ditching Bev and just running away to Brazil right now, before he was on the airport's do-not-fly list. He didn't love Bev and she sure as hell didn't love him, but okay, yeah, he cared about her. Even though he never wanted to see her again, he wanted to know she was safe.

Then Larry saw a big lanky white guy, ruddy face, approaching in, Jesus Christ, a circa-*Midnight Cowboy* fringe jacket and from its odd aroma, it hadn't been washed since Jon Voight wore it. But this guy looked older than Voight, and he looked like the other guy, not Jim Carrey, from *Dumb and Dumber*. Daniel Craig? No, but there was a Daniel in it.

"You Larry?" the guy asked.

Larry had been expecting a Latin guy, like Vegas, but this guy didn't look like Cheech *or* Chong. His breath smelled like whiskey and he looked like he'd been drunk since 1985. Not the *Dumb and Dumber* guy—Nick Nolte, that's who he'd cast. If Nick wasn't busy having a mug shot taken.

"You with Vegas?" Larry asked.

"Why else would I be at a fuckin' In-N-Out Burger?" the guy said.

There was pretention in his voice, the Midnight Cowboy acting like Larry was Ratso Fuckin' Rizzo.

"Cool," Larry said because he wanted to come off as a hip, with-it dude and "cool" was the only word he could come up with. "Can I, um, get you a coffee?"

"Ain't here to socialize, pops," he said. "Mullah's in the case."

Mullah? Larry felt like he was in *Straight Time*, that Dustin H flick about the ex-con. And *pops*? Larry was five years older than this guy, tops. Okay, maybe ten, but *pops*?

Looking at the suitcase, paranoia took hold and Larry wondered if the guy had stuffed a small Arab in there. He couldn't resist and corrected, "Moohla."

Got a blank hillbilly stare, like the bumfucker from *Deliverance*.

"Wanna count it?" the guy asked.

Larry nearly said, *It's ok, I trust you*, but how fucking dumb would that sound? Instead he went dumber, said, "Eddie's family to me."

The guy walked out.

Larry opened the briefcase expecting a) an explosion or b) a red light like in the Tarantino flick. Instead he saw neat stacks of twenty- and fifty-dollar bills.

So far, so good. Larry had the ransom money and while Eddie Vegas would be more than upset when he found out he wasn't buying into a piece of *Bust*, he was buying into a piece of Jack Shit, by the time he connected the dots, Larry and Bev would be on the beach in Ipanema, sipping drinks with little umbrellas in them.

Again the problem occurred to him that he had no way to contact the kidnappers, but even this problem seemed resolved when he saw a new note on his car:

MEET MY GUY AT THE FOUR SEASONS IN ONE HOUR

Larry looked in every direction—nothing unusual. He was glad he had a meeting spot finally, but he was paranoid as hell. How the hell did the kidnappers know that he'd be at In-N-Out Burger? Did Eddie Vegas, or one of his *Winter's Bone* goons, kidnap Bev? Was he about to give the money back to the same guy he'd just gotten it from?

This idea didn't seem to make any sense. It was more likely that somebody else had kidnapped Bev and had been following him all over L.A. But if somebody was following Larry did that mean that person had seen him kill Dr. Hoff?

Without thinking it through any further, Larry drove to Beverly Hills to deliver the money. He could barely control the steering wheel; his hands were sweaty and his heart was on frigging fire.

When Larry arrived he immediately spotted one of the guys who'd abducted his wife—the non-Spanish one. But the guy didn't look like he did last time, like one of the Crowes in that show on FX. No, he was dressed in an expensive suit, oozing bile and confidence.

He opened with, "I do feel at home here."

Larry, across from him now, said, "I am so happy for you… Jo?"

"Mo," Mo said.

"What happened to Jo?" Larry asked.

"Let's just say he checked outta the hotel early." Mo smiled, showing his yellowed teeth.

"You should quit that shit," Larry said.

"Smiling?" Mo asked, still smiling.

"No, smoking," Larry said.

"Who said I smoke?"

"Your teeth are stained."

"Maybe it's from coffee."

"You should visit a dentist every now and then."

"You payin' for me?"

"I think you can pay for yourself now," Larry said and indicated the briefcase.

Mo waved a slim finger almost in Larry's face, said, "Uh-uh, none of that bitterness an' shit, Larry. As my momma used to say, manners cost little, but…" He paused then added, "…attitude cost mo'. Get it, mo'? Like my name?"

Larry was through dealing with freaking lowlife; this was worse than ICM.

"How did you know I was at In-N-Out Burger?"

"Huh?"

"The fuckin' note on my windshield."

"The boss handles that shit, I just follow orders."

"What are you, some kinda Nazi?"

"What's a Nazi?"

"You don't know what a Nazi is?"

"Oh yeah, from *Seinfeld*."

"You been following me around all day or not?"

"Why you care?"

Larry decided that going on about this could only get him into more trouble.

Hoping for the best, he said, "How about we get to down to business?"

Mo smiled. One way or another, Larry was bringing all kinds of weird sunshine into the lives of shitheads today.

Mo said, "So what're you waitin' for? Pass it over."

Larry didn't budge, said, "You're fucking kidding, asswipe. First Bev, then the payment."

Mo shot to his feet, snapped a crisp salute, said, "See you at her funeral then."

Larry caved, gave him the briefcase, said, "Okay, okay, here… but how can I trust you?"

Mo reached over, lightly took the case, turned to walk, said, "Trust is like a dick, usually stuck in all the wrong holes."

As Larry drove home, he couldn't help thinking of a dire script he had once worked on, about a father of a kidnapped girl, the money's paid but no girl and the father goes mad, winds up in an institution and it spiraled into a *Cuckoo's Nest* ripoff. They had Anthony Hopkins penciled in but he fucked off and got an Oscar for playing a cannibal.

Back at his house, he was horrified to see blue lights flashing and a fleet of cop cars strewn around his driveway. He got out slowly, his heart pounding, thinking, "They found Hoff."

He formulated a new plan, because that's what sharp thinks like him did—they planned. When they told him about Hoff he'd go for one of their guns. He wouldn't get his hand near the holster before one of the Fruitvale idiots would shoot him and he'd wind up dead. He didn't know if he believed in life after death or reincarnation or any of that bullshit, but if he lived this life over again he just hoped it would be easier to make it to the top of the movie business next time around.

Two cops approached—why were they always in twos? were they fucking Siamese?—and the taller one said, "You Laurence Olivier Horowitz?"

"Yes," Larry said, eyes aimed at the holster and gun right there, a few feet away.

"We found your wife," he said.

Not what Larry was expecting.

"She okay?" Larry asked, relieved he hadn't gone for the gun. But the relief didn't last long.

"No," the tall cop said.

Larry stuttered, "Y-you mean…"

And the short cop went, "Your wife's dead, Mr. Horowitz."

SEVENTEEN

Do I see sheets of plastic in your future?
DEXTER MORGAN

Mo was jerking off to Season 2, Episode 6 of *Orange is the New Black* when he heard the woman screaming and thought, *Ah, shit, man, makin' me pause fuckin' prison sex an' shit? Damn.*

Headed up into the bedroom to see the woman curled up against the wall, mouth gagged, but her dress hiked up and panties off. Jo had his jeans undone and was sweating.

Mo grabbed Jo by the shirt, dragged him out to the corridor, hissed, "I told you not to be doin' that shit."

But something had given Jo a whole new set of cojones.

He squared up, sneered, "You ain't my boss, yo, I'm sick of you tellin' me how to act an' shit. I go by my own rules, kid, by Colombia rules."

Mo slammed his fist into Jo's chest, harder than he intended. Jo staggered back, tottered at the top step, then crashed down the stairs, Mo would swear afterwards he heard a definite *Ker-ast* as the man's neck snapped.

Mo rushed down but he could see from the angle of Jo's head that Jo was a goner. Mo had killed men lots of ways but he'd never broken a man's neck before. That was kinda cool.

If Jo hadn't disrespected women, Mo may have been upset, or at least concerned, but he didn't give a shit.

The producer's wife was on the floor, mouth still gagged, crawling, trying to get to the window. Mo went and grabbed her, said, "Where you going, sweetheart?"

She was crying 'cause of what Jo done to her. She was suffering and Mo couldn't stand to see her suffer. When a horse is suffering you got no choice, you got to put it down.

"Sorry, I can't have you go on livin' with this shame," Mo said, and he broke her neck. *Ker-ast*.

He hoped it was the last woman he ever had to kill, but it had to be done.

He didn't bother to clean up the bodies, figuring he'd be in Mexico before they started smelling, and then he watched a few more episodes of *Orange is the New Black* in peace and fucking quiet.

Later, he got a text from the boss, told him to go to the Four Seasons to get the money from Larry. Shit, the Four Seasons was fancy, so Mo put on his best suit—okay, his only suit—and went to meet the movie producer.

Mo got a text from the boss: **How'd it go with Larry?**

Mo texted back: **meet me right now at the spot important**

"The spot" was the meeting spot they'd worked out in advance, at a bar in Venice Beach. The boss thought he was meeting to get his share of the money, but Mo wasn't planning to give the man nothin', well, except a bullet it in the head.

EIGHTEEN

On days like today, when they're talking to me like that,
I just feel like killing them. I'm not kidding,
I actually want to murder them.
JASON STARR, *Cold Caller*

Things were finally coming together for Bill Moss. When he came to Hollywood, fucking sixteen years ago, he got hired to write a screenplay for Fox and he was one of the hottest screenwriters in town. But in Hollywood fifteen minutes of fame lasts about fifteen seconds. In a flash, Fox had fucked up the script, bringing in too many writers to do rewrites, and Bill lost his agent and blew most of his money on gambling, eating out, and hookers. Broke and with few other options, he had to get a temporary part-time job selling discount phone service in a telemarketing cubicle.

The temporary job had lasted seven years. During this time, a producer named Larry Reed somehow had gotten ahold of Bill's draft of the Fox script and wanted a meeting with Bill. While Bill thought Larry was full of shit, the guy had some serious credits, had gotten that Garofalo movie made, and it wasn't like other producers were lining up to offer Bill work.

Work. Well, that had turned out to the ultimate four-letter word, as Larry didn't pay Bill a cent to write the script for *Spaced Out.* Bill poured his soul into that script, considered it his *meister verk*, or however the fuck they say it in German. Worse, Bill did free rewrite after free rewrite, believing Larry's bullshit that Travolta and then Tom Selleck were attached. Then Larry stopped taking Bill's calls and it hit Bill that he had wasted years of his life, working for that jackass.

All sorts of people worked at telemarketing jobs, including the occasional ex-con trying to go straight. Enter Mo, stage left. One night at a bar they were exchanging sob stories when Mo said, "Man, there's somethin' I don't get. This producer fuck, Larry, been fuckin' you over for years, right?"

"Yeah," Moss said.

"Then how come you don't wanna fuck him back?"

A plot hatched in Bill's brain—better than any other plot Bill had come up with lately. It sounded easy when he laid it out for Mo. Mo would kidnap Larry's wife, hold her for ransom—the very same seventy-five K Larry had once promised Bill for writing *Spaced Out*. Bill would supply all the information Mo needed, figure out the timing, set the plans, supply the technology they would require, such as it was. Bill would be the boss. Mo would be the muscle.

Mo didn't tell Bill about involving Jo until later, until after the kidnapping. Bill wasn't crazy about changing to a three-way split but, fuck it, you didn't argue with your muscle—not when you were built like Bill was. And twenty-five K would get him out of the telemarketing cubicle for six months. He could try to get a job writing for Nickelodeon. Bill had never written for a kids' show before, and most of his writing was dark as hell, but he could write a kids' show. He could write anything if he put his mind to it.

The kidnapping itself couldn't have gone better, and they were holding Larry's wife in some basement apartment or some shit. The best part—Bill had hidden GPS in Larry's car, and had been tracking him all over the city, leaving notes on his windshield. Bill knew it had to be driving Larry crazy. The old fuck was so technologically challenged, he probably had no idea what was going on. Whoever thought revenge wasn't sweet had never tried to get some.

Then, out of the blue, this chick Brandi Love calls, says she wants to hire him to write *Bust*. Bill did some research saw that *Bust* was a real, big-time book and the dark subject matter was right in his wheelhouse. But why was Darren Becker, a top producer, partnering with Brandi Love, an ex-porn star? Bill rented a couple of the *Brandi with Ginger* movies and there was no doubt she knew how to give head, but did she know how to make a movie?

Figuring the whole thing was worth a laugh, he showed up at the Chateau in an old sweaty sweatshirt and ripped jeans. She fed him some shit about how much she loved his writing, and wanted him on the project, and as the lunch went on Bill started to realize that this deal was real. For some fucking reason Darren Becker and Lionsgate were hell bent on getting him on board.

C.A.A. found out about the deal, and an agent signed Bill and started negotiating the contract. Didn't take long for word to spread. Within days, Bill's career had gone from zero to a hundred. It seemed like every studio in town wanted to be in business with him.

Meanwhile, time was running out for Larry. Bill tracked him on GPS to In-N-Out Burger on Sunset and, watching from across the street with binoculars, saw him receive a briefcase, hopefully one full of money, from some older, shady-looking guy who kind of looked like Nick Nolte.

Bill left a note for Larry to be at the Four Seasons in one hour. He wanted the exchange to happen at a public place where Larry couldn't try anything stupid.

Bill tracked Larry there on GPS, so he knew Larry had shown up. Then Bill texted Mo, asking him how it had gone with Larry, and Mo texted back:

meet me right now at the spot   important

This was weird—Mo changing the plan again? Mo was supposed to release Larry's wife as soon as they got the money and meet at the spot tomorrow. Why did he want to meet at the spot "right now," and why was it "important"?

Bill drove to the spot, about ten blocks from his place in Venice, at a parking lot behind a dive bar. It was late, after midnight, so there weren't many people around. He didn't see Mo's car. He waited. Too late, he wished he'd brought a knife with him or some other kind of weapon.

Then Mo's car pulled up and Bill watched him get out. Mo was holding the briefcase, so maybe the panic was for no reason. Maybe Mo would give Bill his twenty-five K and they'd go their separate ways and Bill would become the next Ethan Coen and never have to see Mo and Jo again.

Bill met Mo in the middle of the lot.

"Yo," Mo said.

Okay, Mo was being polite, that was a good start.

"Yo," Bill said.

Mo handed Bill the briefcase. It was light; felt like there was nothing in it.

"There's nothing in it," Mo said.

Shit.

"What happened?" Bill asked. "Did you get the money from Larry?"

"Yeah, *I* got it."

Bill didn't like the inflection, said, "Did you let Larry's wife go?"

"Can't do that," Mo said.

"Why not?" Bill said.

"'Cause she's dead."

Now Mo had a gun out, aimed at Bill. Bill's heart was pounding —fight-or-flight, mostly flight, kicking in. But he couldn't fly faster than a bullet.

Buying time, trying to figure out what the fuck to do, Bill said, "Why'd you kill her?"

"I didn't *kill* her, man," Mo said. "I'd never kill a woman. I just put her out of her misery is all."

"So is that what you plan to do to me too? Put me out of my misery?"

"No," Mo said. "You I plan to kill."

Bill knew Mo was about to do it, so he swung the briefcase as hard as he could against the side of Mo's head. It didn't do much damage but was enough to distract him, get him off balance, and gave Mo a chance to try to grab the gun.

"Come on, man," Mo said, wrestling with him for it. "Don't make this harder than it is."

The gun fell to the ground and Mo bent to get it. Bill had his hands around Mo's throat. It felt like a chicken's neck, more fragile than he'd thought it would, his hands stronger.

Bill had never killed anyone before, never even close, so he was surprised how good at it he was. Maybe it was because he was pretending that Mo was every exec in Hollywood who'd every fucked him over, but he found himself squeezing harder than he ever had in his life, and within about thirty seconds Mo was dead.

"Hey, what's goin on there?"

A guy, didn't look like a cop, was coming over from the direction of the beach. Maybe he'd heard the struggle or something.

"Nothing," Bill shouted back, and after a moment the guy walked on. Angelenos. Always torn between nosiness and not wanting to get involved.

Moving as fast as he could, Bill dragged Mo's body to his car, strained to get it up and into the trunk, and then peeled out of the lot.

He drove three hours straight, out to the desert. He'd once

read a *Wolverine* comic book where Wolverine chops up a body and leaves it by the side of the road for the coyotes to eat. Bill couldn't chop Mo up—he didn't have time for that bullshit, and also didn't have adamantium claws—but he dumped the body on the side of the road, someplace remote.

"*Bon appetit*, coyotes!" he shouted as he floored it, heading back to L.A.

NINETEEN

No problem can withstand the assault of sustained thinking.
FORTUNE COOKIE

"Who the fuck is Joseph Watkins?"

Larry screaming in the humid, practically airless interrogation room at the precinct in downtown L.A. He sat opposite a squat, bald detective named Brubaker, a desk between them. Larry would cast Telly Savalas to play Brubaker, even though, except for the baldness, the guy didn't look anything like Savalas.

"He went by 'Jo,'" Brubaker said.

"Right," Larry said. "Bad mojo."

"Bad what?"

"There were two guys who abducted my wife, Mo and Jo."

"That some kind of joke?"

"That's what I thought too, like *The Three Stooges*, except with Jo and no Curly." Larry smiled, then realized he shouldn't be smiling, being interrogated about his wife's murder and all, and tried for an appropriately somber, stone-faced look.

"Regarding the *abduction*," Brubaker said, leaning on the word, as if maybe he didn't believe it. "How come you didn't report this to the cops right away?"

"I was afraid," Larry said. "I thought they'd kill her."

"And they did kill her."

"I guess I fucked up."

"You guess?"

"They could've killed her anyway."

"Where were you this evening?"

"What?" Larry had heard, he just wanted to hear it again.

"I said where were you this—"

"In 'N' Out Burger on Sunset."

"All night?"

Shit, this wasn't some bullshit movie script with holes in it, Larry realized. This was real life, with real cops, who could do things like check security footage and other technological shit.

"Most of the night, yeah."

"Define most."

"What difference does it make where I was?"

"'M'I asking the questions or you?"

Larry was about to shit his pants, thinking, *Were these questions about Bev and Jo just decoys? Did the bastard want to nail him for Dr. Hoff?* He thought he'd done a good job cleaning up, but so did every schmuck on *C.S.I.*

"Instead of talking to me," Larry said, "you should be out looking for the killer. It has to be the guy I gave the money to. Mo. Or maybe it was the guy I've never met, the one who's been leaving the notes."

"What's his name?"

"I'm sorry, I forgot to tell you." Larry rolled his eyes sarcastically. "I don't know his name. I just know they call, *called* him 'the boss,' and I'm willing to bet it's not Tony Danza or Bruce Springsteen, so that rules two people out."

"You think this is funny?" Brubaker asked.

"Do I look like I think it's funny?" Larry said, and, of course, fuck, he couldn't stop smiling.

Stone-faced, Brubaker went, "If my wife got whacked, I wouldn't be cracking dumb jokes, I'd be crying."

"Maybe I'm internalizing my anguish," Larry said.

"Yeah, maybe," Brubaker said, "but I fuckin' doubt it."

"Look," Larry said, "instead of this nonsense with semantics…" He knew semantics was the wrong word, but he liked

the way it sounded. Continued, "…let's be a little more produc-
tive, shall we? How about you bring a sketch artist in here and
I'll give you a full description of Mo, down to his yellow teeth?"

"Tell me about Dr. Hoff," Brubaker said.

Larry tried to hide the full-blown surge of panic he was
feeling.

"Dr. Who?" he tried, squinting, going for a completely
confused look, but he was a shitty actor, why he'd gone into
producing. The irony was you have to do *more* acting as a
producer, which was why his career was in the shitter.

"You know him," Brubaker said. "He's your doctor."

"Oh, Dr. *Hoff*," Larry said. "Sorry, out of context, I was thrown
off. What on earth does Dr. Hoff have to do with this?"

Could he sound any more dishonest?

"He was killed earlier today, stabbed to death with a letter
opener."

"Jesus," Larry said. Better, maybe because he didn't have to
act to express shock and horror. "That's awful."

"When was the last time you saw him?" Brubaker asked.

"*I* saw him?" Larry said.

"That's what I'm asking you," Brubaker said. "When?"

"Couple days ago? I had a flesh wound when Bev's abductors
shot at me and I went to the doctor for some…" He almost said
Vike, but he wasn't dumb enough to open that can of worms.
Went with, "Band-Aids."

"Were you aware that Dr. Hoff was having an affair with
your wife?" Brubaker asked.

So Larry had been right all along, and Dr. Hoff had been the
Sam Adams drinker. Larry was glad he'd killed him, the son of a
bitch.

"The news doesn't shock me," Larry said.

"So you knew about it?"

"I didn't have any evidence. I mean a beer bottle, but…"

"We have evidence," Brubaker said. "It's early, but we saw the texts that the doctor and your wife exchanged, and the pictures."

"My wife sent him fucking pictures?"

"They sent each other pictures."

Thinking *Who would want to see a naked picture of Bev?* Larry said, "Jesus Christ."

"Do you think it's possible that Dr. Hoff was this 'boss' you mentioned?" Brubaker asked.

"I think that's very possible," Larry said, though he knew it was impossible, because he'd gotten the most recent note on his windshield *after* he'd killed Dr. Hoff. But he liked that it deflected attention away from him—for the moment, anyway.

After more questions, mainly rehashing and rephrasing what had already been asked, Larry was told to wait in another room in the precinct. It was hard for Larry to not feel like a total moron. He could have ditched his cheating whore of a wife and been in Brazil by now, but he'd tried to do the right thing, the moral thing, and look what fucking happened.

One of Larry's ex-assistants had set up e-mail alerts for Larry from *Variety*. Larry always had trouble logging on to the Internet so the alerts were a way of keeping him up on the major Hollywood news, so he wouldn't sound like an out-of-it jackass at meetings.

Larry was trying to check his email when he saw he'd gotten one of the *Variety* alerts about fucking *Bust*. Lionsgate with Darren Becker and, Jesus Christ, Brandi Love had hired Bill Moss to the write the pilot. Were they fucking kidding? Why did they want Moss, whose claim to fame was the script of *Spaced Out*, which had never even been set up at a studio?

Larry stewed, cursing to himself and pacing. A few more hours went by. Fuck, what was going on? Were they analyzing evidence taken from Dr. Hoff's? Larry thought about demanding a lawyer, but how would that look? It would seem like he was nervous, like he had something to hide. He was nervous and had something to hide, but the trick was not to seem that way. He had to play it cool, get a vibe going of, I'm not worried. I'm a hip movie producer, a Hollywood player, who always comes out on top.

Like that.

Finally Brubaker came to the room and announced that there had been a new development. Brubaker led Larry to another room where there were several other people sitting in front of a big TV. The fuck was this, a screening?

Larry said, "The fuck is this, a screening?"

No one laughed or even smiled.

"Sit the fuck down," Brubaker said.

Larry did.

Brubaker played grainy footage of two guys in, it looked like a parking lot.

"This is from a couple of hours ago," Brubaker said. "Do you recognize these men?"

Larry leaned forward. Looked like the guys were talking, one holding a briefcase, and then there was a gun, a struggle—

"Fuck, that's him," Larry said. "The guy in the suit. The one who gets strangled. It's Mo."

"You sure?" Brubaker asked.

"Positive," Larry said.

"Who's the other guy?"

The other guy looked familiar. Larry wasn't sure why at first, but knew he'd seen him somewhere.

Then it clicked.

It was Bill Moss. But why was Moss meeting with Mo? It was like all the disasters of Larry's recent life were colliding.

"You recognize him?" Brubaker asked.

Larry's brain was churning. Was *Bill* the boss? Shit, it made sense, was adding up. Bill had always seemed a little out there, a little, what's the word? Unhinged. Yeah, unhinged. And seventy-five K. Wasn't that how much Larry had promised him to write the script?

"No, I have no idea who that is," Larry said.

"You sure?" Brubaker said. "Watch it again."

Brubaker replayed the footage.

"I'm sure," Larry said. "I have no idea who that is."

A couple of hours later Larry was released. He was proud of himself for thinking fast, not I.D.'ing Moss and not letting a golden opportunity slide. This was the break Larry had been waiting for, his way back into *Bust*.

Larry went directly from the police station to Moss's bungalow in Venice Beach.

Bill came to the door, surly and disheveled.

Larry, smiling and upbeat, asked, "Miss me, boss?"

TWENTY

Life in the movie business is like the beginning of a new love affair;
it's full of surprises and you're constantly getting fucked.
DAVID MAMET, *Speed-the-Plow*

Angela moaned almost convincingly as Becker drilled her for the third time in two days.

Drilled.

Becker's term. As he slurped all over her he promised, "Gonna drill you, my Brandi Love."

Everything about him repulsed her. He was fake, wore aftershave that would restore hair on Paul Giamatti's head. One thing he apparently wasn't anymore was gay. He'd told his husband Ron it was over and asked for a divorce. Wasn't the first time Angela had gotten a man to ditch his marriage and it wouldn't be the last.

Becker had said, "I never thought I could love a woman again, but there's something about you, baby."

Angela was glad Becker was into her—so to speak—because she didn't think the threat of going public about him at Bryan Singer's pool party was enough to keep her on the project long-term. As Angela knew perhaps better than anyone—seduction was the most surefire way to get what you want in life.

Now in Becker's California king bed, she said with absolutely no tone, "Oh give it to me, big daddy." Making it sound much like *Mary had a fucking little lamb…*

But like most guys who bought their own bullshit, he said, "Whole lot more where that came from, cunt."

Jesus.

"Oh, yeah, talk dirty to me when you drill me," she said weakly.

Saved, almost, by the bell. The doorbell. He gasped, "Leave it."

She made a face of grim reluctance, said, "Might be important, baby," and shoved the dipshit off. He landed in a heap of withered dick and disappointment.

Angela threw on a faux silk robe. It matched the act she was peddling to Becker, all sheen and no substance. Opened the door to Bill Moss, who sniggered, "*Come* at a bad time?"

She had to eat this crap, smiled, said, "Lovely to see you, darling." Get that Hollywood vibe of never actually using anyone's name.

Bill swaggered in, flopped on a sofa, said, "Wet my whistle, bitch."

Using the slur as a sly form of affection, as in, Gee, I'm so *avant-garde*.

Proving he knew nothing about women or *avant-garde*.

This was a different Bill Moss than the Bill Moss she'd met with at the Chateau. He seemed edgier, raunchier, nastier. Had success gone to his head already or was something else going on?

"You been drinking?" Angela asked.

"No, PIMPing." Bill giggled. "Yep, scored some PIMP with my first check from Lionsgate. You know PIMP, the new wonder drug that knows how to take care of you. I don't know how I ever wrote without it."

"Lovely," Angela said. "Does wonders for your personality."

"Thanks for noticing," Bill said. "Am I the only one horny tonight?"

On cue, Darren rolled in, having pulled on a garish pair of Bermudas and a T that read: BONO BLEW ME.

Bill said, "You look like a guy who's had some *coitus inter-ruptus.*"

Angela wisely decided to go make the drinks, saying with a cheeriness she faked, "Dry Martinis good?"

Bill was staring at Becker and nothing he was seeing gave him any joy.

"What is this," Bill said. "Fucking *Mad Men*?"

"Just trying to lighten the mood," Angela said.

"No, thanks, I can party without the company of a couple of Hollywood shitheads," Bill said. Then, "Just so as we're all..." And, Jaysus fuck, made those air quotes. "...on the same page, Larry Reed is now our new producing partner."

Becker was raging, shouted, "Fuck no, not that fucking cunt!"

Bill smirked, went, "Whoa, language, there're ladies present." Glanced at Angela. "Kind of."

Repressing a sudden urge to scratch Bill's eyes out, Angela said, "Why do you want Larry involved? After he fooked you over on S*paced Out*? Had you write all those drafts on spec?"

"Let's just say we resolved our creative differences," Bill said.

"Bullshit," Darren said. "Larry bought him off and there's no fuckin' way I'm going along with this."

"I think we should sit calmly like civilized people and discuss this," Angela said.

"Nothing to discuss," Bill said. "Larry's in or I'm out and Lionsgate's already on board, wanna know why?"

Angela sighed, went, "'Cause they like, *like* you."

He snapped, "Not like, fucking *love*, as in, I call the shots."

Angela went to Becker, "He's right, you know. Lionsgate loves him, so if he and Larry are a package, we're stuck with Larry."

"Larry's a package all right," Becker said. "Good choice of word." He tried for a sneer, managed a poor man's grimace, which made him look like a disappointed groupie, went, "So how's the screenplay coming?"

Bill went up close to Becker, said, "All humility aside, it's fucking awesome, a clusterfuck of ingenious writing."

Angela forced a grin, went, "We're blessed to have you, Bill."

Bill smiled, all teeth and no cattle, went, "Finally, something we agree on."

TWENTY-ONE

People are afraid to merge on the freeways of Los Angeles.
BRET EASTON ELLIS, *Less Than Zero*

In the limo from LAX, riding along the 105 with Kat and Lars, Paula was screaming into the phone, demanding to speak to her film agent, Donna James. Going:

"I don't give a shit if she's in a fucking meeting, do you know who the fuck you're talking to?"

"You said you're Paula Segal." The girl sounded like she was sixteen fucking years old.

"No, not Paula Segal," Paula said, "Paula Segal of *Bust*. You've heard of *Bust*, I hope."

"I'm sorry," the girl said. "What's 'bust'?"

"You don't know what..." Paula's eyes rolled. "*Bust*. B-U-S-T, *Bust*."

"Um, sorry," she said.

"Ohmigod," Paula said. "Have you been living under a freakin' stone? First we have to wait fifteen minutes in the hot sun for the limo, and now *this*. Can I have your name, please?"

"I told you my name."

"And you thought I was actually *listening*? What's your name?"

"Britney."

"Of course it is," Paula said. "Well, Britney, please tell Donna if she doesn't call me back in five, make that four minutes, she's fired, and you're fired too!"

Paula clicked off, loving this. Finally, after years of mediocrity, she was in control of her career again. She had to savor this, relish it.

As Paula was fixing a drink in the limo's understocked bar—she was going to complain to Charles Ardai about this later—Kat said, "Did you really have to speak to her that way?"

"Who?" Paula asked.

"That assistant—Britney?"

"These people work for me," Paula said.

"But you don't have to be, like, such a bitch about it. You're acting like my fuckin' sisters."

"Your sisters are famous, but I'm a star," Paula said. "There's a difference, right, Lars?"

Lars was staring at his iPhone; Jesus Christ, what was it with the Swedes and Apple products? And he wasn't watching porn again, was he? Yes he was—Paula caught a glimpse of a gang-bang.

"For fuck's sake, can you turn that shit off?" she said.

"Vut shit?" Lars asked, practically screaming, because he was listening with earbuds.

"That horrible, sexist crap," Paula said. "It's okay when we're writing about Max Fisher because we're, like, in character, but it's degrading to women."

"I don't think it's so degrading," Kat said.

"Well, aren't you Miss Oppositional today?" Paula said. "If I said I want to fuck Angelina Jolie would you argue that too?"

"I think porn is empowering," Kat said.

"Watching four guys taking turns sodomizing a chick when she's bound and gagged is empowering?"

"If the woman is in control, yes."

"How is she in control if she's bound and gagged?"

"Maybe she wants to be bound and gagged."

"You mean maybe she's drugged? High on PIMP?"

"Most porn stars don't take drugs," Kat said.

"Really, and how do you know? Have you ever been in a porno?"

"Yes, actually."

Lars's eyes bulged. He went, "Vut film? I must know title."

"I made a couple of movies actually," Kat said, "with this rabbi I knew in Israel."

"You made a porno with a rabbi?" Paula asked.

"These were amateur movies, just for Israel."

"Some of the best porn is in Israel," Lars said. "Not many people know this."

"Good, so why don't you watch with Lars, knock yourself out, get your rocks off."

Paula downed the rest of her drink and made another, wondering what she was doing with Kat. She'd been into her because she was a Kardashian and because she was, let's face it, hot, but she was starting to understand why her family had disowned her.

Paula's cell rang, Donna James, going, "I'm so sorry to make you wait, Paula. How was your flight into L.A.?"

"Hideously awful."

"I'm so sorry to hear that. I'm super excited about your reading tonight."

Why were people in L.A. always super excited? Wasn't it enough to just be excited?

"Well, I'm super pissed off with your fucking agency," Paula said. "I'm in town with my entourage on our book tour, and my meeting with Darren Becker and Lionsgate still hasn't been arranged."

"Actually I just got off the phone with Lionsgate," Paula said. "Unfortunately they can't meet today, but I've set up a meeting for you with Darren Becker and his producing partner, for you and Lars, at three p.m. I'll text you the address."

"Whoa, whoa, back up," Paula said. "Producing partner? I thought Darren was the only producer on this project."

"No, that's changed. He's working with Brandi Love."

"Brandi who?"

"Love."

"Sounds like a porno name."

"Vut?" Lars had rabbit ears.

"Nothing," Paula said to Lars. "Go back to your gangbang."

"I'm sorry?" Donna asked.

"Not you," Paula said. "Who's this Brandi?"

"She's a new name for me too," Donna said, "but Darren has been raving about her. Oh, and Darren will tell you the great news about the screenwriter they've hired. His name's Bill Moss and there's a lot of heat on him around town right now."

"I wish someone had informed me about all this," Paula said. "Does Lee Child find out about his screenwriters third-hand?"

"Oh, I'm sorry about that," Donna said. "Next time there's news I'll make sure you're the first to know."

The traffic was so bad that they didn't have time to check into their hotel, and they went straight to the meeting with Becker. It was at Becker's office, on the second floor of a modest building in Westwood. Paula was expecting something more upscale; what the fuck?

Paula, Lars, and Kat entered together. While Paula was still upset with Kat she thought the pros of having her along outweighed the cons.

Darren Becker came out to greet them. He was lean and tan with artificially white teeth, wearing a shirt with only two buttons buttoned, like Hank Moody in *Californication*.

Becker shook hands as Paula made the introductions, empha-sizing that Kat was "Kat *Kardashian*."

"It's great to finally meet you," Becker said, as he led the group along a hallway to his office. "I can't tell you how excited I am to be working on this project. And Brandi, my producing partner, is super excited as well."

In the office, a blonde was waiting. Paula's first thought was, *Holy shit, she's hot*. Her second thought was, *Holy shit, how is this possible?*

"This…this can't be happening," Paula said, staring at the woman.

"What's wrong, baby?" Kat asked.

Becker, with his permanent smile, went, "Brandi Love meet Paula Segal."

"You're…you're supposed to be dead," Paula said.

"Bigfoot revived me," Angela said.

"Lars is confused," Lars said.

"This isn't Brandi Love," Paula said. "This is Angela Petrakos… from *Bust*."

"Wait, Brandi Love, I know your work," Lars said. "You are star of *Brandi and Ginger*, yes?"

"In the flesh," Angela said.

"Wait," Paula said to Angela. "You were in porn too?"

"I've had a dark few years, yes," Angela said.

"It's nothing to be ashamed of," Kat said.

Lars, ready to drop to his knees, gushed, "It is a great honor to be in your presence."

"I still can't believe you're alive," Paula said to Angela. "And I can't believe I'm here, actually *with* you. The next thing you'll tell me is that Max Fisher and that Lee Child wannabe are alive too."

"I don't know about Max," Angela said, "but I actually saw Sebastian the other day at the Chateau Marmont."

"Funny you mention Lee Child," Becker said. "I met his brother at my health club the other day. Get this, he was trying to pitch me to be the screenwriter of *Bust*."

"Over my fookin' dead body," Angela said.

"I've already seen your fookin' dead body," Paula said. "What was this about Bigfoot?"

An old sleazy guy, a squat Latino with a mustache, and a young guy in ripped jeans and a hoodie entered.

"Speaking of the screenwriter," Becker said.

Paula leaned in to Kat, whispered into her ear, "Is this a producing team or the world's ugliest boy band?"

The old guy came over and Paula shook his sweaty hand as he said, "Larry Reed, A-List producer."

The Latino guy said, "Yo, I'm Eddie Vegas, I'm Executive Producer too."

"*Co*-Executive Producer," Larry said to Eddie.

"Excuse me?" Angela asked.

"I'm sorry?" Becker asked.

"He's my partner," Larry said.

"*Co?*" Eddie said to Larry.

"You didn't say anything about him to us," Angela said to Larry.

"He's in or me and Bill are out," Larry said. "You want to tell Lionsgate that you're looking for a new screenwriter? Yeah, I'm sure that conversation will go over well. Why don't you also tell them you want to cast Lindsay Lohan as Angela. Actually, come to think of it, she'd be a pretty good Angela."

"*I'm* playing Angela," Angela said to Larry.

The guy in the hoodie didn't shake, just looked at Paula—she could see the whites of his eyes around his pupils.

Paula had great psycho-dar. It was how she'd written *Bust*, gotten into the heads of so many psychos. Put her in a room with a hundred people and one psycho, she could pick out the psycho. Seriously, the Secret Service should hire her to screen rooms before presidential appearances. But in this room her psycho bell wasn't just ringing, it was fucking blaring.

"Well, it's great to have the whole gang in one room finally," Larry said, smiling. "This is super exciting stuff and I'm super hungry. Who wants sushi?"

TWENTY-TWO

I have two rules: no castration, and no violence to nuns.
CHARLES ARDAI

Max loved to follow the news stories about himself. At Attica, fuck, he must've read the stories about his arrest and trial thousands of times and it always brought him such a rush. The only thing more addicting than PIMP was fame. Max couldn't get enough of himself; he felt the way movie stars feel when they read gossip. Whining about the paparazzi, yeah, right, they ate that shit up—Alec Baldwin probably had TMZ pics of himself hanging over his bed, staring at his own manic face every time he came.

Lately Max had been reading the articles about the search for the mystery man, the Philip Seymour Hoffman-on-a-bad-day figure with an Irish accent, who was responsible for the shootings in Brooklyn and Harlem. It wasn't as satisfying as seeing the Fisher name in the papers, but it was damn close.

He read an article in the *Post* that rehashed what had been in the papers about him lately, how they were describing the wanted killer as "twisted," "heartless," and "cold blooded." He remembered his mother once shouting at him, "You'll never be anybody!"

Well, he'd proven her wrong, goddamn it.

"Look who's the big kahuna now, momma!" he shouted.

He flipped to Page Six. Nope, no mention there, but wait, what was this? Paula Segal and some Swedish guy, reading

from their phenomenal bestseller, *Bust*? Sounded to Max like a
dumb title, God knows why it was selling so well. But that name
Segal? Why did it sound so familiar?

Wait a sec, holy shit. Paula Segal was the writer bitch who'd
visited him years ago at Attica. Max's biographer.

He read the description of the novel again, and realized the
dumb book was about his life. Now, knowing that the book was
about *him*, he decided that *Bust* was a great title, slam-dunk
fucking brilliant. Whoa, and, holy shit, what was this? They
were making a TV show of the book too? Someone was actually
going to *play* him on TV? He had to read this part several times
to make sure he was reading this correctly. Either this PIMP
was better than he thought, or one of his insane fantasies was
actually happening.

Max Fisher, a character? A fucking American icon? Tony
Soprano *who*? This was Max's time, the moment he'd been
waiting for, for like ever. He had to get out to L.A., visit the set,
witness this for himself, but he couldn't just leave town, especially not with a blackmailing nun on his ass.

Max had run through so many scenarios about the nun.
Bottom line, no way was she going away. If he were insane
enough to actually give her the cash now, it would be only a
matter of time before she was back for more. Nuns always
came again, ask the Pope.

Max had been chipping at the PIMP, taking it easy, well sort
of. He just got a new supply and told himself he needed to test-
run it. Whoa fuck, this shit was strong and then some. Gave
him a rush like white speed and his mind, that beast was fucking
electric and, like Richard Pryor on an 8-ball, it was talking to
him. Oh yeah, cajoling him, telling him all the good shit he
always got off on, starting with, "Yo, you the Max."

Better believe it.

Max shouted, "Word!"

And now the PIMP suggested—in its sweetest PIMP voice—"We need a mega flourish."

Max went, "Wotcha…"—sure sign of Max out of control was his use of Cockney—"…got in mind, Homes?"

Heard the plan, whooped. "That is a doozy."

He picked up the phone, dialed.

At first the nun was skeptical, asked, "Why do we have to meet at a church?"

Max wanted to shout, *'Cause, I like say so, bitch*.

PIMP went with, "Fitting we use a sacred place for sacred business."

She was suspicious, but went with it.

They arranged to meet at St. John the Divine on Amsterdam Avenue. How do you dress to rub out a nun? Somberly. Max was in a black suit, black shirt and if he'd inserted the tiny white collar, he could have been De Niro in *True Confessions*. He carried a muted, expensive briefcase, like all top brass in clerical circles. No friggin knockoffs for them unless you were counting altar boys.

The nun had taken center pew and old habits die hard, she was absently polishing the rail.

Max slipped in next to her, noted it was just the two of them in the place, went, "Might we light a candle for those who suffer?"

The nun, dressed in Christian Dior and smelling of Chanel, went, "Cut the fucking shit."

PIMP, loving the mind fuck, said, "Might we least kneel and pray, for world peace?"

She sighed deeply, an old pro at it, as Max opened the briefcase and, in a PIMP-fueled move, took out a nine-inch blade, gutted her as a recorded choir began *How Great Thou Art*.

PIMP asked, "Don't'cha love fucking symmetry?"

Blood splashed all over Max, his black suit showing the spillage like dark martyrdom. The nun was making lots of guttural noises and Max said, "Ah, shut the fuck up already."

When she had bled out, he managed to put her sitting up-right, then wound a rosary round her hands like handcuffs. Nuns do love their beads. As precaution, he slipped the tiny white collar on, getting that priest gig going, he even felt, well, *holy.*

Then giggled, whispered, "Not as holy as this cow."

And stood, stared at the high altar, said, "Lord, accept this humble sacrifice."

Outside, he took a moment to gather his frazzled wits when an old woman stopped and asked, "Bless me father?"

He touched her cheek almost with tenderness. Fuck, he felt... *humble* in his omnipotence, said, "Child, many are called, nun are chosen."

Maybe PIMP had been in control during the whole time because reality didn't hit home till he was back at his apartment and said, "Holy shit, I killed a fuckin' nun."

Down from the PIMP, he thought it was a dream. But he checked his dick, saw it was still tiny—nope, not dreaming.

He flicked on the TV to New York 1 News and it was right there:

NUN MURDERED AT MANHATTAN CHURCH

That pretty much said it all. Max couldn't tear himself away from the TV all evening, watching every station's reports about the murder. There was a description of him, maybe from the old woman outside the church, and talk of video footage.

Somehow living across from Manhattan North wasn't as exciting anymore. He knew it was time to cut his losses and take off—for a while anyway. But where to? He couldn't go back to fucking Portlandia, not when he was on the verge of ruling the world.

Then it hit him; it was so obvious, maybe even destiny.

Next morning, he was on a flight to L.A., the PIMP muttering, "We are so going to own this fucking town."

TWENTY-THREE

There were a lot of terms you had to learn,
as opposed to the shylock business
where all you had to know how to say was,
"Give me the fuckin money."
ELMORE LEONARD, *Get Shorty*

"What the fook are we going to do?"

Angela with Darren, who was eating the last piece of tekka maki from the sushi party platter.

Smiling while chewing, Darren said, "We can get married, elope if you don't want to have a wedding."

"No, I mean about all of these fookin' producers," Angela said. "We don't have any actors yet and the producers are sucking up twenty percent of the budget."

"Whoa, talking about budgets now," Darren said. "My girl knows her shit."

Oh now he was giving her that look again. That oh so romantic look of, *I want to climb on your body and hump you.*

"Yes, I've been reading up on the business side, frankly it's easier to grasp than the porn business. Read a couple of articles online, browse the PGA website, and you get the gist."

"Well, I don't know what those sites are telling you," Darren said, "but when a budget gets too high you have to do one thing. You have to…" He brushed aside the shite from the desk, plopped her down, and began unbuttoning her blouse. "…make some reductions."

Jaysus, how much sex drive did this guy have? And why was she a magnet for guys on Viagra?

"Who are we going to let go?" Angela asked. "Larry and Bill are a package, and Larry and Eddie Vegas are a package."

"Speaking of packages…" Darren unzipped his fly. At least the guy was hung so it wasn't a total loss.

"Including you and me, there are five producers on this project, and that doesn't include producers at Lionsgate and the network. By the time the credits run, the show will be over."

"We can't let that happen." His hand was in her shirt now, feeling her up like a horny teenager. He said, "We have to hold on to our *Bust*…our very, very sexy *Bust*."

Oh, gawd.

Letting him have his fun though she sure as fook wasn't, she said, "God knows why Lionsgate love Bill so much. I said to the exec, 'Maybe we should give Quentin a call,' 'cause I heard he's looking for an edgy pilot to write and direct. Lionsgate says we can't let Bill go because, get this, 'He's the hottest writer in town right now.' I'm talking Quentin T, who's won how many Oscars? And Bill Moss is hotter?"

"I don't want to point the accusing finger of blame," he said, reaching under her panties, "but it is your fault."

"My fault?" Angela said. "How's it fookin' my fault?"

Yanking down her skirt and panties, he gave her ass a hard spank like he thought he was in fookin' *Nymphomaniac*, then said, "You were the one who sent them *Spaced Out*. You were the one who got them hot on Moss."

Angela knew this was true but said, "Well, we're stuck with him, so that doesn't solve the problem, does it?"

"So what do you think about what I was saying before?" Darren asked as he grabbed her ankles.

"About my bust?" she asked.

"No, about our wedding," he said. "I think you'd look so sexy in a wedding dress. Virginal white of course." He was thrusting in her. "I can't get enough of you. You're like a bad habit."

"We have to figure out how to get rid of these gobshites," Angela said.

"How do we do that?" Darren said. "I mean…fuck, your tits are so hot…it's like a game of pick-up sticks right now. If we pull out one stick, we lose…oh my God, baby…I mean we're stuck. There's…shit…no way out."

"There's always a way," Angela said.

"Yeah," he said, moaning. "Oh, fuck, yeah."

Angela had to get away from Darren, just to give her body a break, so she made up an excuse that she was meeting up with an old college friend. Yeah, like she'd even made it through three days of high school. She just wanted to take a ride, clear her head, maybe walk along the beach at night, hear waves crashing. Depressing late-in-act-two-of-a-movie shite like that.

She got in her car, checked her phone for messages. Lionsgate asking about the screenplay, making sure Bill Moss was "happy."

Fookin' A.

Angela responded: *Screenplay's coming along swimmingly*.

She'd seen swimmingly used in a screenplay recently and had been dying to find a good use for it.

Then she saw a Facebook notification—a friend request from Sebastian. The fooker! He shot her, left her for dead, and now he's *friending* her? When she found him she was going to kill him slowly, with maximum pain, make the Drano in a bathtub seem like a warm-up.

She headed past Santa Monica, toward Malibu. The sun had set, but there was a big moon, and there were great views of winding cliffs. Then she noticed that a car with tinted windows was following her.

It took a few minutes to realize that it had to be Sebastian himself. Who else could it be?

He was following *her*? Yeah, right. Fook this.

She hit the brakes hard and he had to swerve to avoid her. Then she was chasing him. She sped alongside him, narrowly missing a head-on collision with a truck, then rammed the side of the car. Ahead the road was turning to the right. If she kept ramming him to the left he'd drive straight off the cliff, fall hundreds of feet, and die in a fiery crash. It wouldn't be the brutal death that she had planned for him, but it would be close enough.

But he must've realized the predicament because at the last moment he skidded to a stop, inches from the cliff.

Angela climbed out of the car, shaken but nothing like how she was about to feel in a moment. She glared at the guy coming towards her, and from her mouth dribbled, "Oh my sweet Jaysus."

She saw what appeared to be Philip Seymour Hoffman, as if he were auditioning for the role of Heath Ledger's bloated corpse. With a ginger beard and, fuck me, a shitload of weight.

But that smirk. Oh Lord! It couldn't be…it could only be…

Max.

And worst of all, her damn treacherous heart skipped a beat. The fuck was with that?

Max, seeming equally dazed and bewildered, croaked, "Angela?"

He explained about how he'd seen the name Brandi Love on a website, and followed her leaving Darren Becker's earlier, but it had been dark and he hadn't gotten a good look at her…

"But…" he said. "You…you were dead."

Angela hadn't seen Max this frightened since he'd found out the murder of his wife had been botched. She told him the Big-foot story, an abbreviated version, and that she'd taken on the name Brandi Love after a sojourn in London. Yep, she used the word "sojourn."

Max kissed her. Angela was blown away by the jolt of pure,

unadulterated joy. It literally felt like time stopped as they held each other. So much history…most if it bad, a lot of it deadly, murderous, ferocious, insane, but oh what a ride. Then— enough with the *Notebook* shite—he had her over the car's bashed fender, his tongue deep in her throat and her gripping at his dick. They would have done it right there, mad and fierce, lost in a carnal frenzy, but a tour bus of old folk passed and the codgers, delightedly leaning out the windows, goaded, "Get a room," "Give her one!" "Ride that rainbow!" and inexplicably, "Free medical for over-70s!"

Angela pushed Max away, attempting to fix her clothing while he, showman supreme, bowed, hollered, "Coming soon to a theatre near you!"

Then he turned to Angela. She expected words of love, got, "Aren't you some cunt?"

Took her a moment, then she posed on her right foot, did a mini pirouette, and blasted him a right hook that lifted him off his feet. He sprawled in the dust, spat out some blood, snarled, "That all yah got, Angie?"

Well, no.

Kicked him in the balls. When he recovered some from that, he held up a hand, gasped, "Can a guy buy a gal a drink?"

He could.

Considerably the worse for wear, they ended up in a small bar that advertised, *Happy Hour All Day*.

Angela sneered. "Just like our respective lives."

They grabbed a back table, dim lit to downplay their bedraggled appearance, and Max tried to put his hand up her skirt.

The waitress, standing before them, noticed and instead of calling the cops, smiled, said, "Second marriage huh?"

Max ordered a Long Island Tea and added, "Don't skimp on the rum."

Angela had a large Jameson with Coors Light.

Max laughed, said, "Light? Gotta watch the waist, eh babe?"

She looked at him, really looked, said, "I guess being schizoid, you're eating for two? One of them Orson Welles?"

He laughed, said, "Love it when you talk dirty, Angie."

The drinks came and Angie raised her glass, said, "*Slainte*."

Max, draining most of his first, burped, said, "To soul mates."

Angela, despite her turmoil of feelings never ever succumbed to sentiment, muttered, "Whoever the fuck they might be."

The waitress smiled, gave Angela a thumbs up, said, "You said it, sister."

Angela, never big on sisterhood either, smiled nicely, said, "Fuck the hell off."

Germaine Greer would have been proud.

Naomi Wolf, hmm, not so much.

After a couple of drinks and reminiscing about the bad old days, the conversation turned to *Bust*.

"It's our baby," Max said. "We should be running the show."

"Trust me," Angela said, "I'd rather it be me and you than these Hollywood fucks I have to work with. I'm sick of their fookin' coconut water and fake smiles and dumb script notes."

"Then what's the problem?" Max said. "Bring me on board."

"It's not that simple," Angela said. "We already have five Executive Producers, not including the execs at Lionsgate and whatever studio gets on board."

"Sounds like we have to take some people out," Max said.

Agreeing, Angela went, "Well, Darren Becker controls the property equally with me right now, so if something were to happen to Darren you could take his place."

"I'll get it done tonight," Max said.

"Too dangerous," Angela said, but she thought his assertiveness was fookin' hot. "You're a wanted felon. But I know the perfect man for the job."

Max got his hand under her skirt now, all the way up, and said, "Maybe we *are* soul mates."

It felt good with Max back inside her; it felt right.

"Mates, yes," she said. "Souls, not so sure."

TWENTY-FOUR

*Noir is the swift kick in the nuts you get
just as you are about to cross the finish line to win the race.*
DANA KABEL

The murder of Sister Alison, in broad daylight in a famous
Manhattan church, was the story of the year. The Mayor and
even the Pope were outraged, and the public wanted justice.

Miscali was on the firing line for his C.O. who opened with,
"The fuck is with nuns being offed on my patch?"

Miscali liked things to be at least technically accurate, dared,
"Actually, sir, just one nun, and it's the church's patch."

His C.O. went ape, screamed, "Freaking sarcasm, from a
dumb flatfoot who's always a day late and many fucking dollars
short."

Miscali saw many things wrong with the sentence but decided
to forgo any further correction, went with, "I'm on it, sir."

Later, Miscali tracked down a witness, an old woman who
claimed she'd seen a heavyset, red-haired man leaving the church
who looked like "Satan himself." Some grainy video of a guy
who could've been the man the old woman had described was
picked up by a security camera near the church. Watching the
video, Joe had a nauseous feeling, something churning in his
gut and he wasn't sure why.

In bed, in the middle of a sleepless, acid indigestion night,
it hit.

He watched the video again and muttered, "Philip Seymour
Hoffman."

Then Joe remembered a guy bumping into him on the street the other day, maybe last week. It was all coming into focus, like a Polaroid he wasn't sure he wanted to see. The party invite, PIMP, the murders in Harlem and Brooklyn. Had Max Fisher been living right across from the precinct?

Joe rushed to the bathroom and threw up the veal parm special he'd had before sleep. Fisher was like Jason from *Friday the Thirteenth*, no end to his sequels. Put even *Rocky* to shame, even if you counted De Niro and Stallone in that lame one-last-pull at the franchise tit.

Joe called Leonard, got him up to speed.

"Jesus Christ," Leonard moaned, half asleep, "not with your Fisher obsession again."

"I'm tellin' you," Joe said. "This time's different."

"That's what you said before you flew to Boca on the Department's dime."

"I'll be by in ten."

Joe and Leonard went to the apartment building across from the precinct, asked about the tenant in the penthouse.

"Sean Mullen," the doorman said. "Lovely man. Moved out yesterday."

Joe and Leonard rode the elevator to the penthouse. Buzzed, no answer. Thanks to 9/11 and ass-fucking civil liberties there was a law in New York that cops could enter an apartment with no warrant if there was a suspicion of drug use.

Joe said to Leonard, "I smell pot, don't you?" and he busted down the door.

The place was huge, but empty.

"Wow," Leonard said, "just the other night the place was rockin'."

But then, in the empty master bedroom, in the middle of the floor, Joe saw it.

"Holy fuckin' shit," he said, bagging the evidence.

"What's holy shit?" Leonard said. "So you found some book."

"Not any book," Joe said. "This is *Bust*, the bestselling book about Max Fisher."

"This *is* shocking." Leonard smirked. "You know how to read?"

"I don't have to read, I read the papers," Joe said. Then, realizing the stupidity of this, covered with, "Don't you get it? That's why Fisher was living here, right across from us, and that's why he left the book. He's trying to fuck with my head."

"And it's working. Joe, seriously, I'm talkin' as a friend here. You need a vacation."

"Fuck you," Joe said.

At the precinct, Joe updated his C.O., starting with, "We have a witness."

The C.O. blessed himself with scorn dripping from every movement, said, "Al-ee-fucking-looyah. Do tell me you at least talked to her, or is that way too much to hope for?"

Joe felt a tiny bit of pride, not much but a shitload more than had been going round, said, "Not only an I.D. but I immediately got on the horn with the airlines and *result*, the alleged perp is not only the one and only Max Fisher but he's on his merry way to L.A."

"Whoa, slow down," the C.O. said. "Max Fisher?"

Joe told him about the book he'd found and said, "I think Max Fisher is the Red Devil, I think he killed that woman in Harlem and those dealers in Brooklyn, and he's responsible for the PIMP epidemic that's sweeping the country."

"Maybe he blew up that Malaysian airplane too."

"I'm serious," Joe said. "I don't have all the evidence yet, but if I go to L.A.—"

"You're not going to fucking L.A.," the C.O. said. "You're gonna stay here and get me a break, a real break, in the Sister Alison case, or you can kiss your pension goodbye."

Joe had his own doubts, thought Fisher might be deliberately driving him insane, but when you're obsessed you're fucked and by late afternoon he was sitting in the middle of a three-seat row on a crowded flight to LAX out of Newark. Crammed in by a fat guy reading a lurid paperback called *The Pack* and a quietly sobbing woman to his right. The AC was on the blink and Joe felt he was drinking the fat guy's sweat. The woman meanwhile had increased her sobbing. Joe, sipping the Fifth he'd brought in a Starbucks container, asked, "You all right, ma'am?"

She stopped instantly, whirled round to glare at Joe.

She asked, "You what, the feelings police? A person can't have a moment of dignified grief without some cocksucker mocking her?"

Joe looked to the fat guy for help, but the guy was engrossed in the novel and making little oh-fuck-me purrs of delight. Joe took a healthy swig of the bourbon, said, "Sorry for caring."

Oops.

Her voice was up, she shrilled, "You care? You know me? Why do you care, you looking for a pity grope, that it, you pervert?"

The flight attendant arrived, all perfume and impatience, demanded, "Everything all right here?"

With a sigh, Joe flashed his gold and everything quieted down. After take-off the woman leaned into Joe, asked, "Wanna join the mile high club?"

To avoid having to field any more such offers, Joe got talking to the guy on his other side. Tongue loosened by the bourbon, he mentioned the nun's murder, the fact that it was the first such slaying in a decade. The guy reluctantly put aside *The Pack*, said, "That is just shocking."

Joe nodded, and in an almost literate mood, said, "Agreed— a nun's death diminishes us all."

The guy gave him a look of utter scorn, said, "You gotta be kidding, Columbo, I meant they weren't killing half enough of the bitches."

It was only later, when Joe, halfway sober again, was unpacking in his two-bit motel near LAX, that he realized he'd nicked the guy's novel.

Joe was enough of a cop to know that in a foreign land, even if that foreign land is L.A., you call in the locals. Not only do they know the ground but you save them burning your ass later.

Joe used a contact back in NYC to hook him up with a detective from the Hollywood Division, a woman named Gaylin. Being a cop in Hollywood, she looked more like a movie star than a flatfoot. Light-skinned black and she was built. Her rack had Joe slightly stupefied.

He went to her, "You're like for real a serious cop?"

Nothing like getting off on the wrong foot. She stared at him for a long minute, a guy in a bad suit, tie askew, a shirt from Primark, and his face reflecting a long line of cheap cigars, rotten coffee, too many jelly doughnuts.

She went, "You get it that for us to deal with the movie crowd, we have to blend."

Joe attempted a hint of humor, said, "I'd say you managed that."

She got right in his face, snarled, "Don't fucking patronize me, dickwad. It's my playpen, you get to ride along. Your job is to stop staring at my tits, it's embarrassing."

Joe, a tiny bit turned on by the reprimand, went, "I'm all yours."

Got, "I try to avoid infections."

Their first call was on Becker, one of the producers of *Bust*. He seemed on edge, far from happy to have cops all over the TV show he was about to film. He said, "Those pictures were Photoshopped, I wasn't at those pool parties."

Joe looked at Gaylin then back at Becker and went, "Pool parties?"

"Oh," Becker said. "That's not why... Never mind. What's this about?"

"Max Fisher," Joe said. "You know him?"

"I know *of* him."

"The fuck's that supposed to mean?"

"He's the subject of my new TV show."

"Have you met him recently?"

Becker smiled. Did this guy putt from the rough? Joe was pretty sure he did.

"What's the smile for?" Joe asked, not sure he wanted to hear the answer.

"Well, I assume Fisher's dead, isn't he?" Becker asked.

"We have reason to believe he may not be dead."

"I'm not sure I follow."

"We think he's been living in New York City," Joe said, "dealing a new drug called PIMP, you may have heard of it."

"It's been in the news," Becker said.

"He altered his appearance," Joe said, "may have had plastic surgery. He's still not exactly going to win any beauty contests. He has red hair, they're calling him the Red Devil on the streets. People say he looks like Philip Seymour Hoffman now—post autopsy."

"Are you fucking shitting me?" Becker seemed excited. "I'm gonna have to work this into the show."

"Fuck your show," Joe said. "Have you met a man named Sean Mullen?"

"Sean who?"

"That may be Fisher's new identity."

"Look, I'm just trying to make a TV show here," Larry said. "At least get a pilot shot. I mean it's been one thing after another on this thing. You should've seen the people involved in this project, stuffed into my office like a fucking Marx Brothers movie. I thought somebody would open the door and we'd all tumble into the hallway. We haven't even started rolling yet and there hasn't been a production with this much drama since LiLo did *The Canyons*."

Joe sighed, then said, "Be a damn shame to shut down the whole operation cause of one douchebag."

Becker got all antsy, moaned, "Look I told you I have no idea where Fisher is and I doubt my producing partner knows either."

"Who's your producing partner?" Joe asked.

"Her name's Brandi Love," Becker said, "but she's gone for the day, personal business."

Joe wrote the name in a pad, muttering, "Sounds like a porno name." Then, "Any more names for us?"

"Bill Moss," Becker said.

"Who's Bill Moss?" Joe asked.

"He's writing the pilot," Darren said. "He's been researching Fisher. He'd know more than me."

"Where do we find this gentleman?" Gaylin asked.

Becker gave her the once over, said, "She speaks. I thought you were here to take notes."

Gaylin smiled and it transformed her, made her looked like Halle Berry, and how great is that?

She asked in a demure tone, "You're an industry guy, ever hear of the Hollywood hop?"

Becker was into it now, going with the mellow vibe, asked, "That a book I should option?"

She let her weight shift to her right then stomped ferociously on Becker's instep. He roared and hobbled over to his desk.

She said, "Get Moss's address and then hop back here with it."

Back in their car, Gaylin pulled out into traffic, a small smile playing on her lips, said, "Like the kids go, let's bounce."

Joe was in love, and almost didn't hear her when she said, "Tell me about this Fisher. I heard some shit but surely no one guy could have caused all the havoc they claim."

Where to begin? Joe said, "This guy is like Keyser, the fuck's his name? Whoozie? You know, that movie. He's like a ghost, but trails mayhem and homicide like bad news."

Gaylin, focusing on her driving, asked, "Keyser?"

"You know, Kevin What The Fuck's His Name played him."

"Costner?"

"You don't see a lot of movies, do you?"

She threw him a look, said, "I work with these fuckheads every day, clean up after them, you think I want to pay twelve bucks for anything they produce?"

Joe smiled. She had a pair, this one.

He said, "Reason Fisher is still in the game, still free, is people underestimate the schmuck, they see this fat jerkoff, in fucking love with himself, and they let down their guard. The tighter, more hopeless the jam, the more bodies he leaves behind."

Gaylin digested this, then went, "Guess we'll have to go the Hollywood route."

Did she mean traffic?

She added, "Shoot the fuck in slow motion."

Joe didn't for a moment think she was kidding.

*

She dropped Joe at his rental, said she had to get back to pick up her kid from daycare.

Joe, feeling the hit in his gut, asked, "You're married?"

"I look that dumb?" she said. "Divorced twice."

Back in business, Joe said, "Join the club."

Was he imagining it or did he and Gaylin have a connection? He had the light, weightless feeling of falling in love; who the fuck cared that this always led to disaster?

He went to see Bill Moss.

TWENTY-FIVE

Noir…all those beautiful sentences telling you the most terrible things.
ROBERT POLITO

In his bungalow apartment in Venice Beach Bill Moss was antsy, big-time. He'd just taken a call from some New York cop who was coming by to "ask some questions about *Bust*." Was that just bullshit and was he really coming to talk about Mo? Yeah, probably.

Bill looked at his laptop, Final Draft open to the *Bust* screenplay, and man, it had been flying. The words tumbling over each other in an attempt to outshine anything he'd ever written before. He was into the Drano scene, but wasn't using the dialogue Segal and Stiegsson had written. They were fucking novelists; what did they know about screenwriting? Even Faulkner and Goodis had gotten the shit kicked out of them out here.

Bill stopped typing for a moment, nearly laughed, saw that image of the Drano melting through the skin of the dead psycho and thought, *Fuckit, I'm the real deal, the big cheese, a Matt Weiner of word alchemy*. Hot on this thought was lurking paranoia. The lingering stench of having offed Mo was like a constant whisper of, *You are so fucked, Jose*.

He crushed some speed ampoules, put them in a blender with pineapple, Red Bull, and sheep urine. The sheep urine was a tip from Gwynne, before she *consciously uncoupled* from the Coldplay dude.

Going *Taxi Driver*, he muttered, "Every muscle must be tight," as he put the concoction on warp speed and watched as the whole mix whirled.

He was dressed in khaki combat shorts and a black T with the words *LET IT BE...LET THAT SUCKER SLIDE* across the chest. His feet were pushed into Huaraches, loose Mexican sandals he'd bought in Cancun while working on his last script. It had been called *Fast Track*, and was, let's face it, a total rip-off of the ill-fated HBO series *Luck*, based on a self-published book by some has-been New York City crime writer. The writer had been e-mailing Bill lately, and contacting him on Twitter and Facebook, trying to arrange a time "to hang out" during his next trip to L.A., but Bill had been blowing the jackass off. Yeah, like he needed to hang out with some hanger-on novelist, when he was finally making it onto the Hollywood A-list, getting rez's at the best restaurants and partying with Nic Pizzolatto.

As Bill gulped the foul beverage, he remembered hanging on the set of *Luck*, for research—writer code for stealing ideas—and shooting the shit with Dusty, that's Dustin Hoffman to the plebs, and what a fucking shame it was that *Luck* had been cancelled just because, get this, a few freaking horses got hurt. Boo hoo, Jesus Christ, did they ever count the death toll after a John Wayne western?

In the large right pocket of the awful shorts, Bill had a long lethal blade with a gold handle and a precious stone embedded in the handle. A gift from a nephew of Ortega's. Oh yeah, Bill knew the players. As in speed dial to the maddest and most juiced honchos, guys Bruce Willis would piss himself to know. The drink shot into his bloodstream, giving his heart a wallop, making him feel like the Irish psycho in the *Bust* screenplay.

The doorbell shrilled, and fuming, wired, murderous, he let the cop in.

"I'm Miscali," the prick hard-assed, then pushed by him, no like, *hello, how you doing*, and insult to fucking injury, walked over to the *Bust* screenplay and, Bill couldn't fucking believe it, began to read.

Bill took a moment of sheer incredulity to assess the guy. Where the fuck did he find that shitty suit? If he'd worn that suit in the eighties it would've been ten years out of style. Was there an auction of the old wardrobe from *Barney Miller*? In L.A., where pretty much anything went fashion-wise—see Brad Pitt—this suit screamed, *Shoot me now.*

Miscali sneered, "So you're glorifying that psycho Fisher, the man responsible for the death of my partner, one of New York's finest ever?"

The drink took Bill for a momentary mellow stroll along his pride in the work. He said, "I'm working on the part where a cop gets iced and dumped in a lot in Harlem—that your partner?"

And Miscali did the worst thing of all, he sneered. You could see the contempt dripping off him. He snarled, "Exploitive sensationalist bullshit. You get off on killing? Are you writing a movie or the script for a snuff film?"

The insult pushed Bill to instant aggression. He fingered the blade, went, "What're you implying?"

"You get ideas in your head, when you're writing this shit, maybe you get the urge to act some of them out."

"That's the way you think it works?" Bill asked. "All writers are killers?"

"No," Miscali said, "only some of them."

Bill lost it, went, "Cut the shit, I never even knew Mo!"

Jesus, he thought, did I really say that?

Miscali was all attention, moved right into Bill's face, pushed, "Mo? What's that story?"

Bill, knowing he couldn't take it back, went on a mad whim, went, "*Love* the suit." And the tiny voice in his head snapped, "Bill....*Bill*, what the hell are you doing, you don't want to antagonize this guy."

But he did, he truly did, and added, "In that outfit, you'd be a natural on Jerry Springer."

Let the insult hover. Miscali eyeballed him, his face red, a mix of shame and rage entwined. He said, "Think you and me, pal, we might take a run down to Hollywood South, drop you in a cell with some Crips, give you some material for the…" Indicated the screen. "…*screenplay*."

The contempt that had just been dripping before leaked all over that word, and then the knife was out and with a Red Bull-fueled ferocity and speed-induced grunt, the blade was above Miscali's groin and was cutting, moving fast, shredding, all the way up to the cop's throat. Miscali let out a howl of sheer and utter shock, and Bill stepped back as a literal geyser of blood shot into the air, splattered his newly art deco'ed ceiling. Then with a slight whimper, the cop collapsed in a bloodied mess on the floor.

Bill muttered, "Holy fuckin' shit." Then, to an unseen audience, "Did you catch that?"

Bill blacked out for a few hours but came to, hours later, in a junk-filled lot in downtown L.A., Miscali's feet sticking out of a nearby dumpster. Jesus Christ, Bill hoped nobody had seen him come down here. Fuck it, he decided, he had to trust his unconscious mind. It was what had gotten him this far, as a writer and as a killer, and it would take him the rest of the way to the top.

As Bill slunk away, he thought of Miscali's Macy's bargain shoes sticking out like a beacon, hearing Hannibal Lecter's line to Clarice about her footwear, and he whispered—to himself, to the world—"No fucking doubt, I'm movie literate."

TWENTY-SIX

I like you, Guy. I'd do anything for you.
PATRICIA HIGHSMITH, *Strangers on a Train*

Fantastic news! Angela had accepted Sebastian's friend request and posted a smiley face on his page with:

BRANDI LOVE: Great to hear from you, Sebs, been way too long!

He knew she wouldn't be able to resist his British charm. He IM'd her:

SEBASTIAN CHILD: I knew you wouldn't be able to resist my British charm!

Rather long pause, then:

BRANDI LOVE: What can I say? Love has no logic.

SEBASTIAN CHILD: So I gather you're willing to let bygones be bygones, my Love? (pun intended)

BRANDI LOVE: You know how I can't resist a Brit with wit.

He was trying to think of the perfect, well, witty response to this, when he got:

BRANDI LOVE: When I can see you? There's so much I want to say.

A moment later, it was

BRANDI LOVE: Is now too soon?

Squeezing his legs in an incompetent attempt at tempering his suddenly burgeoning excitement he typed:

SEBASTIAN CHILD: Not soon enough!!

Sebastian, driving in the latest car he'd nicked on his way to the rendezvous—fittingly a Cougar—was elated. Not only was he eager to give Angela the fuck of her life, he was equally overjoyed about the dollar signs in his future. His stalking of Becker hadn't panned out, but he'd found a way in to *Bust* nevertheless. If he wasn't the most resilient, most resourceful man on the planet, he wanted to meet the man who was.

The meeting spot was a dreary motel on the outskirts of town in God knows where. It didn't occur to him to wonder why she'd suggested meeting in such a remote locale; he assumed it was because she was anticipating a night of uncontrollable ecstasy and wanted to do it in a suitably lurid venue.

She'd IM'd him a room number as well, and he knocked.

When he saw her there, in practically nothing save a lacy garter, it seemed as if no time had passed. They could've been back at Santorini, locking eyes and fates for the first time.

He was pressing her up against the wall, kissing her madly, saying, "I don't know why I shot you. I need you so desperately. I must've been insane."

Was this a dialogue from an old film? If it wasn't, it should have been. One of those gothic stories by a Bronte that he could've written himself if he'd been alive then and put quill to paper.

He ravished her so many times he lost count.

In their blissful exhaustion he whimpered, "You're all I've ever wanted. How've I lasted these years without you?"

Then Angela said, "If you want to prove your devotion to me, and redeem yourself for what you did, you'll do one thing for me now."

"Anything, darling," Sebstian said, wanting her again, feeling once again as if he were in that Bronte story. "Just say it."

✿

Sebastian had to pinch himself: everything was going to be fucking hunky dory. He actually said that aloud, not realizing that nobody had used that expression since Bowie was young.

Google Earth, God bless 'em, provided directions to Darren Becker's house. The small matter of a weapon. He'd gone to a seedy dive off Wilshire, a place where you could buy weapons, dope, and passports. Sebastian could fall in love with this town.

A weasel of a guy slipped onto the stool beside him, asked, "You a Limey?"

Sebastian was gobsmacked. Really now, who since Terence Stamp used *limey*? It was like pre-Hugh Grant hooker days. Sebastian squared his firm jawline, his mother used to say "Boykins, it's your best feature." Dear old Mum, batshit now, thinking she was the Queen Mum, and legless before noon. Sebastian looked at the guy, straight from central casting as a *bad un*. Sebastian moved his accent up a notch, not too much, like an oar length at Henley Boat Race. Ah, those were the days, straw hats, strawberries and cream, fair damsels in white flimsy dresses and croquet in the background. Sebastian had never been within a fart of that event but saw his Merchant Ivory movies. He intoned, "My good fellow, might one tempt a chap to a libation?"

Too much? A tad. The guy who, get this, was wearing a Lance Armstrong bracelet—really, man? The guy went, "The fuck is a libation?"

Yeah.

Long story mercifully edited, Sebastian scored a .9MM and a bag of the new wonder dope, PIMP. Now dressed to assassinate, sweating in black track gear and watch cap, he fingered the nine, a surge of sheer joy, adrenaline, and down-home psychosis shooting through his veins. PIMP rules.

His mind was tick-tripping like a demented cheap watch. He flashed through the first killing he'd done, the details blurred by the drug and only a false elation and a blend of rush and terror lingering. He moved the nine to his left hand, muttered, "You are better than Tim Henman, you are the Federer of murder."

Giggled.

And like a comic-book character, slapped his hand over his mouth, banging his recently capped front teeth with the gun barrel. Spat, "Shit hurts."

Then the front door opened and there was Becker, letting a Lab off a leash, urging, "Good boy, go water the garden," and Sebastian, in a sudden wave of PIMP-induced ferocity, leapt from the bushes, screaming holy heaven, screaming, "Water this, you wanker."

Missed with the first two shots, as Becker, transfixed, went, "Wanker?" Then, "It's you—from the health club!" and the third shot went through Becker's mouth, hurling the back of his head against the stucco Spanish door frame.

Sebastian stopped, "Holy fuck, Jesus, sorry 'bout that, I mean…" and let off two more rounds, taking Becker's legendary groin to Ensenada and parts west.

The sound of the gunfire had momentarily deafened Sebastian and he thought, *Dammit, forgot the earplugs*, then saw two large shapes whirl out from the doorway, big bruising shapes, and he whined, "Jesus, Angela, you didn't mention, like…bodyguards."

He fired off an optimistic round and the guys hesitated, and who knows, Sebastian might have actually got away, but, yeah, the dog. Had a piece of Sebastian's honed ass, sinking deep and hard.

Sebastian roared, "Ah for fuck's sake, that's not fair, that's hardly fucking cricket!"

The second guard, apparently a student of Asian hard-core martial-arts movies, had gone into the house and grabbed a faux Samurai sword, and with one fierce leap and lunge, severed Sebastian's elegant head from his shoulders. His head, doing what his body had failed to accomplish, made it on to Wilshire, where a U-Haul carrying a coyote and his crew squashed it to multicolored paella.

A kid across the street was getting it all on his smartphone, muttered, "Hashtag WayCool, way better than *Grand Theft Auto 2*."

And lest we ever forget, this *is* Hollywood, the kid sold it to the new tabloid show from Jerry Springer's production company and made his first Spielberg steps into the biz.

Everyone a winner.

TWENTY-SEVEN

You're no messiah. You're a movie of the week.
You're a fucking T-shirt at best.
BRAD PITT IN *Seven*

Took Max a while to get Angela to call him Sean. Like, Sean Mullen.

She laughed, said, "Seriously, take it from a gal who has known an Irish guy." Paused. "Like *intimately*, and you have just the worst accent since Dick Van Dyke tried to do Cockney in *Mary Poppins*."

Max was pissed on two counts. The accent bit of course hurt his pride—he loved his fuckin' brogue—and that mention of the Irish prick opened up all sorts of old shit that was best left, well, buried.

He said, "Right, but you, you work it brilliantly as Brandi Love." His tone leaked sarcasm.

She snapped, "The fuck is that, like a slur?"

He'd done just a wee smidgen of PIMP and was feeling the love, went, "Babe, *c'est il est, il est*." He thought this meant *It is what it is*, but his mangled pronunciation and syntax would have confused even Carla Bruni.

A ring at the door startled them both. Angela shot him a look, went, "It's Brandi, remember."

For a mad moment Max thought she was having booze home-delivered.

She opened the door to a tough-looking broad who showed a

badge, said, "Detective Gaylin, LAPD, I'm looking for a Sean Mullen," and tried to see into the apartment.

Angela said, "Oh, of course, come in," and flashed her mega smile. It usually brought wood but with a broad, who knew?

The cop stepped into the room. Max knew he was sweating and couldn't stop grinning like an idiot.

Got, "Something funny to you, sir?"

He launched his hand out, offering friendship, dope, love and—yeah, okay—bullshit. Smarmed, "Sure 'tis only me way, us lads, we do be like over-friendly, to a fault, be-Jaysus."

Max noticed her hand shift—move closer to her holster. If she pulled a gun on him…well, he had his own piece tucked away and nobody beat the Max at quick draw.

Well, in his own mind anyway.

The drug coursing in his blood, on its upward swing, told him, *Chrissakes, stop smiling*.

And he did, abruptly. Throwing off Gaylin a bit, who checked that her gun was easy to pull.

"I talked to the police earlier," Angela sold. "Told them all about how that British lunatic Sebastian had been stalking Darren for days, had even gotten a job at Darren's health club."

"I'm not here about Sebastian," Gaylin said. "I'm guessing you are Brandi Love."

Angela, focused, managed, "Yes, yes I am." Then added, "Last time I checked."

Angela and Max exchanged looks, both realizing this was the very worst thing to say when you're fucking with aliases.

Gaylin absorbed this, then asked Max, "And what sort of freaking stage leprechaun are you?"

Angela, despite the very brittleness of the ground beneath her, had to bite her lower lip to not laugh out loud. Max flashed back to high school now, his friends giggling in the back of the classroom after Max hit their idiot science teacher in the head with a giant spitball.

Sweating profusely, using the best of the Irish he'd learned over the years, he went, "I'm Sean Mullen, from the bould county of Galway, we gave the world Claddagh rings, Aran sweaters and a midlist mystery writer, and you'll have to forgive me, ma'am, but I got stuck into the oul Jay last night." His face contorted in horror as he thought maybe she thought Jay was, like, a guy. Recovered, muttered, "That bin like the Jameson, fierce lethal stuff, and speaking of which, would you like a lad to wet your whistle?"

Angela couldn't contain it, laughed, and added fast, "Sean, you wicked devil, the lady doesn't know that means, Would you like a drink?"

Gaylin, God bless her, seemed a little freaked by the oddness of this bizarre duo. Went, "Mr. Mullen, are you aware that you bear a resemblance to a fugitive named Max Fisher?"

"Aye, I'm not familiar with the name," Max said. "We have no Fishers in Galway. Fishing, yes. Me brother's a fisherman, Declan Mullen. Wonderful man indeed."

"Did you ever live in New York, Mr. Mullen?"

"Thought of moving me own self there, but what would I do?" Max said. "Tend bar, drive a horse 'n carriage? May not be horses soon in Central Park and then what's an Irishman to do? Beg Liam for a role in his next movie?"

The PIMP made Max believe his story was getting more convincing, and maybe it was.

Gaylin asked, "Have you seen Joe Miscali recently?"

Max wasn't expecting this; he thought he'd ditched Miscali in New York.

"Who?" Max asked.

"Miscali," Gaylin said.

"Aye, love, we have no Miscalis in Galway," Max said, "alas, but we have swans though. You should come see the swans sometime soon, good on ya, eh?"

Little too much brogue there?

Gaylin said, "So a New York cop, middle-aged guy, beer belly, didn't come talk to you?"

"No, darling," Max said.

"Can you please tell us, what's this all about?" Angela asked.

"A New York detective, Joe Miscali, came to L.A. the other day," Gaylin said, "and he seems to have disappeared."

Was it possible that Miscali was off the board? This day was getting better and better.

"So what does this possibly have to do with us?" Angela asked.

"Maybe nothing," Gaylin said. "But something doesn't sit right with me about all of this. Miscali went AWOL from the NYPD." She looked at Max. "His trip to L.A. from New York was unsanctioned. Apparently he was obsessed with Fisher, has had a lot of conspiracy theories over the years."

"No offense," Angela said, "but why are you bothering us about it?"

"Miscali thought Mr. Mullen here bore a resemblance to Fisher."

Max went, "Begorrah, no, not I…"

"Miscali may have had issues," Gaylin said, "but it seems a bit too coincidental that Darren Becker gets killed yesterday and then Miscali disappears."

"I'm sorry," Angela said, "but really. There's no connection to us."

"One person dying, one disappearing, and both connected to this TV project you're involved with. *Bust*, right?"

Max was staring at hers. For a cop, she had a great rack.

"I already explained about Sebastian," Angela said. "He'd

been stalking Darren for days. Darren said Sebastian confronted him at his health club. Darren was killed by a madman, end of story. Now, maybe you're right, maybe *Sebastian* had something to do with whatever happened to that cop, Miscali? But it has nothing to do with me or Sean."

Gaylin eyed them both suspiciously for a bit longer. When neither showed signs of cracking, she went, "Well, thanks for your time, Mr. Mullen…Ms. Love. If I have any more questions, I'll be back." At the door she turned, said, "Oh. Mr. Mullen…"

"Aye?" Max said.

"Would you be open to a taking a lie-detector test?"

"Excuse me?" Angela said.

"It could help clear things up," Gaylin said.

"Fook no," Angela said. "What the hell. You have no evidence of anything, except for some story about a New York cop with obvious mental problems. I think you've wasted enough of our fookin' time."

Gaylin looked pissed off as hell, but reluctantly—what other choice did she have?—left.

When she was gone, Max and Angela laughed for a long time. Max knew Gaylin would be back at some point, and a lie detector could lead to disaster. But for right now PIMP was in control, and he wasn't going to let anything ruin the ride.

TWENTY-EIGHT

When things are bad, never complain,
because things can always get worse.
JEWISH SAYING

When Paula woke up in her room at the Sofitel, she knew something was seriously wrong. She had an awful feeling she hadn't felt since she'd found that the promised 20,000-copy print run of her last book at St. Martin's Press had been reduced to 1,000—all library sales. It felt like she was having a nightmare, but she was definitely awake, her face squished into an extra-firm pillow selected from the Sofitel's pillow menu.

She turned onto her side, squinting against the California sun shining through the blinds, and noticed that Kat was gone. Then she noticed the note, handwritten on hotel stationery:

Baby,

You know how much I admire you, but I think success has gone to your head and you know how I just can't deal with that bullshit. I've also discovered that I'm no longer attracted to women. As my rabbi in Israel often said, "Go know!" If you're not shocked already, I know this part will come as a bigger shock to you so please breathe deeply before you read the rest. Have you exhaled the breath? Okay, here we go—Lars and I have gone to Sweden to make amateur porn. He says he can make me a big star in Sweden and I believe that God has a plan for me and this is my time to shine. By the time you read this we'll be boarding our flight, so please

don't try to stop me. Also, please understand that I am not a
person, I am passion. This is who I am and no one will ever
be able to change me, especially not you.
   Shalom,
   Kat

Paula had always had a well, issue, with rejection, and this
time was no different. She went on a rampage that would've
impressed Johnny Depp, and it was goodbye extra-firm pillow
and practically everything else in the room. Lamps were
smashed, chairs broken, LCD TV shattered—Charles at Hard
Case was going to flip when he saw the bill. But only one
thought was careening through Paula's brain at the moment—
I'm going to be alone forever.

   She'd thought that when she'd found Kat her search was
over, that she'd found the one. But now her love was gone, she
was Katless. Worse, she'd lost her co-writer. *Slide, The Max* and
any future books in her Angela-and-Max series were in jeop-
ardy.

   She sobbed into the remnants of her pillow and finally rallied enough to call her agent, Janet Ortiz, in New York. Janet
assured her that there was nothing to worry about, that Hard
Case already had the cover painted for the next book and writers
would be lining up to co-write with her. She texted Paula a jpeg
of the painting.

   "What the fuck?" Paula shouted. "There's no redhead in the
story. Angela is *blonde*."

   "So?"

   "And what's she doing, reaching for a…"

   "A gun."

   "And Mr. Oblivious sitting there smoking doesn't notice?
What is he, a congenital idiot?"

"He's distracted by her legs."

"Who the fuck is he anyway? This is not a scene from my goddamn book! Nothing like this ever happens in it!"

"So what?" Janet said. "Since when has a Hard Case Crime cover ever had anything to do with what's inside the book?" Then added unhelpfully, "Anyway, how do you know what will or won't be in the book? You haven't even written it yet." Which was, after all, the bigger problem.

"Fuck," Paula said. "Who the hell is desperate enough that he'd be willing to step into Stiegsson's shoes? Do you really think you can find someone?"

"Absolutely," Janet said.

Sure enough, within an hour, Janet called back and said Reed Coleman had interest.

"But isn't Coleman currently writing with three other people, including Laura Lippman?" Paula asked.

"Yes, but he said he'd dump those projects, even stop writing Robert B. Parker's books, to get on the *Bust* bandwagon. And Hard Case says whatever's okay with you is okay with them."

Paula liked Coleman's enthusiasm, and if he was really willing to dump Lippman to write with her... This would be a double-whammy for poor Laura, since Paula knew she was already kicking herself for rejecting Paula's initial co-writing offer and letting a max opportunity with *Bust* slide. But she hoped Laura had been around long enough to understand that writing's a business, and sometimes you have to be the pimp.

"Tell Coleman he's in," Paula said.

So things were looking up. Okay, so she'd lost her love, but she'd kept what was dearest to her—her career as a novelist—intact.

Then she got a call from Donna James, her film agent, heard: "Have you been watching the news?"

Staring at the smashed TV, Paula said, "Not today, no."

"Well, I have bad news and I have bad news," Donna said, "which do you want to hear first?"

"I'll take the good news," Paula tried.

"Sorry, I don't have any of that."

Donna told Paula that Darren Becker had been murdered by a delusional man who went by the name Sebastian Child. Sebastian had been killed too, by Becker's bodyguards. "Beheaded," Donna said.

"Oh my God," Paula said. "Sebastian?"

"You know him?"

"Of course I know him," Paula said. "I met him while Max was in Attica, around the time of the prison break. He looks— well, *looked*—so much like Lee Child it's freaky."

"I see," Donna said. "Well, with Becker gone, Brandi Love has a new producing partner, named Sean Mullen."

"Wait, Sean Mullen?"

"You know him too?"

"He was a character in *Bust*. He disappeared around the time Max was at Attica." Paula's mind was churning, trying to figure out what this all meant, if it meant anything.

"Maybe it's just a coincidence," Donna said. "I mean Sean Mullen sounds like a common name."

Now Paula was panicked. She asked, "This won't affect the screenplay, will it?"

"That's the other bad news," Paula said. "Bill Moss has disappeared."

"Disappeared?" Paula was stunned.

"He announced to Lionsgate that he had to exit the project for personal reasons," Donna said. "An exec went to talk to him about it in person and his bungalow in Venice was cleaned out. He cancelled his phone service, credit cards, Netflix account. It's like he doesn't exist."

"Personal reasons sounds like bullshit," Paula said. "Why did he really leave?"

"You're a natural mystery writer, aren't you?" Donna said. "Well, what they're saying on the news is that Sebastian and Bill might've known each other, and Bill had for some reason conspired with Sebastian to murder Darren Becker. I guess it's sort of like the Tonya Harding and O.J. cases combined." Donna laughed. "But I think that's just a theory right now. As they say in the media—the story is fluid. I guess that's a fancy way of saying they don't know jack shit." Donna laughed again.

"Okay, let's cut to the chase," Paula said. "Is *Bust* dead or not?"

"Absolutely not," Donna said. "Lionsgate is one hundred percent committed to the show with or without Bill Moss. Brandi Love and Sean Mullen are co-executive producing now. I don't see anything listed for Sean Mullen on IMDB, but Brandi has vouched for him, so I'm sure he'll be great on the project. Everyone is super excited."

"What about the other executive producers?" Paula asked. "Larry Reed and Eddie Vegas?"

"I haven't heard anything about them," Donna said, "thank God. As an agent here said the other day—Larry Reed could turn shinola into shit faster than Steve Martin in *The Jerk*."

Paula had thought the world of book publishing was a clusterfuck, but it was nothing compared to this. It was a miracle that any TV shows ever got made.

Paula left an apologetic note for the maid and then rushed off to meet with Angela and this Sean Mullen at Darren Becker's old office.

When she arrived she saw Angela with the ugliest, most bloated version of Philip Seymour Hoffman imaginable, with red hair and a red beard. He looked like a ginger version of George R. R. Martin.

But the disguise didn't fool Paula.

"Oh my God, it's you," she said.

"In the flesh, sugar tits," Max said.

With a rush of emotion, Paula went to Max and hugged him tightly.

"This is surreal," she said. "It's like you came out of my brain or something. My book's coming to life."

"Hey, easy with my fiancée," Angela said. "We Irish girls can get jealous, you know."

"Wait," Paula said. "You two are…"

Angela stuck out her hand, displaying a massive diamond, and went, "Yes, engaged, and not with a fookin' claddagh ring. It was Darren's ex-wife's, God bless both of them, and God rest Darren."

Paula was dazed—the events of the morning hitting her. "I'm dizzy," she said. "I think I should sit down."

"Here, take one of these," Max said.

He gave her a little pill, something white, looked harmless as a Tylenol.

"What is it?"

Max smiled, said, "It knows how to take care of you."

Angela handed her a cup of water and she swallowed the pill.

"Does anybody else know that you're Max Fisher?" Paula asked.

"Not anybody currently living," Max said.

"A cop came around asking questions, but we got rid of her," Angela said.

"Even you two can't pull this off." Paula was looking at Max. "You're on the FBI's Most Wanted List, for God's sake."

"Yeah, but number six," Max said. "What's up with that shit? Cocksuckers."

"Still," Paula said. "You're taking a big risk."

"Hey, look how long it took them to find Whitey Bulger,"

Max said. "L.A.'s the best place in the world to hide. Everybody has their head so far up their own ass, nobody notices anything."

"But somebody will recognize you eventually," Paula said. "I mean, I know who you are. How do you know I won't go to the police?"

"We'd sue you for defamation of character," Angela said. "Basing a novel on living people isn't exactly kosher, you know."

"I didn't know you were alive when I wrote it."

"Would a judge buy that?"

She laughed. "A judge. That's ridiculous. Like either of you would willingly go anywhere near a courtroom. If people knew who you were you'd spend the rest of your lives in jail. Especially Max."

"I have the best lawyer in the business," Max said.

"I know, Darrow," Paula said. "I put him in *Bust*."

Something was affecting Paula's mood; was it the pill Max had given her? She couldn't tell if she was aroused or angry, didn't know if she wanted to fuck somebody or kill somebody. All she knew was that suddenly she felt fucking great.

"Can I have another one of those?" she asked.

"Anything for my favorite writer," Max said.

Paula swallowed another pill, went, "So what does this all mean for *Bust*? Who's going to write it?"

"First of all," Angela said, ducking the question, "so sorry about Kat and Lars. We heard about it through the grapevine. If it's any consolation, Lars makes the worst porn I've ever seen and he's hung like a peanut. I know they'll bomb out in Sweden."

"That's okay, I already have a new co-writer for the novels," Paula said, "and I want to make out with you. Wow, Jesus, I don't know why I said that. I feel like it's not me who's talking, like something's taken control of me... So, wait, about a new writer for the pilot to replace Bill Moss..."

"Our first idea was Bret Easton Ellis," Angela said. "Author of my fave fookin' book ever, *American Psycho*, and also the giver of A-list cunnilingus."

Paula assumed this second part was a joke.

"But unfortunately Bret can't do it," Angela said. "Something about how he's too busy writing a show about a stalker for Showtime."

"So who's next on the list?" Paula asked.

"One of the hottest writers in the country right now," Angela said, "though not thus far known for her screenwriting, she's immensely qualified for this project."

Was it the pills Max had given her or was Paula getting *thisclose* to an orgasm? Paula had an urge to reach out and grab Angela's breasts, so she did.

"Sorry," Paula said. "I…I…I don't know…"

"It's okay," Angela assured her. "I've been felt up by worse."

"Who?" Paula asked.

"Well, one of them is in this room."

"Fuck you too, sweetheart," Max said.

Max and Angela kissed.

"No, I mean, who is this hot writer?" Paula asked.

"You," Angela said. "We want to hire you, Paula."

Paula writing the TV pilot? It was ingenious; after all, who knew more about *Bust* than her? Angela was the sexiest woman Paula had ever seen and she didn't give a fuck about Kat.

"You can pick up where Bill left off or you can write it from scratch," Angela said. "We have total faith in your abundant talent."

"I'll show you some abundant talent, bitch," Paula said, and kissed her.

Her awful morning was a distant memory.

Thanks to those little white pills, life was all good.

TWENTY-NINE

A man is his job, and you are fucked at yours.
JACK LEMMON IN *Glengarry Glen Ross*

"Make it real," Larry said.

"Bill Moss is gone."

Larry, in his car, in traffic in downtown Hollywood, didn't even know who the fuck was calling, said, "Who the fuck is calling?"

Larry had been supposed to meet Eddie Vegas at a strip club, to update him on the project. Larry didn't have an update—fucking Darren and Angela had kept him out of the loop—but he had some good bullshit prepared.

Then this call from a private number.

"Lionsgate told Eddie he's not a producer anymore," the voice said. It was a guy—old, a smoker, or both.

"I don't know who I'm talking to," Larry said.

"Make this right," the guy said, and clicked off.

"You there? You there?" Larry said, feeling like some idiot in a movie who says, *You there? You there?* even when it's obvious he'd been hung up on.

"Fuck me!" Larry screamed.

He called Becker's various numbers—got voicemail at all of them. Same when he tried to reach Angela. All the execs at Lionsgate were either out of the office or in meetings.

Cut to an hour later—Larry arrived at Becker's office in Westwood. The kid at the door tried to stomp him as he stormed into Becker's office. But Becker wasn't there—just Angela, alone.

"Sorry, I'm in meetings," Angela said.

"Meeting with who?" Larry said. "There's nobody here."

"I'm busy, Larry."

"Yeah, too busy to answer the phone," Larry said.

"I learned how to produce from the best." Angela smiled.

"Look," Larry said. "I'm just here to resolve a little misunderstanding. Lionsgate's telling my producing partner that he's not on the project anymore, do you know why that is?"

"Maybe because he isn't," Angela said.

"Huh?"

"Bill Moss quit the project, so since he's out, you're out, and your friend's out as well."

Knowing he was fucked, that this would never fly with Eddie Vegas, Larry said, "Quit? What do you mean quit? He can't quit."

Angela smiled, bust fully expanded, and said, "Welcome to Hollywood, sweetie."

Larry knew he had officially passed his expiration date and it was time to get the fuck out of town. He went home, packed a suitcase, and returned to his car. As he was getting in, he felt a gun against the back of his head, heard:

"Goin' somewhere?"

It was the guy from In-N-Out Burger who looked like Nick Nolte's mug shot.

"Make a sound, it'll be your last," Nolte said.

He led Larry into the back of a black sedan. There were two younger guys in the car, up front.

When the car started moving, Larry said, "I didn't call for a car service, but it's nice of you guys to take me to the airport."

Larry going for humor to lighten the situation, the way the victims at concentration camps told jokes to distract themselves from the horror. Anyway, that's what he'd heard.

They went up to the hills, not far from the Hollywood sign.

"Get out," Nolte said.

Were they going to shoot him here? Larry was ready to start begging for his life, when he noticed another car, a BMW, off to the side. Eddie Vegas got out of it. He was in jeans, a white T-shirt, a black blazer. He looked sharp.

"You look sharp," Larry said to him.

"You got my money?" Eddie asked.

"Is that what this is all about?" Larry said. "Jesus, why didn't you just say so instead of sending half of *48 Hours* to come get me?"

"You got the money or not?" Eddie said.

"I don't have it *yet*," Larry said. "But I'm working on it."

"Sorry, ain't good enough, man." Eddie took off his blazer and handed it to Nolte. Said to Larry, "I told you, you had two strikes, and I told you Eddie Vegas don't strike out."

"You didn't strike out, okay?" Larry said. "You got a foul tip. You're still alive."

"I ever tell you how I got the name Vegas?"

"'Cause you like to gamble?" Larry asked.

"No, I hate fuckin' gambling," Eddie said. "I got the name Vegas 'cause one time in Vegas when I was coming up, I had to deliver some product to a warehouse and the deal went bad. Guy I was with got blown away, my gun, shit ran out of bullets, but I fought, you know how? With my bare hands. Killed six guys with my fists. Mano a mano is the way I like to do shit. Keeps it more personal."

"You're kidding, right?" Larry asked, as the first punch connected with his face and something cracked, probably his jaw.

Nolte and another guy held Larry up, as Eddie continued to assault his face like a punching bag.

"P-please," Larry said through a mouthful of blood. "M-make it quick."

Eddie didn't. But eventually the pain went away and numbness set in. Larry couldn't believe this was how he was going to check out, never getting that big hit. He'd always thought his luck would turn eventually, but the credits were rolling, and he was looking for his name, but it wasn't there. There were other names, and then he couldn't remember what his name was, what he was searching for.

Then the credits stopped rolling altogether, faded to black.

THIRTY

I should find Ford attractive, everyone else does.
"He's too good looking," one of my sorority sisters groaned.
"I can't even look at him without feeling like
I'm being punched between the legs."
ANITA NUTTING, *Tampa*

It had been a long time—what, couple months?—since Eddie Vegas had taken somebody out with his hands and it only got him warmed up. It was like when you get a blow job but it ain't enough 'cause a few minutes later you want another one.

Maybe Larry Reed was gone, but that didn't mean the debt was dead. Eddie didn't care how many Hollywood *putas* he had to take out, he was gonna get his money back.

So Eddie was at the house in Brentwood, banging on the door, going, "Sean Mullen. Yo, Sean Mullen, open the fuck up!"

Eddie's boys were in the car; he'd told them to hang out there. He was cool, he'd said. He wanted to do this one alone.

Brandi Love, one of the other producers of—what the fuck was the show called? *Bust*, yeah, *Bust*—opened the door.

"Look who it is," Eddie said. "One of my co-executive producers. The chick who used to make pornos, which is a good thing, cause it means you used to gettin' fucked."

"Sorry," Angela said, "I think you have the wrong address."

Bitch tried to slam the door in his face. Yeah, right. He pushed it open hard, almost knocked her down. She was lucky he didn't turn her face into hamburger meat, and maybe he would when he was done with Mullen.

That's when a guy came over. Ugly, big, fat, red motherfucker with a beard. He was in some kinda black silk kimono with dragons spitting shit on the sleeves. Man looked like Mickey Rourke with red hair on the most fucked-up day of his life.

Guy went, "What'cha carrying, dude?"

Dude? Shit, who was this white boy? If it was Mullen, soon he was gonna be a dead white boy.

"You Mullen?" Eddie asked.

"You a wetback cunt?" guy said.

Did he have some accent? Yeah, sounded British or Irish, Eddie could never tell that shit apart.

"You think you tough, huh?" Eddie said. "That, or you the dumbest-ass motherfucker in Los Angeles."

"If it's multiple choice, I pick A," the guy said.

Eddie had to smile, what else was he gonna do? Some dumb foreign fuck off the boat didn't know who he was talkin' to.

The guy went to the drinks cabinet, started making a pitcher of margaritas. Serious? Eddie couldn't say anything—this shit was too funny, he had to see what happened next. Brandi was standing there too. Wait, was she fucked up, on something? Eddie thought so. Man, these movie people, they're fuckin' crazy.

He watched the guy pour two drinks, handed one to Eddie, went, "You didn't answer my question?"

"I ain't no cunt," Eddie said.

"No, about what you're carrying," the guy said. "You packing a Heckler 'n Koch, a Nine, or the prissy cop shit, a Glock?"

Jesus Christ. What a fucking moron. From now on, Eddie was only gonna invest in movies if his own kind was in charge. He was gonna give Jimmy Smits a call.

"You really wanna see my piece?" Eddie asked.

"I'll show you mine if you show me yours," the guy said and he took out his, looked like a Browning.

Then the crazy white nigger put two rounds in the ceiling.

Eddie jumped a foot, going, "The fuck, man, chill."

Then he was lookin' down the barrel of the gun at the fat man's face.

The guy asked, "What do you want, asswipe?"

Shit, they was both fucked up. On coke? Nah, somethin' harder.

Eddie had enough, went, "I'm a patient man…" and had his own piece out, aimed at the guy's head, "…till I'm not."

Brandi pulled a gun out of her garter or some shit and aimed it at Eddie.

Just what Eddie needed—some fuckin' Tarantino bullshit, everybody aimin' guns at each other. Or was that John Fuckin' Woo?

"Yo, I don't know what you on, but you both fucked up," Eddie said. "I gave Larry Reed seventy-five grand to be executive producing a TV show, the next *Prison Break*. Now Larry ain't giving me my money back, so if you're Sean Mullen you got two choices. Make me executive producer or give me my fuckin' money back in cash, same cash I gave Larry Reed."

"A man with a gun aimed at his head shouldn't be making demands," Brandi said.

Eddie knew he could take the guy out and then take Brandi out too. Ain't no porno bitch gonna outshoot Eddie Vegas.

He was about to do it, too, when the guy held out his hand—not the one with the gun—and had a white pill for Eddie to take, asked, "PIMP?"

"Oh, shit, so that's what y'all on," Eddie said. "Yo, I don't take that crazy shit."

"Yeah, well the rest of the country does," the guy said. "PIMP is the new E, the new Lodes, hell, the new Nirvana, and… ready for this…it knows how to take care of you."

Eddie had heard that *It knows how to take care of you* shit on the street, said, "I don't need no PIMP lesson, man. I need my fuckin' money."

"Guess it's time to fess up," the guy said. "My name's not Sean Mullen."

"Oh yeah, it ain't?" Eddie thought he was full of shit.

"It's Max Fisher."

"What?" Eddie said.

"You know me," Max said. "You were a co-executive producer of the TV show based on my fucking life."

Eddie stared at the ugly guy and now he saw it. Under the fat and all that red. Under the surgery scars.

Shit.

"Man, it's really you," Eddie said, lowering his gun.

"Yep," Max said.

Eddie, awestruck, went, "I heard about you for years. Man, you a motherfuckin' legend on the street. How you broke outta Attica, said fuck you to all them Aryan bitches."

"Yeah, 'tis been a wild ride," Max said, talking weird again, with that accent.

Max and Brandi had lowered their guns too.

"Damn, I should be gettin' your autograph," Eddie said. "Nobody believe it when I tell them I met Max Fisher." Then he had his iPhone out. "Can I get a selfie?"

"Sorry," Max said. "No pics."

"I get it, I get it, it's cool," Eddie said. He was so nervous around Fisher it was hard to talk. Like that time he'd met Ricky Martin.

"I want to make a deal with you," Max said. "The truth is I'm not only a TV producer, I'm a PIMP dealer. In fact I'm responsible for the PIMP explosion around the country."

"Wait," Eddie said, "so you're tellin' me that's what you been doing all this time when the cops are lookin' for you and you most wanted? You're dealing PIMP?"

"Yep," Max said.

"Most wanted and dealing PIMP?" Eddie said. "Oh, shit, that's cold."

"I need a guy like you in my operation," Max said. "If you forget about *Bust* and the seventy-five grand I'll give you PIMP distribution rights for all of the west coast. Does that put wood in your chinos?"

Eddie thought it over for maybe a few seconds, then asked, "Will I be like, *Scarface*?"

Max smashed a glass, cut into Eddie's face, straight line down his cheek, then cold-ass as shit went, "Yeah, but not as good looking."

THIRTY-ONE

The next day all hell broke loose, and the thing is
I should have seen it coming.
ROBERT WARD, *Red Baker*

Max had known he'd hit it big in L.A.—'cause he hit it big wherever he went—but he hadn't known he'd hit it, like, this big. His life, alas, had been like a fairy tale, and like a trip to the VIP room at a strip club, it had a happy ending.

It was like he and Angela had dreamed it up, years ago in Manhattan, when she was his secretary and he was CEO of a computer networking company. He'd thought all they'd have to do is off his bitchy wife and they'd live happily ever after, and okay, okay, things hadn't been exactly happy, and they'd left dozens of bodies in their wake, but they were here happy now, living the dream, and that was all that mattered, right? Fuck the past. Didn't the Buddhists say that?

Bust had been picked up by Netflix, who'd already greenlit three full seasons of the show. Paula had written a great pilot and early buzz was that the series would be a surefire hit. Max and Angela, still known to the world as Sean and Brandi, had been taking meetings with executives. Thanks to years of hiding out, watching TV shows and movies, Max was like a fookin' natural in the movie biz. As it turned out, dealing PIMP and making television had lots of similarities. It was about the product, all about the deals. And he knew as much as these studio fucks about dealing. Maybe more.

On the first day of principal photography, Max and Angela

were on the set, holding hands and getting goosebumps, while hearing the director, Bryan Singer, scream, "Action!"

The set was the pizza place in Manhattan, where Max hires the hit man, Thomas Dillon, to kill Max's wife. Ah, memories. Colin Farrell was Dillon and Paul Giamatti was Max. Max had thought George Clooney would be more of an aesthetic fit but he had to admit Giamatti had him down cold.

Angela—still known to the world as Brandi Love—had been cast as Angela. Max thought Angela looked the part, and those tits looked better than ever, but in her first scene with Giamatti, in a recreation of Max's old office in Manhattan, she delivered her lines in such a stilted way everyone winced. The fucking gaffers, even. It didn't get better as the day wore on. It was obvious that Giamatti was frustrated with her and that everybody thought she was awful.

During a break, execs from Lionsgate and Netflix met with Max in private, telling him that they all thought Angela had to be taken off the show.

"We already have a yes from Lindsay Lohan's people," the Lionsgate exec said, "and Colin refuses to work with Angela anymore."

"I hate to put it so bluntly," the Netflix exec said, "but Brandi sucks. Either she's off the show or we can't continue with the production."

Max didn't like the disrespect from the Netflix exec, or the threat, and made a mental note to hire somebody to kill the guy's dog or cat at some point to send a message. But he told them he agreed that Angela had to go and he'd break the news to her tonight.

Max waited till later that evening when they were home at their new estate in Beverly Hills. After their nightly routine of sex and P—he had taken to calling the drug P, a single letter like some stars just used a single name, like Madonna or Rihanna—he broke the news to Angela that she was off the show.

He cut to the chase with, "You're gone, girl."

Okay, okay, so Max had done perhaps a wee bit more P than he'd intended and was bumping in his mind from elation through paranoia to outright delusion. He was dressed in a pair of white chinos, a white T with the words YOU GOTTA KILL THE FLING YOU LOVE, and a white windbreaker with gold trim, not unlike Elvis before he bought the farm on a toilet seat. He looked in the mirror and what P showed him was Tony Manero. The reel of *Saturday Night Fever* looped in his head. He said, "TCB." If Elvis hadn't quite left the building, he would soon.

Max was so out of it he failed to remember that Angela was right along with him on the P train. If the shit made him crazy, it wired Angela to a whole new level of batshit nuts.

"Gone girl?" Angela said, scratching herself like a gorilla with jock itch. "Who's gone girl?"

Max, under a giant disco ball, said, "You, you're off the show. Lindsay Lohan's replacing you." He flashed back to his time as a CEO and said, "You're terminated, my sweet bitch." Then he was at a pub in Galway and Angela was the shite-slow barmaid, and he went, "Ya old cunt, get me like, double Jameson on the rocks and you know, like, maybe before the fooking sun sets," and he snapped his fingers.

Even off in the stratosphere on P, he knew he'd made a huge mistake. Not by firing her, but by snapping. He'd forgotten the golden rule of never, ever snap at an Irishwoman.

Sure enough, Angela moved right in his face, went, "Hey, cocksucker, have a drink of this," and Max felt the jolt in his head, his neck snap back, and knew the cunt had shot him.

He emitted a tiny, "Duh?" and, like a deflated balloon, crumpled to the floor.

❖

The P said to Angela, *It is what it is*. And she answered, "Ah, shit the fook up."

She had the double Jameson, her mind a mix of utter blankness and fierce practicality, urging, *Get....get....get rid of the body*.

She answered aloud, "Okeydokey."

In a purple haze, she got Max in the front seat of her car, propped him up like a passenger, blood only slightly leaking down his jaw. But some Dark Gods were minding her, it was dusk and she got him to the L.A. River, humming, *Drop kick me Jesus tru the goalposts of life*.

A fuck of a tune to hum.

Then in a P-fueled surge of energy, humped him over the bridge and into the river, where he made an almighty splash, something he'd always wanted. Then she dumped the gun she'd used, the dainty .22 she'd bought for protection and been carrying strapped to her thigh—'cause you always gotta watch your back in this town—in there with him.

As she drove off, she crooned, "He got the goldmine and I got the shaft."

The moon played out over the surface of the water and later Angela realized if she hadn't been so far gone on P, and had been playing real close attention, she might have seen the slight bubbles hitting the surface and easing out like sad credits on a sadder movie.

THIRTY-TWO

I wasn't actually in love, but I felt a sort of tender curiosity.
F. Scott Fitzgerald, *The Great Gatsby*

Angela was living the dream. She was helming *Bust*, the hottest TV show in the country, which had been nominated for nine Golden Globe Awards, including Best Television Series—Drama, and she was part of the hottest gay couple in Hollywood. Yep, Angela and Paula were an item, the last lesbian power women of Hollywood, the Ellen and Portia du jour. They'd been featured in all the major mags and had had an exclusive, invitation-only wedding back on Lesbos. She had been to rehab to get off PIMP and tearfully told her story of overcoming her addiction to Oprah. She made Oprah cry when she talked about the abuse she'd suffered from Max Fisher and the other men in her life, and how the experiences had driven her to porn and prostitution. But when Angela talked about her meteoric rise to the top of Hollywood the audience gave her a standing O and Oprah shed tears of joy. Book rights to Angela's life story had been sold at auction to St. Martin's Press with Paula as the ghostwriter, and a film was in development at Universal with Angela —AKA Brandi Love—executive producing.

Speaking of Love, Angela was in love with Paula, considered her her latest soul mate, but Angela also loved that she was taking a break from men, who'd caused so much havoc in her life. As Angela often told her new A-list friends, the best part about Paula was she didn't have a dick, and without a dick you can't get fucked.

On Golden Globes night at the Beverly Hilton Hotel, Angela

and Paula were making a big splash. They'd already told the fashionistas at E! what they were wearing—Angela in Herrera and Paula in Dolce & Gabbana. Arm in arm during their entire stroll along the red carpet, they stopped for photos every few seconds and to do an interview for Ryan Seacrest. Then they posed for cast photos with Paul, Lindsay, and Colin, waved to John Stamos, Tom Hanks, and, of course, Jodie Foster, and chatted with other celebs including Jennifer Aniston and her new ex-boyfriend—both huge *Bust* fans—and with Robert Downey Jr. and his wife, Susan. Angela had a new movie project in development with Robby so it was all smiles but, the truth was, she was planning to dump the project in the morning. Robby was hot but not hot enough to get in on the Brandi Love bandwagon.

Angela didn't want the night to end; she wanted the red carpet to stretch on for eternity. It was hard not to get emotional as she flashed back to the journey that had gotten her here: New Jersey, Dublin, New York, Greece, Attica, Butt Fuck Canada, London, and finally Hollywood. Her life had been like the most challenging maze in the world with so many dead ends, but she'd finally found a way out and emerged onto the red carpet of the Golden Globes. It felt a lot like destiny.

It felt a lot like destiny. Great line, she'd have to remember to remind Paula to include this in the book.

Then Paula said: "Oh my God, I can't believe who I just saw."

Angela was smiling for a paparazzo, maybe the image for the next cover of *People*, and then noticed Paula staring at something in the distance.

"Who?" Angela asked. She couldn't see for herself, more flashes blinding her.

"It's impossible, of course," Paula said. "I have to be imagining it."

"Who?" Angela asked again, hoping Paula had spotted Brad

Pitt. Angela imagined convincing Brad to ditch Angelina later at the after-parties. Would Angela swing back the other way for Brad? Hell, yeah. For all her big talk, she was getting bored with being a lesbian, and writers could be depressing as hell. Besides, it was about time to reinvent herself again and fook Brangelina. Brangela had a better ring to it.

"Brad Pitt?" Angela asked.

"No…"

Angela was smiling for another photo and only turned to look after Paula said:

"…Phil Hoffman."

out of it, pushing his lips out with the cube so
hem. Then, finally, he stuck the cube in his
nunk and asked, "You'll be Max?"
1 what had happened to no names. He was
ething about it, but then figured this guy was
head games with him so he just nodded.
1 over, whispered, "You can call me Popeye."
uld say, You mean like the cartoon character?
startling Max, and then said, "Fook, call me
early in the morning." Popeye smiled again,
1 the money up front."
r—negotiating was *his* thing—and asked, "It's
an, isn't that what Angela…?"
widened and Max thought, Fuck, the no-name
out to say sorry when Popeye shot out his hand
x's wrist. For such a bone-thin guy he had a

he hissed.
cared shitless but he was angry about the money
free his wrist, couldn't, but managed to say,
leal, you can't just change the terms."
putting the skinny little mick in his place.
e let go, sat back and stared at Max, sucking on
ore, then in a very low voice he said, "You want
wife, I can do whatever the fook I want, I own
ited prick."
t in his chest, thought, Shit, the heart attack his
gist told him could "happen at any time." He
Diet Pepsi, wiped his forehead, then said, "Yeah,
I guess we can renegotiate. Five before and five
t?"
he wanted Deirdre gone. It wasn't like he could

WANT MORE
OF THE MAX?

Try These Other Hard Case Crime Novels
From KEN BRUEN
and JASON STARR…

BUST

When Max Fisher hired Angela Petrakos as his assistant he was an
unhappily married man. But the two of them had a plan to put an
end to that situation: Pay an ex-IRA hit man to put Deirdre
Fisher out of her misery.

SLIDE

Max tries to reinvent himself as a hip-hop drug dealer, while
Angela finds herself hooking up with a would-be world-record
holder…in the field of serial killing.

THE MAX

Arrested by the NYPD for drug trafficking, Max is headed for
the cell blocks of Attica—but it's Angela who's in for the bigger
surprise, in a quaint little prison on the Greek island of Lesbos.

Read On for a
Sample Chapter From
BUST!

People with opinions

In the back of Famiglia
Fisher was dabbing his
up as much grease as he
across from him with
nothing like the big, stro
he looked more like a
weighed more than 130
blue eyes, a thin scar d
gray hair. And somethi
looked like someone ha
gled his lips.

The guy smiled, said
me mouth."

Max knew the guy w
be *so* Irish, that talking
those Irish bartenders
understand a fucking w
Light and they'd stare b
thing was wrong with t
Who's the potato eater j

Max was about to an
boss, and asked, "Are yo

The man put a finge
"Sh…sh," then added, "

a big produc
Max had to
cheek like a

Max wond
going to say
just trying to

The guy le

Before Ma
the guy laugh
anything exc
then said, "I

Max felt be
eight, right?

The guy's e
rule, and was
and grabbed
grip like steel

"Ten, it's te

Max was sti
too. He tried
"Hey, a deal's

He liked th

Finally Pop
the ice some
me to kill you
your arse you

Max felt a j
fucking cardio
took a sip of his
okay, whatever
after. How's th

Bottom line

hold interviews for hit men, tell each candidate, *Thank you for coming in, we'll get back to you.*

Then Popeye reached into his leather jacket—it had a hole in the shoulder and Max wondered, Bullet hole?—and took out a funny-looking green packet of cigarettes, with "Major" on the front, and placed a brass Zippo on top. Max thought that the guy had to know he couldn't actually light up in a restaurant, even if it was just a shitty pizzeria. Popeye took out a cigarette; it was small and stumpy, and he ran it along his bottom lip, like he was putting on lipstick.

Man, this guy was weird.

"Listen closely yah bollix," he said, "I'm the best there is and that means I don't come cheap, it also means I get the whole shebang up front and that's, lemme see, tomorrow."

Max didn't like that idea, but he wanted to get the deal done so he just nodded. Popeye put the cigarette behind his ear, sighed, then said, "Righty ho, I want small bills and noon Thursday, you bring them to Modell's on Forty-second Street. I'll be the one trying on tennis sneakers."

"I have a question," Max said. "How will you do it? I mean, I don't want her to suffer. I mean, will it be quick?"

Popeye stood up, used both hands to massage his right leg, as if he was ironing a kink out of it, then said, "Tomorrow…I'll need the code for the alarm and all the instructions and the keys to the flat. You make sure you're with somebody at six, don't go home till eight. If you come home early I'm gonna pop you too." He paused then said, "You think you can follow that, fellah?"

Suddenly Popeye sounded familiar. Max racked his brain, then it came to him—Robert Shaw in *The Sting*.

Then Popeye said, "And me mouth, a gobshite tried to ram a broken bottle in me face, his aim was a little off, happened on The Falls Road, not a place you'd like to visit."

Max never could remember if the Falls were the Protestants or the Catholics, but he didn't feel it was the time to ask. He looked again at the hole in Popeye's leather jacket.

Popeye touched the jacket with his finger, said, "Caught it on a hook on me wardrobe. You think I should get it fixed...?"

Don't Let the Mystery End Here.
Try These Other Great Books From
HARD CASE CRIME!

Hard Case Crime brings you gripping, award-winning crime fiction
by best-selling authors and the hottest new writers in the field.
Find out what you've been missing:

FIFTY-to-ONE
by **CHARLES ARDAI**

Written to celebrate the publication of Hard Case Crime's 50th
book, *Fifty-to-One* imagines what it would have been like if
Hard Case Crime had been founded 50 years ago, by a rascal
out to make a quick buck off the popularity of pulp fiction.

A fellow like that might make a few enemies—especially after
publishing a supposed non-fiction account of of a heist at a Mob-
run nightclub, actually penned by an 18-year-old showgirl with
dreams of writing for *The New Yorker*.

With both the cops and the crooks after them, our heroes are
about to learn that reading and writing pulp novels is a lot
more fun than living them…

ACCLAIM FOR CHARLES ARDAI

"A very smart and very cool fellow."
— Stephen King

*"Charles Ardai…will be the next me
but, I hope, less peculiar."*
— Isaac Asimov

Available now at your favorite bookstore.
For more information, visit
www.HardCaseCrime.com

SONGS of INNOCENCE

by RICHARD ALEAS

Three years ago, detective John Blake solved a mystery that changed his life forever—and left a woman he loved dead. Now Blake is back, to investigate the apparent suicide of Dorothy Louise Burke, a beautiful college student with a double life. The secrets Blake uncovers could blow the lid off New York City's sex trade…if they don't kill him first.

Richard Aleas' first novel, LITTLE GIRL LOST, was among the most celebrated crime novels of the year, nominated for both the Edgar and Shamus Awards. *But nothing in John Blake's first case could prepare you for the shocking conclusion of his second…*

PRAISE FOR SONGS OF INNOCENCE:

"An instant classic."
— Washington Post

"The best thing Hard Case is publishing right now."
— San Francisco Chronicle

"His powerful conclusion will drop jaws."
— Publishers Weekly

"So sharp [it'll] slice your finger as you flip the pages."
— Playboy

**Available now from your favorite bookseller.
For more information, visit
www.HardCaseCrime.com**